# LUCIFER'S TEARS

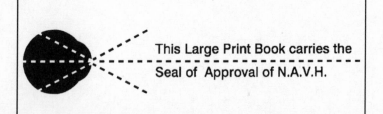

This Large Print Book carries the
Seal of Approval of N.A.V.H.

# LUCIFER'S TEARS

## JAMES THOMPSON

**THORNDIKE PRESS**
*A part of Gale, Cengage Learning*

GALE
CENGAGE Learning·

Detroit • New York • San Francisco • New Haven, Conn • Waterville, Maine • London

Copyright © 2011 by James Thompson.
An Inspector Vaara Novel.
Thorndike Press, a part of Gale, Cengage Learning.

Thorndike Press® Large Print Thriller.
The text of this Large Print edition is unabridged.
Other aspects of the book may vary from the original edition.
Set in 16 pt. Plantin.

LIBRARY OF CONGRESS CATALOGING-IN-PUBLICATION DATA

Thompson, James, 1964–
    Lucifer's tears / by James Thompson.
      p. cm. — (Thorndike Press large print thriller)
    ISBN-13: 978-1-4104-3886-7 (hardcover)
    ISBN-10: 1-4104-3886-4 (hardcover)
    1. Police—Finland—Fiction. 2. Homicide
investigation—Fiction. 3. Helsinki (Finland)—Fiction. 4. Large
type books. I. Title.
PS3620.H675L83 2011b
813'.6—dc22                                              2011013361

Published in 2011 by arrangement with G. P. Putnam's Sons, a member
of Penguin Group (USA), Inc.

Printed in the United States of America
1 2 3 4 5 6 7 15 14 13 12 11

For Nat Sobel and Judith Weber
And, as always, for Annukka

# 1

The baby kicks against my hand and rouses me from my nap. Kate and I sleep spooned up. Her head in the crook of my shoulder, my head buried in her long red hair. Her tall, pale body pressed against mine. My hand draped over her, resting on her pregnant belly. Kate doesn't stir. As she's gotten further into her pregnancy, she sleeps deeper, and I sleep lighter. Now that she's eight and a half months along, I barely sleep at all, just doze under the surface of waking consciousness. The sonogram said we're having a girl.

I pull on a robe, wool socks and slippers, light a cigarette and go out to the balcony of our Helsinki apartment. Illuminated by streetlights, snow pours through the dark in wet, blinding sheets. Fierce wind buffets me, blows up under my robe, freezes my nuts, takes my breath and makes me laugh. I hang on to the rail to keep from being blown off to the sidewalk below. It's minus twenty Celsius.

My home, Finland. The ninth and innermost circle of hell. A frozen lake of blood and guilt formed from Lucifer's tears, turned to ice by the flapping of his leathery wings. I limp back inside. This kind of cold makes my bad knee go so stiff that I drag my left leg more than walk on it.

My head is splitting. I hobble to the bathroom, shake a couple Tylenol out of a bottle, chew them up to make them work faster, stick my mouth under the spigot and chase them with water. I don't know why I bother. They don't help anymore. The migraines started not long after Kate miscarried the twins a little over a year ago, and have gotten worse over time. I've had the same headache without a break for almost three weeks now. It's starting to make me crazy.

I sit in a rocking chair by the bed and watch Kate sleep. As Dante's Beatrice was his object of unconditional love, Kate is mine. Kate: my cinnamon-haired, fair-skinned snow queen. Kate: my beautiful American. Since I met her, Kate has been my beginning and my end. For me, there is only Kate.

Pregnancy has made Kate more radiant

than ever. I feel a pang of guilt for our dead twins, and wonder again if I caused her to lose them. I wonder if she thinks about them as often as I do, and if she blames me for their loss. Kate begged me to give up the Sufia Elmi case. She said the stress was too much for both of us. I refused.

I managed to solve the murder, but the attrition rate was high. Five dead bodies piled up before the case was over, including my friend and sergeant Valtteri and my ex-wife. Two women were widowed and seven children left fatherless.

And I was shot in the face. The bullet left an ugly scar, which could have been corrected with minor plastic surgery, but I refused. I wear it as a symbol of my guilt for failing to solve the case sooner. I could have spared all those people so much death and misery. In my mind, I see Valtteri pull the trigger. His blood and brains spray across the ice. The shot echoes around the lake. He looks at me with dead eyes and falls. His blood stains the pearl-gray ice and looks black in the murky light. I still refuse to talk about it. Kate believes I suffer from traumatic shock.

I pursued the Sufia Elmi case to the exclusion of everything and everyone else. Even Kate. She miscarried two days later, the day after Christmas, and lost the babies. I blame myself. I believe the stress I caused her sparked the miscarriage. I've never told Kate about my guilt, can't make myself vocalize it.

Kate was unhappy in the Arctic Circle, in my hometown of Kittilä. She wanted to move to Helsinki and start over. As a reward for solving the Sufia Elmi murder, I was decorated for bravery and offered the job of my choice. I lived in Helsinki years ago, but left for a reason. My memories of this place are bad. Still, I owed Kate this, so we moved here and I took a slot in Helsinki homicide.

Kate's brother and sister, John and Mary, are arriving from the States tomorrow evening. She hasn't seen them for a few years, and I'm glad she has the opportunity, but they're going to stay for weeks, to see Kate through the final days of her pregnancy and help out after the baby is born. Who the hell does that? I never heard of a family doing such a thing. I can't say it to Kate, but I don't want them here. It will change the dynamic of our household. And besides, I want Kate all to myself during this intimate time. I don't need any help taking care of my wife and child.

After a while, I go back to bed. I slide my arm under her head and she turns toward me, gives a sleepy little snort, then wakes up enough to look at me and grins. "Want to make love to me?" she asks.

"Yeah," I say. "I do."

Pregnancy and the attendant hormonal changes have lent a sharp edge to her libido, and despite the migraines, I'm happy to accommodate. I suffer an irrational fear that sex will hurt our child, and take her more gently than she might prefer. Afterward, she lays her head on my shoulder, continues her nap.

I wait until I'm sure she's asleep again, before I move. She likes it if I stay awake in bed until she's asleep. It makes her feel safe. I have the night shift, check the clock. It's seven p.m. I have to be at work in an hour. I take a shower and dress. Kate is still asleep. I pull back the blanket, kiss her belly and cover her up again on my way out.

As I drive to Pasila police station, the streets are almost empty. I use my Saab for a winter play toy in the snow, cut the wheel hard to make the car slip sideways, accelerate to straighten it out again. Reckless endangerment.

# 2

It's Sunday night, ten p.m. I'm working the graveyard shift, usually the province of rookies. I may have only been in homicide for a little while, but counting my time spent as a military policeman while doing my mandatory service in the armed forces at nineteen, I have twenty-two years in law enforcement. The slight of being assigned these bullshit shifts isn't lost on me. I'm working with Milo Nieminen, the other new guy, recently promoted to detective sergeant. My status in Helsinki homicide is further reinforced.

Rauha Anttila, age seventy-eight. Found dead in her sauna by her son. Said son couldn't take it and left. A lone uniformed officer watches over the house, waiting for us to arrive. I dismiss him. Milo and I are alone in her apartment. We don latex gloves, walk through the bathroom and open the sauna door. I'm not sure if Milo can take it either. He makes gagging sounds, is on the edge of vomiting.

Milo and I haven't really gotten to know each other yet. He's in his mid-twenties, on the short side and thin. His hair is shaved down to stubble. Under piercing dark eyes, he has shadowy circles that look permanent.

"You could try a face mask," I say. "Some cops use them in these situations."

"Does it help?"

"No."

I estimate that Rauha has been dead for about ten days. Her sauna is electric and has a timer on it with a max of four hours, so she didn't cook too long, but the heat set the process of decomposition into action faster than normal. Her body has passed through the bloating period and is toward the end of the black putrefaction stage. She's taken on a darkish green hue. Her body cavities have ruptured and gases are escaping. It must have been worse a couple days ago, but the smell of decay is overwhelming.

Milo looks a little better, must be getting used to it. "Jesus, why didn't a neighbor call this in days ago?" he asks.

"The sauna door was closed, and so was the bathroom door. Most of the stench passed through the sauna stovepipe and out the roof. They probably smelled something,

13

but just thought it was a dead mouse or something in the ventilation."

The formation of gases in her abdomen has driven fluid and feces out of her body. The gases moved up into her face and neck and caused swelling of her mouth, lips and tongue. Her face is disfigured, almost unidentifiable. Water blisters have formed on her skin. Milo screws up his courage and moves in for a closer look.

"Watch out," I say.

"For what?"

"Vermin. They've been laying eggs in her for days."

Rauha is slumped over, lying on her side. Milo makes an effort to examine her. He moves Rauha, tries to look under her for possible signs of violence. Water blisters burst and run. Rauha's skin is stuck to the sauna's wooden seat, slips through his fingers and comes off. Maggots wriggle out of her ass and drop squirming onto the bench.

I watch him try to be tough. He shudders but keeps going. He moves her head. Scalp slides off her skull. He jerks his hands away in disgust. I suppose because he can't think of anything else to investigate, he uses a tongue depressor to look in her mouth for an obstruction of her airway, a sign of intentional suffocation. When he opens it, little newborn wasps fly out from between her teeth into his face. He loses it, starts to flail and bat at them.

"Warned you," I say.

He glances at me and turns away fast. If we stay here in the sauna with the body, he might break down. I spare him the humiliation. "Let's do the legwork," I say.

We search Rauha's house for medicines, prescriptions, hospital documents, anything that might clue us in as to why she died. Nothing stands out. When we finish, I call Mononen, the company that transports bodies for us. The dispatcher says we have about forty-five minutes to wait.

We sit in the kitchen, at opposite sides of Rauha's table, bowls of stale cookies and rotten fruit in between us.

"Want a cigarette?" I ask.

"I don't smoke."

Milo stares at the bowl full of moldy oranges and black bananas.

"I take it this is your first bad one," I say.

He nods without looking up.

"Don't worry about it," I tell him. "It gets easier."

He makes eye contact. "Does it?"

I lie to make him feel better. It doesn't get easier, it's just that people get used to anything over time. "Yeah."

"We haven't examined her," he says.

"Sure we have, as best we're able. They'll have to shovel her out of there, and if she's a crime victim, the autopsy will turn it up."

I take a coffee cup from Rauha's cupboard and run a little water in it so I can use it for an ashtray, then sit back down and light a cigarette.

"The other homicide members don't like me," Milo says, "and now I investigate a routine death and act like a pussy."

I dislike the sharing of emotion from strangers. It's a sign of weakness and makes me uncomfortable. But he needs to talk and I don't think we'll be strangers for long, so I give him what he needs and let him open up. "You just got your homicide cherry busted," I say. "Don't be so hard on yourself."

He only stares at the rotten fruit again, so I prod him. "What makes you think the team dislikes you?"

He sits back in his chair, taps out a cigarette from the pack I set on the table and lights it.

"I thought you don't smoke," I say.

"I quit. I guess I just un-quit." He takes a couple drags, and I see him hit by the rush of satisfaction that only un-quitting smok-

16

ing can give.

"They had a 'welcome to the new guy' party for me a couple days ago. Bowling and then drinking. They think I'm an oddball geek brainiac, not a detective."

I was on duty, couldn't attend the party. I know a little about Milo from the newspapers. He was promoted over others with long-standing careers marked by accomplishment, so it's easy to understand resentment toward him. Milo is smart, a member of Mensa. He got his job on the homicide unit because as a patrol officer, he solved one case of serial arson and two cases of serial rape. They weren't his investigations. He did it for fun, as a hobby, by triangulating the likely areas of residence of the criminals. Once within a third of a mile, once within two hundred yards, once to the exact building.

"What makes you say that?" I ask.

The dark circles under his eyes look like charcoal smudges. He smirks. "Because I'm a people person, and my extreme powers of empathy allow me to look into the hearts and minds of others." This makes me laugh, and he laughs a little, too. "Believe me," he says, "I could tell they don't like me."

"How did you solve those cases that got you promoted?" I ask.

17

"A couple psychologists-slash-criminal-profilers developed a computer triangulation program. Police departments are reticent to use it because it's expensive, and because a lot of cops are convinced that their brilliant crime-solving techniques, also known as hunches, are superior to scientific method."

"If it's so expensive, how did you get it, and how come I didn't hear how you did it?"

"I pirated the software, and since I stole it, I lied about it."

I laugh again. He's odd, but I have to admit, he's an entertaining little fucker. "You're one up on me," I say. "I didn't even get a 'welcome to the new guy' party."

"They don't like you either," he says.

"Is this more of your people-person intuition?"

"After they got drunk, they bitched about you. The team doesn't trust you because you got a job in an elite unit for political reasons. That's not supposed to happen. You shot one man and have been shot twice yourself. That speaks of carelessness. You got medals for both those fuckups. That pisses them off. As an inspector, your pay grade is higher than the rest of us detective-sergeants. You make more money than we do. That pisses them off even more. They don't want to work with you. I remember hearing the phrase 'dangerous Lapland redneck reindeer-fucker.' "

I thought they were just standoffish because I'm new and haven't proven myself yet, that it will pass when I do prove myself. Maybe I was wrong.

"Actually," Milo says, "Saska Lindgren said some good things about you. He told the others he thought they should give you a chance."

Saska is half Gypsy. An outsider by race. It stands to reason he would be more receptive to someone like me. According to many, including my boss, he's one of Finland's best homicide cops. He's served as a UN peacekeeper in Palestine, worked for the ICTY — the International Criminal Tribunal for the Former Yugoslavia — investigating war crimes, executions and mass graves in Bosnia, and identified bodies in Thailand after the tsunami of 2004 that devastated the region. The numerous certificates of achievement lining the walls of his office attest to the many educational police conferences he's attended worldwide. He's also one of Finland's leading experts in bloodstain-pattern analysis. Additionally, he's involved in many works that benefit the community. He's such a do-gooder that, up to now, I found him annoying. Maybe I'll try to readjust my opinion.

"Since we're the black sheep," Milo says, "by default, we may find ourselves working together a lot."

The guys from Mononen show up for Rauha Anttila's body. We watch them scrape up her corpse — then we move on.

# 3

We drive back to the Pasila station through a torrent of snow, get there at eleven thirty p.m.

Milo and I walk down the long corridor. I open the door to my office. The national chief of police, Jyri Ivalo, is sitting at my desk, in my chair. Milo gives me a look of quizzical respect and meanders down the hall toward his own office.

Jyri and I have spoken on the phone several times, but I haven't seen him in person since 1996, when he decorated and promoted me for bravery after I was shot in the line of duty.

I was a beat cop in Helsinki and answered an armed robbery call at Tillander, the most expensive jewelry store in the city, on Aleksanterinkatu, in the heart of the downtown shopping district, in the middle of June. My partner and I arrived as two thieves exited the store carrying backpacks weighted down with jewelry. They pulled guns. One of them fired a shot at us, then they separated and ran. I chased the shooter down a street crowded with shoppers and tourists. The thief stopped, turned and fired. My pistol was in my hand, but he surprised me. I was running when the bullet hit me and blew out my left knee, which I had already wrecked playing hockey in high school. I fell hard to the pavement. The thief decided to kill me, but I got a shot off first and the bullet hit him in the side. He went down, but raised his pistol to fire again. I told him to lower his arm. He didn't. I blew his head off.

Jyri looks snazzy in a tuxedo, holds an open flask in his hand. He's mid-fiftyish and handsome, maybe a bit drunk. Judging by the scent, he's sipping cognac. "Inspector Vaara," he says. "Please come in."

"How kind of you," I say and enter.

"How's your lovely American wife?" he asks. "I understand she's pregnant."

I know Jyri well enough to doubt he gives a damn, and I don't want his false pleasantries. "Kate is fine. What brings you here?"

"We have business." He looks around. "Your office furnishings are nonstandard. I'm not sure they comply with regulations. What did Arto say about it?"

He means my boss, Arto Tikkanen. The atmosphere of standard-issue office junk suffocates me. I decorated with my own stuff, most of it from my office in Kittilä, up in Lapland, from when I headed the police department there. A polished oak desk. A Persian rug. A reproduction of the painting *December Day,* by the nineteenth-century Finnish artist Albert Edelfelt. A photo I took myself, of an *ahma,* an Arctic wolverine facing extinction, on the back of a reindeer, trying to get at its throat.

"I didn't ask Arto," I say, "so he didn't have a chance to say no."

Jyri doesn't give a damn about office furniture. He's just playing big dog/little dog, establishing his authority. He lets it go. "Go easy on Arto," he says. "You and he share the same rank. Technically, that's not supposed to happen. He may find it disconcerting."

"Arto is a good guy. I don't think my position here is a problem for him." I'm less than certain about that.

He takes a sip from his flask. "I promised you this job in homicide. How's it treating you?"

His tone implies I should thank him. He promised me this job a year ago, so Kate and I moved to Helsinki last March, and I expected to start in homicide right away. He stuck me in personnel and I pushed papers for all that time because, he said, I needed to wait until a position opened up. That was a lie. The Helsinki homicide team — *murharyhmä* — was undermanned, they could have used me. "You fucked me on that deal," I say. "You made me sit on my ass for eleven months."

"I had reasons, some of them for your benefit. That's an ugly scar on your jaw, by the way. Why didn't you get it fixed?"

My sergeant in Kittilä accidentally shot me before blowing his own brains out. I was trying to talk him down. When his pistol went off, the bullet passed through my open mouth, took out two back teeth, and went out through my right cheek. Bad luck. The exit wound left a ragged, puckered scar. "Like you," I say, "I had my reasons."

"Probably good for business. I bet it intimidates the hell out of bad guys."

I sit down in the chair for visitors beside my desk and say nothing.

"What you went through was traumatizing," he says. "I wanted you to have a chance to decompress, and I thought a healthy dose of therapy would be good for you before beginning a new and stressful position."

24

He pulls out a cigarette. I take an ashtray from a desk drawer. We both light up. Smoking is forbidden in the station. Except for the prisoners. They can smoke in their cells.

"In the future," I say, "trust me to look after my own emotional well-being."

"I had the good of the team to consider, and that's a little more important to me than hurting your feelings. Helsinki homicide employs some of the most efficient police in the world. Maybe as a group, the world's best. A murder hasn't gone unsolved in Helsinki since 1993. A perfect track record for going on two decades. That's a lot of pressure. Nobody in the unit wants that perfect track record ruined, and I wasn't about to let you come in here and fuck it up because you're fucked up. And besides, Helsinki's *murharyhmä* is my pride and joy."

Jyri has a way of getting under my skin. I change the subject. "What's with the tux?"

He leans back in the chair and props patent-leather oxfords up on my desk. He must know it pisses me off. Big dog/little dog again. "I attended a black-tie affair," he says. "The interior minister was there. He asked me to come here this evening and have a chat with you."

I assume this has something to do with

the way the Finnish police marketed me to the public as a hero cop after the Sufia Elmi case. "I didn't know the higher echelons have an interest in me."

"They don't. You came to their attention because of your grandfather."

Now I'm baffled. "Nice intro. Why don't you tell me about it after you take your feet off my desk."

He smiles at me and does it. "Bear with me. It's a bit of a long story. You know much about Finnish-German relations in the Second World War?" Jyri asks.

"I read history books," I say.

"Until a short time ago, this wasn't in any history books. In September 2008, a historian named Pasi Tervomaa published his Ph.D. dissertation, 'Einsatzkommando Finnland and Stalag 309: Secret Finnish and German Security Police Collusion in the Second World War.'

"He claims that in 1941, our security police, Valpo, and their Gestapo set up a special unit, Einsatzkommando Finnland, to destroy ideological and racial enemies on the far north of the German Eastern Front."

"So what? Finns volunteering to fight for Germany on the Eastern Front is well-documented. The SS Freewill Nordic Battalion. SS Viking. Others. It made sense.

For Finland and Germany, Soviet Russia was a common enemy. And it wasn't just Finland. The SS took in soldiers from all over the Nordic area."

"This is different," Jyri says. "Germany opened a prisoner-of-war camp — Stalag 309 — in Salla. It's in Russia now, but at the time it was part of northern Finland. Tervomaa claims Valpo and Einsatzkommando Finnland collaborated in the liquidation of Communists and Jews. Lined them up and shot them and buried them in mass graves. If his accusations are true, Finnish actions constitute war crimes."

"What does this have to do with my grandfather?"

"Apparently, your mother's father worked in Stalag 309."

"How would you know if a guy who worked in a stalag was my grandfather?"

Jyri sighs. "Me. The interior minister. We're plugged into the intelligence community. We learn things. We know things."

"Even if he was, again, so what? He's dead."

"As are all the other Finns who worked in it, except for one. Arvid Lahtinen, age ninety. Eyewitness testimony states that he, among other Finns, personally took part in executions. The Simon Wiesenthal Center

27

sent a formal request that Finland investigate the matter, which we haven't done to their satisfaction, and now Germany has requested extradition. They want to charge Lahtinen with accessory to murder."

"How the fuck can Germany charge him with anything? The claim is that he worked for them."

"Ah. But you see, therein lies the rub. Germany granted general amnesty for war crimes to its own citizens in 1969, so it has to expiate its sins by punishing others. They recently filed similar charges against another old man, accused him of being a guard at Sobibor and involved in the killing of twenty-nine thousand Jews. They extradited him from the U.S."

"How can the world not have realized that Finland had a stalag on its soil until sixty-five years after the war ended?"

"Potential Finnish culpability has been largely ignored because of language lockout. We don't want to talk about it, and very few people in this world besides us can read our documentation. It seems someone at the Wiesenthal Center learned to read Finnish and noticed Tervomaa's book."

"I still don't see what this has to do with me."

"Finland and Germany have an extradition treaty. The Interior Ministry has to at least investigate the matter. The minister wants you to interview Arvid Lahtinen."

Now it all becomes clear. "Because if I find the old man took part in the Holocaust, it means my grandfather did, too. I'll give you credit, that's conniving."

"I liked it. Lahtinen is notoriously irascible and has a habit of telling people to fuck off. We need him to cooperate. You charm him, tell him your grandfather served with him, get him to talk to you. Either come back with proof that he's not guilty, or the two of you concoct a convincing enough lie to get the Germans off Finland's back."

"If he's guilty, why lie?"

"Arvid Lahtinen is a Finnish hero. Every December sixth, on Independence Day, he's invited to the gala at the Presidential Palace. The president shakes his hand and thanks him for his service to his country. Lahtinen was in the Winter War in 1939 and 1940. He took out six Soviet tanks, charged them and destroyed them with Molotov cocktails. He fought in almost minus-fifty-degree weather and personally shot and killed hundreds of Russians. He slaughtered Communists at the Battle of Raate Road and helped save this country. Finland needs its heroes. Pay the man a visit, and keep that in

29

mind while you interview him."

Jyri sucks down a last sip from his flask, stands up, takes a sheet of notepaper from his pocket and lays it on my desk. "Here's his contact information. I'll report to the interior minister that you promise full co-operation. Keep me informed. I'm going back to the party. Some grade-A pussy was there, and I'm dying to stick my dick in it. Welcome to *murharyhmä*."

He gives me a grin and a wink on his way out the door.

# 4

As if I don't have enough to think about, Jyri, never the bearer of glad tidings, has forced me to consider the possibility that my *ukki* — grandpa — was a mass murderer. I loved him dearly. Before he retired, he was a blacksmith. He gave me ice cream when we visited in the summers, and always let me sit on his lap. He used to put salt in his beer. He never mentioned the war. I remember somebody asking him about it once — I guess hoping Ukki would share some heroic tales — but Ukki kept mum.

I don't give a damn about political agendas, but Jyri did a good job of manipulating me. Desire for the truth about Ukki will force me to talk to Arvid Lahtinen.

No doubt there are corpses to be examined. I turned my phone off while talking to Jyri. I wander down the hall to Milo's office to see if the dispatcher has called, but can't stop thinking about Ukki. The throb of the migraine renews itself. I open Milo's door. He's got a look on his face like I caught him jerking off.

"You could knock," he says.

I have no idea why I just walked in on him. It's unlike me. "Sorry," I say. "My mind was somewhere else."

His service pistol, a 9mm Glock, is field-stripped, in pieces on his desk. Beside it are a Dremel tool and a box of ammo. A few loose semi-jacketed soft-point rounds are lined up in a row beside a little jar. A desk drawer is open. I get the impression he left it that way so if someone knocked, he could scoop the stuff into it and hide it quick.

Milo's scowl is justifiable. "Well, get your head out of your fucking ass," he says.

Milo's shirtsleeves are rolled up, and I see that despite his small stature, he's built out of ropey muscle.

"What are you working on?" I ask.

"None of your business."

Whatever he's doing must be at least against police procedure, maybe against the law. His discomfiture amuses me. I suppress a grin and wait for him to tell me. We stare at each other for a while.

"I'm trying to figure out if it's possible to install a three-round-burst selector switch into a Glock Model 19," he says.

"Why?"

"Because, as every soldier knows, three-round 9mm bursts take men down, single shots usually don't."

"Three-round bursts often kill, not part of our mandate."

He gets a cocky look on his face. "Show me where it says that in the police handbook."

There is no police handbook or detailed set of rules and codes. He's fucking with me. "Don't be a jackass," I say.

He says nothing.

"Well, can you?" I ask.

"Can I what?"

"Install the selector switch."

"Yes."

"If you shoot someone, they might examine your weapon. If they see the selector switch, you'll lose your job, maybe get prosecuted."

"The switch can be removed and the drill tap filled with a small screw, which no one will ever notice."

I can't hide my amusement any longer. I shake my head and laugh. "And what about the bullets?"

He grimaces. This must be even worse than modifying his weapon. "I'm drilling cavities in the lead tips and filling them with glycerin. When a bullet collides with flesh, it slows down. The liquid inside retains its inertia and releases excess energy by ripping through the front of the bullet. It leaves a jagged slug, and lead fragments continue to tear up tissue. It creates a larger wound than a normal round and causes severe hydrostatic shock."

I've heard of this somewhere before. It comes to me and I tease him. "In a thriller called *The Day of the Jackal,* an assassin fills his bullets with mercury. Why not do the same? That way, when you shoot crooks, you can poison them, too."

He doesn't see the humor. "Obviously because when they autopsied the body, I'd get caught."

This kid has a few screws loose. "Why not just shoot hollow-point rounds?" I ask.

"They expand on penetration but tend to remain intact. Glycerin is more effective."

"I see. Let me show you something. Give me a bullet."

He tosses one to me and I catch it. I take out a pocket knife, notch a cross in the soft lead tip and show it to him. "It's called cross-hatching," I say. "Some people call them dum-dum rounds. On impact, the bullet deforms and breaks into chunks along the cut lines. You get your big wound channels, multiple exit points, severe blood loss and trauma, and someone would have to look for it in order to detect it."

He looks both impressed and disappointed. "My way is more fun," he says, "but I have to admit, yours is more practical. Where did you learn it?"

"My grandpa showed it to me while he taught me to shoot."

My own words take me by surprise. My *ukki,* now an accused mass murderer, taught a child how to dum-dum bullets. I suppose a man from his generation — born just after the Finnish Civil War in 1918, and then later a combat veteran of the Second World War — must have thought the generation to come should be prepared for wars of its own.

"Your grandpa must have been a cool guy."

"Yeah, he was."

I fold up the knife and put it back in my pocket. I think about where I got it, and whatever amusement I feel at Milo's expense disappears. Valtteri's son used it to butcher Sufia Elmi. Valtteri said he hid the murder weapon by keeping it in his pocket, because no one would ever look for it there, and so he would have a constant reminder of his failures. After the inquest, I stole the knife from the evidence locker, and like Valtteri, I keep it in my pocket so I won't forget my own failures.

"Are you going to tell anyone about my hobbies?" Milo asks.

"You realize that, even if you remain a policeman until retirement age, the odds of you having to fire your pistol in the line of duty are about a thousand to one."

"You did," he says.

Point taken. "Just stop doing it," I say.

He nods.

With agile fingers, Milo reassembles the Glock in under a minute. He practices field-stripping it. "What did the head honcho want?" he asks.

"Too much," I say.

The visit from the chief intrigues him. I can see he wants to press the issue, but restrains himself.

"Any dead bodies to look at?" I ask.

"Yeah. Some."

Helsinki homicide is a body factory. I check out three to four corpses during a normal shift. Always understaffed, the three teams in *murharyhmä,* the homicide division, a total of around twenty-five detectives, look into about thirteen hundred deaths a year. Most of them, as homicide cops call them, are grandmas and grandpas, the natural deaths of the elderly. A fair share of the remaining deaths are accidental. About a dozen of those twelve hundred will be ruled homicides and investigated, down from about three dozen murders only a decade ago, due to improved on-site trauma care and response time. It's saved a lot of lives. Also, I figure because of the massive volume of death investigations, some of the more subtle premeditated murders go undetected.

We also look into an average of a hundred and twenty-five suicides each year. Helsinki has a higher rate than the rest of Finland, partly because of sexual minorities. They come from all over the country to the nation's largest city, seeking the acceptance and promise of happiness that they lacked in smaller communities. Since they have higher rates of depression and mental illness than the city's norm, and hence a greater propensity toward self-destruction, I presume many of them don't find what they're looking for. In the couple of weeks that I've been working in homicide, I've looked at twenty-seven dead bodies, but I've yet to investigate one as a possible murder.

Over the next hours, Milo and I examine an overdosed junkie, a middle-aged man who died of a heart attack while watching television, and a teenage girl who got drunk, passed out in the snow and froze to death. It's eight thirty a.m. We should have gotten off work a half hour ago. My phone rings. It's Arto, my boss. "I know your shifts are over," he says, "but we're shorthanded. I've got a murder for you if you want to take it."

This takes me aback. I didn't think he was prepared to trust either me or Milo with a murder and risk the precious *murharyhmä* winning streak and reputation, unless we stumbled upon one in a normal death investigation and he couldn't take it away from us.

"Do tell," I say.

"A woman was beaten to death in Töölö. The responding officers say it's bad."

I ask Milo. He's about to jump up and down from excitement. If I take it, it means I won't get a chance to sleep tonight, but solving a murder might go a long way toward quelling the misgivings the other homicide unit members have about me. What the hell. I probably wouldn't be able to sleep anyway.

"Yeah," I say, "we'll take it."

Arto gives me the address and says, "A forensics team is already on the way. Get over there now."

# 5

Milo and I take the car we signed out from the police garage earlier. The department is big on economy. We get a Ford Fiesta. Milo wants to drive, and given the icy road conditions, he does so faster than necessary. The murder scene is only a few minutes away. A time and temperature sign on the side of a building reads eight forty-four a.m. and minus twenty-four degrees. Snow cascades through the darkness.

Europe is experiencing its worst winter in thirty years. Even Helsinki, eminently well-prepared for cold-weather conditions, is in chaos. Hoarfrost coats everything. Constant plowing has created mountains of snow and buried cars. The central railway station is out of commission. Trains still running have to be frequently deiced, and it's wreaking havoc on their timetables. Water mains have burst and flooded the streets. The water has turned into vast sheets of ice and brought the tram lines to a standstill. Traffic accidents abound.

This is the antithesis of the normal Helsinki winters I experienced living here years ago. Usually, in January, the temperature hovers around zero. Helsinki is like that most of the winter, although sometimes the temperature dips down to as much as minus twenty or thirty. We get some snow and it melts. Snow melt snow melt snow melt. Makes it like walking around in icy gray mud for most of the winter. Still, at a certain point some snow piles up. Then the spring thaw exposes a winter's accumulation of dog shit, and the city is overwhelmed by the stench for a week or two. I missed Arctic winter during my seven years here, the meter or two of snow reflecting moon and starlight. The beauty of snow-laden forests. This year, we get to experience real winter in Helsinki, and it brings joy to my heart.

Töölö is a fashionable district. It's not tremendously expensive, but has a reputation for a better class of residents. We pull up behind a police van, next to a snowbank in front of a pretty yellow apartment building at the address Arto gave me. My phone rings. The forensics team's pathologist tells me their vehicle was involved in a minor collision with another car. One of the crime-scene technicians wasn't wearing a seat belt and his head hit the windshield. He needs stitches. They have to take him to the hospital, and we have to wait until he's patched up.

"Fuck that," I say.

"Excuse me?"

"The investigation starts now, without you."

"That's against procedure."

"Time is wasting. We're setting a new procedural precedent."

Pause. "Do you have the right gear to wear?"

"Yep."

"Okay, we'll be there as soon as we can."

Milo and I enter the building and take the elevator to the fourth floor. A uniformed officer stands in the hall. "You the detectives?" he asks.

"That's us," I say.

"Where are the crime-scene techs?"

"Late. They had a car wreck. Fill us in."

"This apartment belongs to Rein Saar, an Estonian citizen. He called in the murder himself. He claims an unknown assailant struck him from behind and knocked him unconscious. When he woke up, he was in his bed beside his lover, Iisa Filippov. She was beaten to death, and he was covered in

41

her blood."

"Where is he?"

"In the back of our van."

Something is amiss here. "Where's your partner?" I ask.

"He went to get us coffee."

So much for police procedure. "You left an injured suspect, alone and unsupervised, in the back of your vehicle?"

He reddens. I let it go.

"What's your impression of the situation?" I ask.

"Rein Saar has a bad cut on his head from a blunt instrument. It looks to me like a lovers' quarrel ended badly. She hit him with something, he killed her and hasn't been able to think of a better lie."

"Does he need stitches?"

"At least not immediately. The bleeding stopped. He might be concussed."

Milo and I don surgical gloves and paper suits, complete with head and foot coverings, to prevent our fingerprints, hair and clothing fibers from contaminating the crime scene, walk into the apartment and take a look around. The home is neat and clean, in large part decorated with inexpensive furniture from Ikea. The kitchen is off the living room.

I go back out into the hall and hand the

patrol officer the keys to the Ford Fiesta. "There are more gloves and paper suits in the trunk of our car. Get some for yourself and the suspect, put them on and sit in the kitchen. Just don't touch anything."

"That's not going by the book," he says.

I use Milo's line. "Show me where it says that in the police handbook."

The uniform doesn't know how to respond.

"It's fucking freezing outside," I say, "our suspect is injured, and I'll want to talk to him before he's processed and treated for his injuries. I would prefer he not be angry, miserable and traumatized while I do it."

The uniform shrugs. "It's your case." He goes downstairs to fetch Rein Saar from the van.

Milo and I examine the kitchen, to make sure the victim can sit in it without contaminating evidence when he comes back inside. I see Rein Saar in the hall while he and the uniform put on paper suits. He looks like he took a shower in blood.

Milo and I walk over to him. "I'm Inspector Vaara. This is Detective Sergeant Nieminen. Do you feel that you require immediate medical attention, or can you stay here for a while so I can talk to you?"

He nods. He can wait. I instruct him and

43

the uniform to sit at the kitchen table.

I turn to Milo. "Let's go look at Iisa Filippov."

"The bedroom is a fucking mess," the uniform says. "Have fun."

We go to the bedroom. The uniform wasn't exaggerating. Blood soaks the bed around the corpse. Fine mists of blood feather the walls and ceiling. Her murder speaks of both method and rage. The smell of fresh blood and scorched flesh, menthol cigarettes, as well as urine and feces, is strong.

We need duplicate documentation so there's no chance of evidence from our initial investigation being lost. I take a digital audio recorder and notepad out of my coat pocket. "Which one do you want?" I ask Milo.

"I'll write," he says.

I start recording. "The victim, identified as Iisa Filippov, is located in the bedroom of a man identified as Rein Saar. The bedroom itself is about a hundred and thirty square feet and unexceptional. It contains a standard queen-size bed in a corner, headboard and left side of the bed against walls. The victim's body lies on the right side of the bed. Other furnishings include a dresser, a single wooden chair, and a nightstand with a reading lamp and a woman's purse on it. There's one closet, not yet inspected. About halfway up, the closet door has an approx two-inch hole bored through it. The room shows no damage to indicate struggle."

I open her purse and rifle through it. "The purse contains a Finnish passport issued to Iisa Filippov. From the photo, I believe the victim is indeed Filippov. It also contains a wallet, makeup and related cosmetic accessories, a pack of Belmont cigarettes and orange Bic lighter, a cell phone and a compact Samsung camcorder." I unfold a sheet of paper. "And a copy of Rein Saar's work schedule."

I give Milo a moment to write and catch up, then continue.

"Filippov appears to be a woman approx age thirty, five foot five inches tall, athletic build, about a hundred and twenty-five pounds."

I'm careful about what I say, because the recording may be entered into evidence, but before being beaten to a pulp, she must have been damned good-looking. Tanned. Long black hair cut in bangs. One eye is burned through, I guess by a cigarette, but the other is open and also nearly black in color. Great figure, something like 36-23-36.

"She's nude and lying face-up on the bed.

Her feet are bound tight with several wraps of duct tape. Her hands are behind her back, underneath her. I kneel down and look. They're bound in the same manner. The remainder of the roll of tape is on the nightstand. Her mouth is stuffed with women's socks. Her clothes — jeans, sweater, panties and bra — are wadded up in a pile on the chair, but I don't see her socks there, so I think the ones in her mouth belong to her.

"Care to add anything?" I ask Milo.

He shakes his head. "Not yet."

Although this murder scene is gruesome, Milo doesn't seem fazed by it, shows no sign of coming unglued, like he did last night when we investigated Rauha Anttila's death.

"Filippov has been struck multiple times with a blunt instrument. Her forehead is split open. Her left arm is broken just above the elbow. Bone protrudes through the skin. Her chest, on the right side, is flattened, suggesting that multiple ribs are caved in. Nothing in the room seems heavy or hard enough to have inflicted this kind of damage."

Milo takes a look around. The place hasn't been dusted for fingerprints yet, so with one gloved finger, he opens the closet door. We look in. I see only men's clothing and shoes on the floor. A stool is inside, a closet seems a strange place for it. "Nothing here either," he says.

Then I notice equestrian clothing on the shelf overtop the clothes rack: shirts, breeches, a jacket and helmet. Interesting.

We go back to Iisa's body. "Filippov has in the neighborhood of fifty burn marks on her body. Most are located on her abdomen, her genital area, her nipples, her face, and one through her left eye. The diameter and circular shape of the burns indicate she was burned with lit cigarettes. The wounds could have been inflicted after death, but I think they were probably used as a method of meting out pain. She voided her bowels either while being murdered, from fear or pain or both, or maybe upon death. Feces and urine are on the sheets between her legs."

"It's enough to puke a dog off a gut wagon," Milo says.

I point at the audio recorder, press a warning finger to my lips and continue. "The blood pool pattern around the victim indicates that another body lay next to her while she bled. The outline of a head, arm and torso are clear. The resident of the apartment, Rein Saar, claims to have woken up next to the victim and found her dead.

This lends some credence to his story. Most unusual is that Iisa Filippov has been struck dozens, perhaps more than a hundred times, with a light instrument at high velocity. It's notable that her face around the lips was beaten with particular severity."

The tone of my description is neutral, but the scene reeks of torture, horror and agony. Iisa's face is nearly destroyed by cigarette burns, whipped to pieces, scored by marks and welts. Deep and wide-open wounds that ooze.

"She was struck on the same surface areas, mostly on the face and torso, multiple times. It appears that the first lash abraded flesh, and that subsequent strikes deepened the wounds. This resulted in significant blood spatter. The walls and ceiling are misted with patterns of thousands of blood droplets that I estimate are an average of two millimeters in size."

I hear the front door open, then voices. The forensics team is here.

Milo points. "Look at this little spot on the wall," Milo says. "Whatever the killer used to hit her smacked it and left a small tongue-shaped bloodstain. Given the clothes in his closet, I'd say Rein Saar beat her to death with a riding crop."

"A good guess," I say.

I go to the closet, get down on my knees and look at the floor. A bloody crop is propped up against the inside wall. I don't touch it, leave it in place for the forensics team to photograph it. "Found it."

Milo comes over and takes a look.

I speak into the tape recorder. "In the bedroom closet, we discovered the probable weapon used in the lashing attack. A riding crop, a little over three feet in length, with a leather tongue on the end. It appears to be made of fiberglass, has a leather-wrapped handle, and a loop on the end to secure grip."

We return to the bedside. Both of us stare down at her for a moment. Milo asks me, "What do you think was the cause of death?"

"She took a terrible beating, but there's no arterial spurting. I doubt if it was blood loss. She's got those socks stuffed in her mouth. I think he beat her with the horse whip until he got bored with it, then maybe just held her nose until she suffocated and died."

"I tend to agree," Milo says.

"Maybe we should call Saska Lindgren and have him come take a look," I say. "He's the bloodstain-pattern expert."

Milo shakes his head. "No fucking way."

"Why not?"

"This is my first big homicide case and I'm not sharing it with anybody."

I raise my eyebrows.

He flushes, embarrassed at his gaffe. "Except you, of course. Listen, I'm going to tell you something personal."

Not again. I wish he wouldn't. I wait.

"You've probably heard that I have a high IQ. People make a big deal about my being in Mensa."

"Yeah. So?"

"I have advanced development of spatial relations and mathematics. The forensics guys are going to come in here, make detailed measurements and photographs, then enter it all into a computer program that will more or less re-create the attack. I don't need the computer program. I can do it in my head."

I don't quite believe him. "Then do it."

Somebody knocks on the bedroom door frame. I look. A member of the forensics team says, "Sorry we're late. You guys want to let us in there?"

"Give us a couple more minutes," Milo says. "Can you loan me a viewing loupe magnifier and a measuring tape?"

She brings them.

Milo looks close up at blood droplets at

various points on the walls, measures distances. He stands on the chair and examines the ceiling. This feels silly, like I'm Dr. Watson to his Sherlock Holmes.

My phone rings. It's Kate. "Where are you?" she asks.

"At a murder scene."

"The weather is so bad, I was worried."

I made a mistake taking this case. I want to be at home with Kate right now and I could be. A fuckup. "I'm fine. I should have called, but I got caught up in this."

"John and Mary will be here this evening. How are you going to be able to spend time with them if you haven't slept?"

She sounds peeved, doesn't realize I seldom sleep. I haven't told her. While she sleeps, I lie in bed beside her and think. "I'll be fine. We'll have a nice evening, and I'll get home as soon as I can."

"Please try. I miss you."

I ring off. Milo is waiting, smiling and expectant. I guess I'm supposed to share his joy.

"Okay," he says. "I got it."

"I'm bursting with anticipation."

"Trajectories are three-dimensional and so have three angles of impact. I calculated gamma, the easiest angle, which is the angle of the blood path measured from the verti-

51

cal surface and extended angle. Then I calculated alpha, the angle of blood spatter moving out from the surface. Then finally beta, the angle of blood pivoting around the vertical. The three angles are connected through trigonomic equations that determine the major and minor axes and angle of impact."

I interrupt. "Please get to the point."

"The tangential flight path of blood droplets is determined with the angle of impact and the offset angle of the blood spatter. They converge at the intersection of two blood-spatter paths, and the stains come from opposite sides of the impact pattern. The area of convergence is formed by the intersection of stains from opposite sides of the impact pattern."

"Get to the point."

"I'm trying to. The area of origin is the area in three-dimensional space where the blood source was located at the time of the attack . . ."

The dark circles around his eyes seem to have taken on a dull shine. I've noticed this happens when he gets excited. "Milo, please. The goddamned fucking point."

He purses his lips, frustrated. I've ruined his fun. "The killer didn't beat her at random. He chose small points on her body, hit the target areas repeatedly to cause maximum pain and damage, resulting in the great number of blood-spatter patterns, then chose a new area of flesh to whip."

I sigh. "Thank you."

He's miffed. "And in case you didn't know, most of the blood spatter isn't the result of the riding crop striking her. When the whip recoils away from the body at the bottom of the striking arc but still at high velocity, that's when the blood really flies."

I did know, but I'm still not certain if I believe he can work it all out without a computer. I'll talk to Saska Lindgren after we get photos and data from forensics, and see if he confirms Milo's version of events.

"He hit her with the riding crop a hundred and twenty-six times," Milo says.

I'm curious about the extent of his capabilities. "What's your IQ?" I ask.

He's embarrassed, flushes again. "A hundred seventy-two."

"Let's go talk to Rein Saar," I say.

We turn the crime scene over to the forensics team. We didn't inspect the other side of Iisa Filippov's body, because the front of it hasn't been photographed yet. I ask them to let us have a look when they flip her over.

Rein Saar's elbows rest on the kitchen

table, his chin on his hands. I sit across from him, start the audio recorder and lay it between us. Milo remains standing. "Mr. Saar, how are you holding up?" I ask.

"My head hurts," he says. "You can call me Rein."

"All right, Rein. You can call me Inspector Vaara." He blinks, nonplussed by my cold manner, which was my intention. "Tell me what happened," I say.

I see a handsome man beneath his bloody face. Athletic medium build. Swarthy and dark-headed. On the tall side.

"Iisa agreed to meet me at seven thirty this morning. When I walked in, I was attacked from behind. I blacked out and don't know anything else. Somebody hit me on the head. When I woke up beside her, she was already dead."

"Where were you this morning, prior to coming home?"

"I spent the weekend in Estonia, in Tallinn, at my sister's wedding. I came home on a ferry with some friends and family. We partied the whole way, and kept the party going all night in Helsinki."

"So you haven't slept and you came home drunk."

He nods. "I'm still drunk. Thank God." He points at a cabinet. "There's a whiskey bottle in there. Can I have it?"

His hangover will kick in soon and it might make it harder to interview him. Besides, some truth serum might not hurt. I nod to Milo. He gives Saar the bottle and a glass. Saar pours a healthy drink and slurps. A pack of Marlboro Menthol Lights is on the table in front of him. He lights one. I note that there's a carton of them in the cabinet where Saar keeps his whiskey. The killer had to go through at least a few cigarettes to inflict that many burns. I get up and check the kitchen and bathroom trash cans. No cigarette butts. The killer took them with him.

I sit down again. "And the purpose of meeting Iisa Filippov was what?" I ask.

He lifts his face from his hands. He folds them in front of him on the table, looks into my eyes and sighs.

"You may think it's a stupid question," I say, "but all information pertinent to this case must be directly stated."

"We were meeting for the purpose of engaging in sex," he says.

The Finnish and Estonian languages are closely related. So much so that even if he spoke Estonian, I could understand some of what he said. His Finnish is good, but his Estonian accent makes him sound silly, like a child in the process of learning how to speak.

"Tell me about your relationship."

"I met Iisa about two years ago at the Equestrian Academy. I was her teacher. She is — was — married. We started an affair almost right away. You should be questioning her husband, not me. He's the only one who would want to do something like this."

"Trust me, I'll speak with him, but that's not your concern. Right now, I want to give you my undivided attention. You should know that it looks bad. She's dead, in your bed, and she was beaten with a riding crop I found in your closet."

According to the nonexistent police handbook, I shouldn't have related this nugget of information, but I wanted to see the look on his face when I said it.

He's on the verge of panic, starts to twitch. "With my riding crop?"

"Yep."

"Somebody broke in and attacked us both. I can't help it if the person used something that belonged to me."

"Who has keys to your apartment?" I ask.

"Just me and Iisa."

I tell Milo to check the front door for signs of forced entry. He leaves the room. We still haven't found the blunt instrument used in the murder. I stand up and look around the kitchen. It's immaculate. Saar is a good housekeeper. An iron skillet is on the stove. It's weighty, a good weapon of opportunity. I try to pick it up, it's stuck to the burner it rests on. I tug, it comes free. I feel its heft, then turn it over and look at the bottom. It's smeared with blood that has hair stuck in it. I show it to Saar. "Looks like this is what you and Iisa got whacked with."

Milo comes back in. "No forced entry," he says.

I show the pan to Milo and sit down with Saar again. "Your story doesn't hold water. It looks to me like you two fought, she hit you on the head with a frying pan, then you lost it and killed her — with gusto," I add.

He shakes his head hard, his eyes turn wild. "That's not what happened. Iisa and I got along great. We never fought. I had no reason to hurt her."

"A married woman and her riding instructor. This reads like a romance novel. I can picture about fifty scenarios that would cause you to fight, maybe even get angry enough to murder her. Make me believe you."

"We had no differences. Our relationship was open and simple. We met a couple times a week and had sex. And we weren't in love, we never used the word. It was just sex. We had fun together."

I admit, as bad as it looks for him, it's convincing, as explanations go. "Who was her husband?" I ask.

"Ivan Filippov. He's originally from Russian Karelia. He owns a construction business that specializes in asbestos removal and industrial waste disposal."

When the borders were redrawn at the end of the war, Russia annexed a part of Karelia that was previously Finnish territory. Stalag 309, where my grandpa supposedly collaborated with the Nazis and participated in Holocaust, is also in that region.

"Was Iisa born Finnish or Russian?" I ask.

"She was a Finn, from Helsinki. She took her husband's name when they got married."

"Did Filippov know about you and Iisa?"

"I didn't think so, until today. She said he didn't."

"If your version of events is true and Filippov is the killer, why are you alive? Why didn't he murder you along with Iisa? Killing you as well would have been more expedient."

He chugs whiskey, frightened. "Obviously, he wanted to frame me. If I go to jail for the murder, he gets off scot-free."

A member of the forensics team comes in. "We turned the body over. Want to take a look?"

I thank Saar for his cooperation and tell the uniforms to take him first to the Pasila station for processing, then to the hospital for examination.

Milo and I go back to the bedroom. A digital Nikon D200 and a Sony video camera are on tripods. Fingerprint dust covers surfaces. Scales and tape measures are scattered about. I check Iisa's phone and find a text message Saar sent her yesterday morning, asking her to meet him here at seven thirty a.m. this morning. Her sent messages confirm the tryst. I'll reserve judgment about Saar's guilt or innocence. So far, I've found no evidence that he's been less than forthright.

The victim is on her stomach. Her reverse shows no signs of violence. I ask Milo, "See anything noteworthy?"

He shakes his head. "No. We're done here."

"Then let's go talk to Ivan Filippov," I say.

## 6

A Lutheran pastor, Henri Oksanen, often accompanies police to give the bad news to family members of the departed. I give him a call, he agrees to join us. Milo and I pick him up. We start out at just after noon and drive through heavy snow to Filippov Construction, in an industrial park in the Helsinki suburb of Vantaa.

The business is in a large, corrugated-metal building. We walk in. Construction tools and materials line shelves and lie on the floor: everything from jackhammers to face masks and other protective clothing necessary for asbestos removal and industrial waste disposal. A gorgeous secretary greets us from behind a battered metal desk. She's a dead ringer for the 1950s soft-porn and pinup star Bettie Page. Tanned. Longish black hair cut in bangs. Black eyes. Curvy figure. Girl-next-door smile. A dark angel. She reminds me of someone else, too, but I can't put my finger on who it is. Sleep deprivation is screwing with my memory.

We ask to speak to Ivan Filippov. She buzzes an intercom and announces our arrival. He tells her to send us in.

The office is nothing fancy. Concrete floors. Basic white walls and filing cabinets. A computer sits on a worktable. Filippov sits behind it. He stands to greet us. He's maybe six-three, age fifty-something, high-cheekboned and clean-shaven. His suit, shoes and haircut are expensive. His attire doesn't mesh with the practical atmosphere of his business and speaks of vanity. "How can I help you?" he asks.

We introduce ourselves. Pastor Oksanen takes the lead. He practices this on a regular basis and is better at it than we are. "Mr. Filippov, perhaps you should sit down. We have sad news."

Filippov's expression turns quizzical and concerned. He regains his seat behind the desk, motions for us to sit. There are only two chairs on the other side of his desk. Pastor Oksanen gestures for Milo and me to take them.

"It's about Iisa, your wife," Oksanen says.

Two detectives and a pastor have come to bring bad news. Filippov must suspect the worst, but his voice is controlled. "What about Iisa?"

"I regret to inform you that she is no longer with us."

He cocks his head to the side. "Then, pray tell, who is she with? I'm not a child, spell it out."

"She has passed on. Her body was discovered earlier today."

Filippov makes eye contact with Oksanen. His face registers nothing. "How did she die?"

The pastor goes around the desk and places a comforting hand on his shoulder. "She was murdered. She's with God now."

Filippov ignores the hand. "I'm an atheist."

Odd first words to utter upon being informed that his wife was slain. He looks at Milo and me. "Who killed my wife?"

It's always difficult to inform someone about the murder of a family member, but because she was planning to commit adultery when she died, this is even harder than usual. "Brace yourself," I say. "This is unpleasant."

"You come in here and tell me that Iisa was murdered, then warn me about unpleasantness. Quit fucking around and get on with it."

His abrasiveness takes me aback. I give

him his way and tell it straight. "She was having a long-standing affair with her riding instructor, a man named Rein Saar. They planned a tryst. She was found dead in his bed, beaten with an iron skillet and a riding crop, and burned with cigarettes."

"Did this Rein Saar kill her?" His accent betrays his youth spent in Russian Karelia. It sounds like Donald Duck speaking Finnish.

"We don't know yet. Saar claims she had a key to the apartment and was waiting for him to arrive. He maintains that he came home, was struck from behind and rendered unconscious. When he came to, he was in bed beside her and she was already dead. He says he never saw the assailant."

Filippov has yet to demonstrate sorrow, only impatience. "Do you believe him?"

"Certain facts contradict his story, others support it."

Filippov leans back in his chair and folds his arms. "I want Iisa's killer found and punished."

"I realize this is a shock and painful for you. Are you able to answer a few questions?"

"Of course."

"Were you aware of your wife's affair?"

"No."

"It had been going on for two years. You had no clue?"

He shakes his head. "None."

"They met a couple times a week. You never inquired about her comings and goings?"

"Iisa maintained an active schedule. She participated in various organizations and had many hobbies, riding among them. She was — or at least I thought she was — a good and faithful wife. I had no reason to invade her privacy or interrogate her."

"Did she work?"

"She had no need. I earn a comfortable living."

Filippov is a cold fish, but businesslike and seems candid. "Forgive me," I say, "but I need to ask you about your whereabouts last night and today. Please understand that this is in no way an accusation, but a part of standard procedure."

He waves his hand, gestures for me to get on with it. I'm senior officer here, but Milo is a new detective and needs experience. I don't want to disregard him. Also, there's something to be said for the good cop/bad cop routine. I nod, signal for him to take over.

"Where were you last night?" Milo asks.

"At a party. In fact, the national chief of

police, Jyri Ivalo, was in attendance. He can serve as my alibi."

Filippov was drinking with Jyri while he and the interior minister discussed me, and here I sit. Interesting.

"And you left the party and arrived home when?" Milo asks.

"I left at around one and was home in bed asleep by two a.m."

"Were you drunk?"

"No. I'm not given to excess."

"Tell me about your morning," Milo says.

"It was like every other workday. I arrived here at nine and haven't left since."

"Not even for lunch?"

He takes a receipt from a file on the tabletop and hands it to Milo. "Lunch was delivered pizza."

Milo pauses, looks thoughtful. "What time did your secretary arrive?"

"Also at nine."

"Can you verify your times of arrival?"

Filippov sighs. "What sort of verification are you looking for?"

"Do you have a security camera and video record?"

Filippov offers a wry grin. "Detective, you're playing games. A camera is mounted over the entrance and you saw it when you came in. You doubtless also saw the video

65

recorder in the outer office." He pushes a button on his intercom. "Linda, would you please eject today's video surveillance tape and bring it in here."

We wait. Linda enters. My memory kicks in. She reminds me of Filippov's dead wife. She looks much as I picture Iisa Filippov did before the cigarette burns and riding crop disfigured her face. Ivan Filippov has precise taste in women. He asks her to give the tape to Milo. She hands it over and departs.

"Inspector Vaara was being euphemistic when he said your wife was beaten with a riding crop," Milo says. "It would be more accurate to say that first, the killer used her for a human ashtray, then whipped her, focusing on her face, until she was nearly unrecognizable. She was systematically tortured, and for the coup de grâce, we suspect smothered to death."

That was way too harsh. I feel an inward cringe, but Filippov doesn't flinch. "I see," he says.

The dark circles around Milo's eyes take on the dull gleam that says he's enjoying himself. "Who might have a reason to do such a thing to her?" Milo asks.

"No one," Filippov says. "Iisa was a gregarious and pleasant person. She enjoyed other people and they enjoyed her. I would say her priority in this world was simple. She liked to have fun."

Simple and fun. This fits in with Rein Saar's assessment of their relationship.

"I would consider a two-year sexual relationship with her riding instructor having fun at your expense," Milo says.

We have to ask questions, but we just informed Filippov of his wife's death. His detached demeanor makes me dislike him more with every passing moment, but still, Milo is pushing too hard. He doesn't relent.

"So you have no alibi to account for your whereabouts between the hours of one and nine this morning."

"No," Filippov says, "most people don't."

"When did you last see your wife?"

"Yesterday morning at about eight thirty, before I came to work."

Milo smiles and raises his eyebrows. "Iisa wasn't home when you got back from the party?"

"No."

"And you found nothing unusual about that?"

"I repeat. Iisa liked to have fun. And I might add that, unlike myself, she was somewhat given toward excess. So no, I found nothing unusual about it."

Milo and Filippov stare at each other, adversaries, for a long moment.

"I've heard about both of you," Filippov says, "and I'm honored to have two such distinguished detectives investigating my wife's death. Your reputations precede you." He looks at me. "You for your tenacity and bravery," and then at Milo, "and you for your intellectual investigative achievements."

He looks at me again. "In fact, your name was mentioned at the dinner party last night."

And then Arto hands me the high-profile murder of Filippov's wife, which I thought he would be reticent to do, only hours later. This strikes me as less than coincidental.

"No doubt my wife's murder will be swiftly solved," Filippov says. "I assume you want me to identify Iisa's body. Isn't that the procedure? I can do it this afternoon."

"That's not necessary," I say. "Your wife's identity has been established. However, I would like to come to your house and examine her belongings. Something among them might provide evidence of who killed Iisa and why."

"Absolutely not," he says. "I won't dishonor her memory by having her intimate possessions pawed at."

"I can get a subpoena if necessary."

"You can try. I'll have it quashed. That's within my power. Let's compromise. I'll go through Iisa's belongings. If I find something I believe helpful to you, I'll deliver it to you myself."

What an arrogant prick. "You're not a detective. You might overlook something crucial."

"You'll find that thoroughness is among my better attributes."

He smiles at me. Given the circumstances, it's disconcerting. "I read in the newspaper," he says, "that your wife is the general manager of Hotel Kämp. Their restaurant is my favorite."

This bewilders me. I say too much. "We just informed you that your wife was murdered, and you're thinking about food?"

"I mourn the loss of my wife, but we must all grieve in our own way. Mine is to carry on with life as usual."

I stand. Milo and the pastor follow my lead. I find Filippov repulsive, can't bring myself to offer my hand or parting condolences.

When we get outside, I ask Milo, "What do you think?"

"Motherfucker butchered his wife and framed her lover," he says, "and he's so goddamned haughty that he doesn't even try to hide it."

Pastor Oksanen pretends he hears nothing.

I'm less certain than Milo — being a bastard doesn't make him a murderer — but I'm inclined to agree. "If he framed Rein Saar," I say, "he did a good job. It'll be difficult to prove."

"I . . ." — he realizes his fuckup — "we will."

Likable as he is, in his own way, Milo has a fundamental character flaw that he'll have to pay for eventually. Arrogance.

On the drive back to Helsinki from Vantaa, Jyri Ivalo calls. "I understand you're investigating the murder of Iisa Filippov," he says.

"That's right."

"I further understand that she was found dead beside her lover, some Estonian fuck."

I haven't filed a report yet, so Filippov must have called Jyri as soon as we left and filled him in. "Also correct."

"Ivan Filippov is a good acquaintance of mine, and he's well connected in the business world. This sounds open-and-shut, but you're given to leaps of imagination. Close the case fast. And defer to Filippov whenever possible."

I say nothing.

"I've got a vicious hangover and I'm not in the mood to be nice. Let me make this clear. You solved the Sufia Elmi case, but it dragged on too long and turned into a fiasco. Not this time."

Fuck Jyri. "Filippov cites you as his alibi. Care to confirm it?"

"Confirmed. He left the party around one. I see no need to relate his whereabouts of last night to the press. I and some others would prefer to be distanced from the investigation. Somehow, the media would invent a conspiracy theory and create a scandal."

Yes, they would. "I don't intend to handle the media at all. I'll leave it to Arto and the police PR folks."

"Good thinking. Media relations isn't your strong suit. And the discussion we had last night about Arvid Lahtinen. You on that yet?"

"I've been working for twenty hours straight. Of course I'm not on it yet."

"You can sleep when you're dead. Get on it." He rings off.

I've always felt that Jyri is excellent at his job but a real fuckwad as a human being. Every interaction I have with him confirms it. I'll handle both the investigation and

Arvid as I see fit.

We drop Pastor Oksanen off at his house and drive back to the police garage. I tell Milo I want him to get some sleep, ask him to look at the tape Filippov gave him, check out evidence from forensics and write the initial report in the morning.

## 7

It's two thirty p.m. I don't have much time, but want to check on Kate. We thought her pregnancy was going well, but found out a couple weeks ago that she's suffering from hypertension and preeclampsia. Placental abruption is a danger, and with it, a risk of maternal mortality. I could lose not only another child but Kate along with her. It scares the shit out of me.

I find a parking space a couple blocks from our apartment on Vaasankatu and walk the rest of the distance home. The snow has stopped, the wind died down. The street is quiet. A white snowscape, lovely and hushed.

Vaasankatu, here in the district of Kallio, is nicknamed *Puukkobulevardi* — Hunting Knife Boulevard. Years ago, this was a dangerous place, and it still has a bad reputation, although largely undeserved these days. The area has its bars and drunks, some Thai massage parlors, but many of them were recently shut down. Prostitution in itself isn't a crime, but various moralistic lobbies raised a stink, so the police cited illegal residency by workers, pimping — which is a crime — whatever they could come up with, to get rid of the parlors and stop the debate. The street is fairly gentrified now, many residents are upscale professionals.

Kate had misgivings about moving to Kallio, but it's the only area in Helsinki that, to my mind, has a feeling of genuine community. And besides, even in this modest area, our nine-hundred-and-ninety-square-foot apartment, which I have to admit is gorgeous, cost us a cool three hundred and fifty thousand euros. A similar place in another part of town could run a million and a half. As general manager of Kämp, Helsinki's only five-star hotel, Kate earns good money, and for a cop, I make a fair wage as an inspector, but not enough for a seven-figure apartment. In the north, a million and a half would buy us a palace. Helsinki is one of the most expensive cities on the planet.

I find Kate lying on the couch, reading a book about child-rearing. I give her a kiss hello. She sits up, rubs her back. At this late stage of her pregnancy, she's having a hard time staying comfortable. "I can't wait to get this child out of me," she says.

I sit beside her, put an arm around her. She looks at me, scrutinizing. "I don't know how you can function without sleep."

It's not like I have a choice. "It doesn't bother me much."

"How is your headache?" she asks.

"It's been worse."

"Your eyes wander when it's bad," she says, "and they're doing it now. You need to go to the doctor again."

"There's no point. The stuff she gave me makes me too dopey. I won't take it."

"Then go see your brother. He'll help you."

Jari is a neurologist here in Helsinki. I haven't seen him since we moved. I guess it's about time to pay him a visit, and anyway, Kate isn't going to let me wriggle out of it. I hate doctors. They'll put me through a series of tests. I don't want to take them, just to find out they don't know what's wrong with me. "I'll call Jari," I say. "Have you given any more thought to staying home with the baby?"

She snuggles up close, I think trying to soften her answer. "I've been on maternity leave for two weeks already, and I just don't think it's for me. And besides, I don't think it's fair to my employer."

This is a source of contention between us. "Kate, I'm sorry to put it this way, but fuck your employer. Nine months of leave after the baby is born is your right as a mother in Finland."

"When Hotel Kämp hired me, they entrusted me with a great deal of responsibility. If I stay home for nine months, I'll feel like I'm betraying a trust."

It's true that employers get pissed off when they lose workers to pregnancy, and sometimes don't want to give young women jobs, because they're considered investment risks. Pregnant women receive full salaries from employers for the first three months of leave.

"You should realize," I say, "that in this country, a lot of people feel that not spending that time at home is betraying a child's trust."

I could dig deeper, explain the unwritten societal rules about what good mothers are expected to do. Good mothers breast-feed, or their competency as mothers will be called into question. Good mothers stay at home for two or three years, that time subsidized by the government. If they don't do these things, whispers and innuendo about whether they deserve the gift of a child will come from other mothers, whose lives revolve around living up to these conventions. It's ridiculous and unfair.

She's getting pissed off. "You want me to sit at home because of what people might think? Kari, I thought you had more substance than that."

"I don't care what people think, but it pays to be aware of cultural perceptions. They also affect your career. I want you to stay home with our daughter because I believe it's the best thing for her."

"So now I'm a bad mother."

I came home to spend some time with Kate and I'm wrecking it. Sometimes it's hard to think, because of the headache, and it causes me to make blunders. I've hurt her feelings. It shows on her face. "I didn't mean that the way it sounded. You're going to be a wonderful mother."

She goes quiet for a moment. I wonder if she's thinking about our dead twins right now. "Maybe you should take fatherhood leave and stay home with the baby yourself. You have all of the same so-called rights as me. And I don't think you like your job anyway."

She's said this before, and she's right, I'm less than enamored with my job at the moment. The truth is that I would like to stay home with our child, but my migraines have gotten so bad that I'm afraid I'm not capable of being her full-time caregiver. I don't want Kate to know this. It would only worry her. I change the subject. "I'm looking forward to meeting your brother and sister tonight."

This is a half-truth. I don't want to be saddled with them for weeks. I'd like to meet them, but under different circumstances. Maybe for dinner and a chat, and then we go our separate ways. But Kate needs this. She and her siblings had it rough growing up. It made them closer than most brothers and sisters, and they've been apart for too long.

What began for Kate as a normal middle-class upbringing in Aspen, Colorado, came to a halt in 1993, when she was thirteen, when her mother, Diane, was diagnosed with breast cancer. At the time, her brother, John, was seven. Her sister, Mary, was eight. Her father, Randy, was unable to cope. Faced with the death of his wife, he went into a depression that left him increasingly incapable of functioning as a husband and father. As Kate's mother grew sicker from chemo and radiation treatments, Kate was forced to become de facto head of the household and to grow up almost overnight.

Kate cared for her mother while she watched her die slow. She spoon-fed her, changed her sheets, cleaned up her vomit — and at the same time cared for her two younger siblings. When Diane finally died, her death broke Randy and he became an alcoholic. He managed to hold down his job, but was blitzed every minute he wasn't working. He paid the rent and basic bills, then spent most of the remainder of his paycheck in bars. He gave the pittance left over to Kate, to clothe and feed herself, John and Mary.

Randy was a mechanic, maintained the lifts at a ski resort, and he got Kate free skiing lessons and lift passes. She has never said it, but I think seeing her mother's helplessness while she battled cancer turned Kate into a control freak. She excelled at everything, got perfect grades at school. She let go of her pent-up anger and frustration on the slopes and became a fantastic downhill skier.

By age fifteen, Kate was winning all of the junior events she entered. She began competing as an adult at age sixteen. She kept winning. She made up her mind that she would compete in the Olympics. When she was seventeen, she was in a race and going nearly a hundred miles an hour. She took a fall, broke her hip, and spent her eighteenth birthday in traction. End of dream. She still walks with a limp because of it.

Kate told me that during her weeks in the hospital, she took stock of her life. She had no close friends — had never had a boyfriend — had devoted her teenage years to raising John and Mary, to her studies and to skiing. It had never entered her mind that she might not become a world-class ski champion. For her, falling had been a mistake, a kind of failure. Kate didn't allow herself failure. She swore to herself that she would rebuild her life and never fail again.

When Kate completed high school, her perfect grades, high scores on aptitude tests and dismal financial situation guaranteed her college scholarships. She first studied at the Aspen community college extension of Colorado Mountain College, where she earned an associate's degree in ski-area operations. Then she worked at a ski resort for two years, where she gained lower-level management experience.

By that time, in 2002, Kate was twenty-two, Mary seventeen and John sixteen. Kate wanted to continue her education. Randy was still a useless drunk, but Mary agreed to look after John until he graduated from high school. Kate got a scholarship from Princeton University. Randy died of liver failure about the time she completed her bachelor's degree in economics. I think his death was a relief to Kate in a way, and that relief brought her guilt.

When Randy died, Kate had been in a steady relationship for two years and engaged for six months. She broke it off. She said something about her father's death made her unable to commit. Kate graduated from Princeton with her master's in economics. She returned to Aspen, this time as upper management at a ski resort, and after a year and a half was running the place. Profits doubled.

In spring 2007, Levi Center, Finland's largest ski resort, located a hundred miles inside the Arctic Circle, asked Kate to interview for the position of general manager. John had moved to New York to attend New York University. Mary had dropped out of college to marry a doctor and settled in Elkins, West Virginia. Kate had no reason to stay in Aspen and decided it was time for a change.

In June of 2007, Kate traveled to Finland. The owners wanted Kate's help in expanding the resort into a massive operation. The Arctic seemed exotic. They offered her a six-figure income. She took the job. She met me at a midsummer barbecue party. We were married nine months later. She got pregnant a few months after that, discovered she was carrying twins, but miscarried. I believe, for Kate, losing the twins was another kind of failure, something unacceptable to her. She wanted a clean start, to put all the sorrow and misery behind us, so we moved here to Helsinki.

But I had left Helsinki years ago for a reason. I was never happy when I lived here as a younger man. Helsinki reminds me of my failed first marriage and of a man I killed in the line of duty. Helsinki isn't a clean start for me. Just old bad blood.

I don't like big-city life. I don't like the memories. I don't like the so-called international atmosphere. *Kaamos,* the dark time, is short-lived. The light coming and going so fast depresses me. I miss the long Arctic darkness. Already now, in January, we have daylight from around nine a.m. until four p.m. This winter is nice, but most years it's not cold enough in Helsinki, the snow doesn't stick. Makes it like sloshing around in a bucket of shit all winter. I'm homesick for the North.

Kate's eyes meet mine for a moment. She understands I'm trying to stop the argument and lets me. "I'm a little nervous about seeing them because it's been so long," she says. "The last time I saw John was in 2006. The last time I saw Mary was 2005. They're grown up now, and I wonder how they've changed. Still, who would have thought that three poor kids like us would have done so well. I'm running the best hotel in the city and John is becoming a university history teacher. Mary is a doctor's wife. I more or less raised them. It makes me proud."

"You have a right to be proud," I say, "and I'm proud of you." I check the time, it's a little after three. My therapy session begins at four. I've been attending counseling for eight months now, and dread it more and more as time goes by.

I hesitate. Apologies are difficult for me. "Kate, I meant what I said. You're going to be a great mother. I was out of line and didn't mean to imply otherwise. It just came out wrong."

She squeezes my hand. "I know."

# 8

I limp through the snow toward my Saab. It's parked near the taxi stand on Helsinginkatu. The street is nicknamed Raate Road, after the scene of a decisive and bloody battle in the Winter War, for the same reason that Vaasankatu is called Hunting Knife Boulevard. It has a bad reputation from bygone days, but not much real wickedness goes on here anymore. It's true that Kallio has its fair share of the permanently unemployed that live on welfare and spend their days in *räkälät* — snot bars, as they're called — drinking cheap beer, but most towns in Finland have their welfare drunks and dives for them to booze in.

I hear shouting down the street. As I close in, I see a man in front of Ebeneser School, a special-needs place for kids with dysphasia. The students there have speech disorders of one kind or another, difficulties with language comprehension or production, most often the result of varying degrees of brain damage. Some can speak but not write, others write but don't speak. Very occasionally, a child will be able to sing but not speak.

The school is a beautiful off-peach Art Nouveau building constructed around the turn of the twentieth century, fronted by a chain-link fence interlaced with a growth of decades-old ivy, now wreathed in frost. I get closer and see that the screaming comes from a young man waving a half-empty bottle of Finlandia vodka. His rant is biblical and apocryphal in nature, and he has a bad speech impediment.

"Thpawns of Thatan, damned at biddth, you have fawen fwom da Towew of Babel. Bettew dat you had nevew been bodn!"

I get up close to him and look through the fence. Four little bundled-up children stand on the other side of it, terror-stricken but fascinated. I see no supervising adult. It pisses me off. "Listen kids," I say to them, "I'm a policeman. Would you please go inside."

The guy bellows an incoherent howl and screams again. "Bettew dat you had nevew been bodn!"

They don't move. I make shooing motions with my hands. "Run along now," I say.

They scramble toward the front door. The guy isn't making any noise now, but he flails his arms, makes frantic gestures, waves the bottle and claws at his face.

"What's your name?" I ask.

"My name is Weejun. Away fwom me, thpawn of hell."

"Well, Mr. Legion, why were you scaring those kids?"

He gulps a drink from the bottle, wraps his arms around himself, rolls his head back and forth and shakes. He's coming apart at the seams. He shrieks like a hurt animal, then manages a shrill, understandable utterance. "To save deir souws! Dey awe damned unwess I thave dem!"

I'm tempted to ask him why, if his name is Legion, aka Satan, he wants to save the children rather than see them spend eternity in hell. Then I decide I'm not interested in the logic of the insane. My head throbs — hate boils up in me.

I grab Legion by the neck, smack his face against the snow-covered fence. It gives me a modicum of satisfaction, so I do it again. He's a skinny little bastard, maybe a hundred and thirty-five pounds. I've been working out hard for most of the past year, since we moved to Helsinki. It takes my mind off the headaches. I bench-press more than twice his weight. He starts to cry, his knees start to give way. I grab him by the neck with one hand, hold him up by his head so that his feet barely graze the ground and look close at him. He's in his mid-twenties and has a bad, close-cropped haircut that looks like a home job. His longish beard is unkempt. His coat, pants and shoes are neat and clean though. I'm guessing his parents take care of him.

His left eyebrow is cut, blood runs into his eye. His nose bleeds. My satisfaction from banging his face off the fence dissipates. He's crazy as a shithouse rat. I ask myself what to do with him. A final lesson and punishment for his treatment of defenseless children seems appropriate. "You like vodka," I say. "Enjoy yourself to the max."

He doesn't get it. His eyes radiate alarm and bewilderment.

"Bottle to lips, drink until empty," I say.

He's done screaming now. Frightening learning-disabled children comes easier to him than dealing with able-bodied adults. He gets the point. "I don't want to. Don't make me. It'th too much."

I pull out an old Finnish proverb that teaches the virtue of patience. *Kärsi kärsi, kirkkaamman kruunun saat*" — "Suffering

suffering, makes the crown glow brighter."

He shakes his head no.

I let go of his neck. "Did I offer you a fucking choice?"

He understands now. Drink, or I'll keep beating him. He's in a bad situation. The booze is his best chance for escape. He lifts the bottle, sucks it down as fast as he can. I wait thirty seconds. Alcohol poisoning starts to hit. The bottle drops from his hand and shatters on the icy sidewalk. Another ninety seconds pass. He drops to his knees and looks at me with uncertain eyes. Another minute goes by, he falls backward. Head hits frozen pavement. Scalp splits. Blood runs in a thin trickle onto the ice.

I reach under him, into his back pocket, and find his wallet. His ID reads Vesa Korhonen, age twenty-three. I put the ID card back into his wallet and throw it onto his chest, then call for a police van to cart him off to the drunk tank. I leave him there on the sidewalk, don't wait for them to arrive. Good afternoon and good night, Vesa Korhonen, alias Legion.

# 9

I'm seeing a psychiatrist named Torsten Holmqvist. I didn't choose him. The police department assigned me to him. His office is in his home, in the fashionable district of Eira, near embassy row. The house, which he told me he inherited, looks out over the sea and must be worth at least a couple million euros. We sit in big leather chairs, on opposite sides of a glass coffee table. I've eschewed his couch.

Torsten is a wealthy Swedish-speaking Finn, and certain mannerisms betray his roots. A casual yet confident way of sitting, an affable comportment and easy laugh that I think feigned. A yellow pullover sweater is draped over his shoulders and loosely knotted in front of his pink button-down shirt. He's in his fifties, his thick hair combed up and back and hair-sprayed, politician-style, a dignified gray at the temples. He smokes a briar pipe. His aromatic tobacco is apple-scented.

His manner and appearance irritate me, or maybe he's good at his job and knows how to push my buttons, and that's why he puts me off. Either way, I've been in therapy before, and I didn't like it then either, but it helped me, so I try and work with him. Besides, I promised Kate I would do this. I'm further agitated because I have a murder to investigate, need to speak to a Finnish hero — now an accused war criminal — and I can't do either of those things while I'm sitting here.

"So," Torsten says, "you assaulted a mentally ill person. Do you consider that a reasonable and responsible action?"

"He terrified defenseless children — disabled children — it seems entirely reasonable and responsible."

"You beat him up and poisoned him."

"He'll get over it."

"As a police officer, you know that you can't rationally defend appointing yourself judge and jury, no matter how reprehensible you found his actions."

"Listen," I say. "If it was a situation involving adults, I would agree with you. But no fucking way I'm letting him get away with ranting a frightening, insane tirade at kids. They might be traumatized. Mentally ill or not, he needed to understand that his actions have consequences."

"You don't seem to have considered the possibility that the young man may have screamed at the children in order to seek punishment."

He's right. I hadn't considered it. "I did nothing that, under the circumstances, most men wouldn't have done."

"I wouldn't have," he says. "Do you think that reflects on my manhood?"

I sigh. I have no interest in his holier-than-thou attitude.

Torsten lets the question about his manhood go and offers me coffee, makes himself a cup of herbal mint tea. He lights his pipe. I light a Marlboro Red. "Would you consider your protective feelings toward children excessive?" he asks.

"Is such a thing possible?" He hates it when I answer his questions with questions.

"Your answer is an answer in itself. Could we discuss why that might be?"

I look out his bay window at the sea. The harbor isn't quite frozen solid yet. Chunks of ice float in it. Beyond them, I watch the whitecaps break for a moment. "If you like."

"Your sister, Suvi, froze and drowned when you were skating on a lake together and the ice broke under her. Your father had placed her under your protection. Do you still think of it often?"

"Daily."

"Yet, your father was on the scene. He was drunk and failed to come to her aid. He was the adult, the caregiver. The blame resides with him."

I light another cigarette. "I blame him, too."

"He let your sister die and he beat you as a child. You've never expressed hatred for him. Not even anger."

"I used to be angry," I say, "but at a certain point, I grew up and recognized my parents' humanity. My father is emotionally damaged. His parents beat him far worse than he ever did me."

"How do you know? Has he told you?"

Dad's parents were the antithesis of Mom's folks — Ukki and Mummo — whom I loved so much. "He didn't have to, some things you don't have to be told. When we visited them, which wasn't often, his father — my grandfather — hurt me, too. The atmosphere in the house was morbid. My father's parents were Lutheran religious fanatics. Laughter was forbidden, and they kicked — literally — us children out of the house for laughing. I can only imagine what they did to him."

He makes some notes on a pad. "Perhaps you're making excuses for him."

I look out at the sea again. It comforts me. I say nothing.

"How is your wife's pregnancy going?" he asks.

I'm glad to change the subject. "She has preeclampsia, but she has no headaches, visual disturbances or epigastric pain — symptoms that suggest imminent danger — so given the circumstances, it's going okay."

"Could we discuss her miscarriage? You've been reticent to do so in the past."

No, we can't. I thought I had made that clear to him. "I thought we were here to talk about a duty-related incident."

"I'm sorry, Kari, but indirectly, we are."

"How so?"

"You're here because of severe trauma. You pursued the Sufia Elmi investigation — forgive me for imposing my opinion — and it was beyond your emotional ability. You told me that you believe your errors in judgment led to deaths that could have been prevented."

He's right. It was beyond my emotional ability. The case taught me several things about myself and life that I don't like. I found out I'm obsessive and reckless. I discovered that justice doesn't exist. I solved the crime, but failed all the people involved, including myself. I thought I had escaped my past, but found out that a part of me remained a beaten child who believed he killed his sister.

I picture my ex-wife's little scorched body. Hairless. Faceless. "Facts are facts," I say. "I fucked up. We've covered this ground before."

"Yes, but we haven't covered other related ground. Your wife begged you to recuse yourself from the investigation, but you refused. I'd like you to consider the possibility that you blame yourself for her miscarriage, and that this, more than what you consider your failures during the investigation, is causing you extreme guilt."

He makes more notes.

For reasons I don't understand, he's pissing me off even more than usual. "You think you know something about me," I say. "You think you can manipulate me into some kind of self-revelation, but you don't and you can't."

He looks at me, appraising, and rubs the top of his pen against the side of his head. Another tiny action that seems feigned. He's careful not to muss his suave politician hair. "Why not?"

"We're in the same business," I say. "We

look beneath surfaces for the truth. If you're going to do that with me, you're going to have to work just a little bit harder, because I see through you."

He takes a second and sits back in his glossy leather chair, puffs his pipe, sips his mint tea. "Please explain."

"People are easy to decipher," I say. "Listen to what's said on the surface. Ask yourself why they said it. Ask yourself what they didn't say, then ask yourself why they didn't say it. When all those questions are answered, the truth becomes evident."

"Simplistic perhaps, but nicely put," Torsten says.

I feel like reversing our roles and watching his reaction. "Let me give you a little lesson about people," I say. "Look at them as well as listen to them. Check out their hands and their feet. Hands tell a life story. Muscle and scars speak of hard work and usually outdoor life or the lack thereof. The condition of fingernails, whether they're clean or dirty or well-kept or maybe bitten goes toward self-esteem. The shoes people wear give away their taste, hence self-perception, and usually reveal their socioeconomic status."

I got him. He tries not to, but he glances at his Gucci loafers, then his thin, lily-white hands and manicured nails. Then he looks at my boots and stubby hands, almost as thick as they are long, and I'm certain he pictures those hands bouncing Vesa Legion Korhonen's face off the fence in front of Ebeneser School.

A gift box of Fazer chocolates and a bowl of chestnuts with a nutcracker sitting in it, left over from the holidays, rest on the coffee table. I take a nut from the bowl but leave the nutcracker, give it a one-handed squeeze and break it open. He winces. I'm not sure why I intimidated him. I munch the nut, place the shells in a neat pile on the table.

He's left speechless for a moment, then says, "Well done."

I made him feel like an effeminate fop and a fraud. I feel awful and find myself apologizing twice in the same day. A rarity for me. "Shit," I say, "I'm sorry. That was uncalled for. You didn't deserve it."

He nods acknowledgment of my regret.

"The truth is you're right," I say. "I feel terrible guilt because I'm afraid I traumatized my wife to the point that it caused her miscarriage, and I'm terrified that she'll lose this child, too. I'm scared that she'll die."

"Kate is medicated for the hypertension associated with preeclampsia, the odds of

96

her losing the child are slim. Your child is safe inside her."

"The odds aren't slim enough. The statistics don't make me less petrified."

He leans forward and locks eyes with me. For the first time I view him as someone trying to help me instead of as an adversary. "Kari," he says, "I think we've made a breakthrough. Our first one. What do you say we start again, and now really begin your treatment."

I nod.

"How are your headaches?" he asks.

"Bad. A migraine is killing me right now. It hasn't stopped for weeks."

"Describe the symptoms."

"They vary. Sometimes my temples pulse and throb. Sometimes it feels like I'm being stabbed deep in the head with a hot knife and an artery is about to explode. Most often though, I feel like my head is being squeezed, like a weight is on me, pushing me to the ground."

"This feeling of being stabbed deep in the head is medically impossible, because there are no nerves in that area. If you were about to have an aneurysm, you would never know it."

I hadn't thought of that.

"It's possible that your migraines are

caused by the gunshot wound to your head or another physical problem, but I would like you to consider the possibility that they're psychosomatic, and that what you're really experiencing are sublimated panic attacks generated by guilt over your wife's miscarriage, and consequently, current fear for your wife and unborn child. That might be why the nearer she comes to term, the worse the headaches get."

"My headaches are panic attacks that last for weeks?"

"Possibly. Still, I think you should have tests run to rule out physical problems."

"I already promised Kate I would."

"Good. Our time is up, and anyway, I think we should call it a day now."

"Me too."

For the first time since our initial meeting, we shake hands.

## 10

Kate will have picked up her brother and sister from the airport by now. I agreed to meet them at five thirty, at a bar in our neighborhood, for a drink before dinner. I'm running late.

I find a parking space on Vaasankatu and walk into Hilpeä Hauki — The Happy Pike — a little bar Kate and I enjoy and consider our local. Most of its sales are from imported designer beers. Its prices are higher than most of the other bars in the neighborhood, but because of it, Hilpeä Hauki has a better clientele, a low-key and less than roaring drunk atmosphere. Kate also likes it because the bartenders are a well-educated bunch, and she can speak English with them. It's a nice place for us to get out of the house and chat.

Kate, John and Mary are sitting at a corner table. The family resemblance is apparent. All three are tall, thin and rangy, have pale complexions and cinnamon-red hair — Kate's in a chignon, Mary's long and pulled back into a ponytail, John's shoulder-length and also pulled back. Mary is twenty-four but looks older, except for young, dancing eyes. John is twenty-three, but looks younger, except for old, unwavering eyes.

I lean over, give Kate a peck on the lips and introduce myself to the others. John stands, shakes my hand and grins. He's got a rebel style with a pricey slant to it. He wears a leather jacket, jeans and cowboy boots, but the leather jacket is soft, expensive and Italian, the jeans Diesels, the boots Sedona West full-quill ostrich. Fancy garb for an academic. I take it he pictures himself a ladies' man. He's a little unsteady, appears to have had a few drinks on the plane. Mary shoots John a disapproving glance because of his wobbling, but her smile toward me is warm. She stands, too, leans across the table and hugs me.

Mary is more understated than her brother. She has on a long, dark dress and no makeup, but her excited smile says she's thrilled to be here. Her plain wool coat hangs on a wall hook beside a Ralph Lauren overcoat, which I assume is John's. "So you're the man who stole my sister's heart,"

Mary says.

She seems pleasant. Maybe my misgivings about having them here for an extended stay were misplaced. "I think it was the other way around," I say.

Kate has her hands folded on her pregnant belly. Her chair can't quite fit at the table because of it. She's resplendent in a green dinner dress. She worked hard at finding clothes she likes while she's pregnant. She smiles. "No, it wasn't."

They must have just arrived, they don't have drinks in front of them yet. "What can I get everyone?" I ask.

"A Jaffa for me," Kate says.

"What's that?" Mary asks.

"Orange soda," I say. "It's Finland's most popular soft drink."

"I'll try one," she says.

I hang my coat up beside Mary's. "And for you, John?"

"What are you having?" he asks me.

"A lager and a Koskenkorva, Finnish vodka affectionately known to most of us as *kossu.*"

"I'll have the same," he says.

Now Mary's disapproving look is for me. "You order two portions of alcohol at the same time?"

"It's a Finnish habit, particularly of

middle-aged rednecks like me. Why?"

"I don't agree with the use of alcohol in general."

What I drink isn't her business. I shrug and smile. "Mary, you may have come to the wrong country."

Her half smile at my half joke is only a politeness.

I make two trips to the bar and bring our drinks. I ask how their trip went. We chat about Kate's pregnancy. We make the small talk of strangers.

Mary sips Jaffa. "This is good. And Kate, you look ravishing. Motherhood agrees with you."

"The baby is kicking now," Kate says.

"Can I feel it?"

Kate nods. Mary lays a hand on her belly. Mary smiles, and tears come to her eyes. "I adore children," she says. "You and Kari are truly blessed."

I'm sipping my *kossu,* but John knocks his back in one gulp. He's also chugging his beer. "This place is a tad on the drab side," he says.

It's not extravagant by any means, but simple and pleasant, furnished with dark wood. The beer taps and bar fixtures are polished brass. "Why do you say that?" I ask.

"There isn't even any music."

"The customers here prefer it that way," I say. "We can hold conversations without shouting."

He knocks off the rest of his pint of beer. "Whatever. The vodka is good. Let's have another round."

Kate and I exchange a fleeting look. "I'll get it," I say.

"I'll go with you," Kate says. "I haven't said hi to Mike yet."

I offer Kate my hand to help her up, and we go to the bar together. She's graceful, having learned to move in a way that makes her limp almost invisible, but pregnancy has changed her balance, and she lurches a bit when she walks.

The bartender, Mike Davis, has a Finnish mother and a British father. He grew up in the U.K., but has lived here since his late teens. He's a big, outgoing guy in his mid-twenties. He's heavily tattooed, is taller than me and runs a little better than two hundred pounds. Despite his good nature, he doesn't look like the kind of guy you want to fuck with. "Hi, guys," he says. "How are things?"

"Pretty good," I say. "Long day at the office."

An older man has had too much to drink. Mike shuts him off. The man yells, *"Minä olen asiakas, minä olen asiakas"* — "I'm a customer, I'm a customer" — the standard bitch of drunks when refused service. Mike pretends he's not there, the standard Finnish-bartender method of dealing with such situations.

"Yeah," Mike says, "I'm having a long day at the office, too. And you, Kate?" Mike asks. "You feeling well?"

"Things are great, couldn't be better," she says. "My brother and sister just arrived from the States. That's them sitting at the table with us."

"I'll make sure to take good care of them," he says.

Mike gets John's beer and *kossu*. The drunk leans on the bar and sulks.

Kate and I sit back down. The bar is about half full, the murmur of conversation low. The drunk screams, *"Vittu saatana perkele jumalauta!"* The anthem of angry Finns announcing aggressive intentions. Kate's eyes open wide. She's been in Finland long enough to understand the gravity of the situation. Conversation ceases. Everyone stares. Mike puts his hands on the bar, raises up to his full height but keeps his face expressionless.

"What did he yell?" John asks.

"It's untranslatable," I say, "but something

104

like 'Cunt devil devil goddamn.' "

John laughs. Mary winces.

The drunk yells some more. Mike's answer is calm. Around the bar, jaws drop. The drunk realizes he's gone too far, turns and walks out the door without another word.

The exchange was beyond Kate's Finnish language abilities, even though they've improved over time. "What was that about?" she asks.

I explain in such a way that Mary and John can understand as well. "Mike's mother tongue is English, so like yours, his accent is soft when he speaks Finnish. When Russians speak Finnish they also have a soft accent. Most Finns have never heard a person with English as a mother tongue speak Finnish, so the drunk made a natural assumption and called Mike a goddamned fucking Russian. A bad mistake. Mike, not a Russian and displeased to be called one, got pissed off and said, 'Yeah, I'm a god-damned fucking Russian, and I hope my grandfather killed your grandfather during the Winter War.' That's the point when the drunk knew he was in serious trouble and left while he could."

"Isn't Finland somehow related to Russia?" Mary asks.

Now I wince. "No, it's not."

John sighs, drinks his second *kossu* in one go. "Mary, Finland is neither part of Russia, nor is it part of Scandinavia proper. It's classified as a Nordic country and is an entity of its own."

"I take it Finns don't care for Russians," Mary says.

"No," I say, "in general, we don't."

"Why?"

Kate has told me John is a Ph.D. candidate in history and a graduate teaching assistant. An educated man. He explains. "Finland was a long-standing Swedish possession, but twice during the eighteenth century, Russia invaded. Thousands of Finns were killed or forced into slavery. In 1809, Sweden ceded Finland to the Russian Empire. In 1899, the czar embarked on a policy called the Russification of Finland. Russian was made the official language, Finnish legislative bodies were rendered powerless, its army was incorporated into Russia's. The czar tried to destroy their culture and Finland resisted."

John's knowledge surprises me. It speaks to me that, historian or not, he spent the time to acquire it.

I take up the story. "We declared independence in 1917, but had a civil war the following year — Bolshevik Reds backed by Socialist Russia versus anti-Socialist Whites, as they were called, backed by Imperialist Germany. Like your own American Civil War, it was sometimes brother against brother. The Whites won, but the result was tens of thousands dead, poverty and starvation."

"You sound passionate about it," John says.

"You would be surprised, even after nearly a century, what strong emotions the Civil War still dredges up in us."

"What was the Winter War?" Mary asks.

"Kari," John asks, "would you allow me to pontificate?"

"Be my guest."

"During the Second World War, Finland fought three separate wars," he says. "In the Winter War, Finland fought alone and it kicked Russian ass, but in fact lost, because it ceded territory in the peace agreement. The Soviets invaded Finland on November 30, 1939. The Soviets had thousands of tanks, Finland had thirty-two. The USSR attacked with upwards of a million men. Finns slaughtered them, killed five Russians for every Finn and beat them back. Finland signed a peace treaty with the USSR in March, but was at war with them again in 1941."

"I'm impressed," I say.

He continues. "Finland sided with Germany against the Soviet Union in what is known as the Continuation War. The Finnish hope was that the German invasion of Russia would allow Finland to regain lost areas and to annex some Soviet territory in the realignment after the Germans beat them. When it became clear that Germany would lose, Finland signed another armistice with Moscow. Finland ceded more territory and agreed to drive German troops out of their country. The consequence was the Lapland War." He asks, "Kari, have I gotten it right?"

I finish my *kossu* and chase it with beer. "In every detail. The German scorched-earth policy as they withdrew resulted in the burning down of Kittilä, my hometown, among many others. Again we starved, did without even the most basic necessities. If you can imagine, in this snowy country, citizens wore shoes made out of paper. After the end of the Second World War, even though they had invaded us, among other humiliations, we were forced to pay war reparations to Russia. On a visceral level, we're still pissed off about it."

I didn't realize the people at the table across from us were listening to us. A woman recites a common Finnish sentiment. *"Ryssä on aina ryssä, vaikka voissa paistaisi."* A Russian is always a Russian, even if you fry him in butter.

Kate looks at her watch. "We should leave for the restaurant soon."

I nod agreement. I'm certain that she's thrilled to see her brother and sister, but John is drunk, and Mary seems a touch strange and dour. The family dynamic and vibe are weird. I'm sure Kate is hoping a change in venue will improve them. I signal Mike for the check and ask him to order a taxi for us.

# 11

Our taxi stops in front of Kämp, alongside an XJ12 Jaguar and a McLaren F1. When the hotel opened in 1887, it was palatial. Over the years, it suffered structural damage, more from wars than anything else, and finally the ballroom dance floor started caving in. In 1966, the original facade had to be torn down and rebuilt. In deference to the part the hotel played — and continues to play — in our cultural heritage, great efforts were made to conserve as much as possible of the original architecture, and it retains its Old World splendor. During the prewar years, our great composer Jean Sibelius threw parties here that sometimes raged for days. In recent years, among other notables, Vladimir Putin and Jacques Chirac have been guests.

We exit the taxi. On the sidewalk, in front of the grayish-green marble entrance, the frigid wind is strong and drives snow into our faces. The doorman wears a traditional top hat and red jacket. He offers a slight bow and deferential greeting, in keeping with Kate's status as general manager.

"Good evening, Sami," she says. The hotel has a huge staff, but Kate has learned each and every one of their names. I'm terrible with names and can't imagine how she did it.

Inside, we pass down a long run of carpet, through a second set of doors and into a large lobby. Its rotunda, supported by massive marble pillars, is dominated by a magnificent chandelier. John turns in a circle. "Damn, Kate," he says. "Quite a place you're running here."

The hotel screams wealth. The mosaic floors — also marble — art and elegant furnishings seem more to John's taste than our local bar. "Thank you," Kate says. "I'm proud of it."

The receptionists, concierge and bellhops also offer Kate smiles and quiet greetings. Again, she calls them all by name, a distinctly un-Finnish habit, and asks how their evenings are going. It's evident that they like her, and equally so that she's comfortable here. This pleases me to no end. The hotel is international and the staff speaks fluent English. At least when she's at work, the cultural isolation Kate suffered living in Kittilä, in large part caused by the language barrier, is gone. Kate is in her element.

We stroll through a lounge, past the bar — which is dark wood and brass, much like the one in dreary Hilpeä Hauki, which John fails to note — into the dining room, and a gracious maître d' seats us. On the other side of the room sit Ivan Filippov, the audacious prick, and his so-called assistant, Bettie Page Linda. Maybe I should be surprised, but I'm not. He catches my eye and nods acknowledgment.

A waiter in a white jacket comes to take our drink orders. "We're celebrating something special," Kate says. "A bottle of Tattinger please."

"And one of those Finnish vodkas for me," John says.

"He'd like a Koskenkorva," I say.

The waiter leaves a wine list on the table. John asks where the restroom is and excuses himself. He weaves a bit as he walks away. When he comes back, he weaves no longer. His eyes are sharp and darting. He's had a little pick-me-up in the men's room. I wonder if Kate notices.

The waiter arrives with the champagne and pours. Mary places a hand over her glass.

"I didn't know until today that you're a teetotaler," Kate says.

"My husband and I are religious people. Alcohol doesn't fit in with our beliefs. And after you saw what it did to our father, I'm surprised you touch it either. Especially in your condition."

Kate reddens. "Mary, I don't intend to drink the whole glass. I just thought a toast to celebrate us being together, for the first time in more than five years, would be nice."

Mary checks the wine list. "The bottle cost a hundred and five euros. Can you afford it?"

"I think my family is worth it on this special occasion. And besides, as general manager, I'm expected to eat and drink here occasionally, so that I know our guests are enjoying their dining experiences. The hotel will pay for it."

Mary concedes defeat, allows Kate to pour a glass for her. Kate raises her champagne flute and we follow suit. "To our family," Kate says.

We clink glasses and drink to the family. John gulps. Kate sips. Mary allows the champagne to brush her lips, but no more. The waiter brings menus and John's *kossu*. I glance at Filippov. He and Linda hold hands and exchange intimate looks.

"John, how do you like being a teacher?" Kate asks.

His pick-me-up has animated him. He gestures with his hands while he talks. "I love academia," he says. "I specialize in Renaissance history. Teaching about the sins of the Borgias is a bit of a guilty pleasure, like watching pornography."

"You said you were on a one-year renewable doctoral fellowship. I was afraid that it might not be continued because of the world financial crisis and funding cutbacks."

He grins. "No. I may be just a Ph.D. candidate, but I'm such a popular teacher that the students would go on strike if the university let me go."

The waiter takes our appetizer orders. Mary takes crayfish soup. Kate carpaccio à la Paris Ritz. I order a Stolichnaya and a half-dozen raw oysters.

Mary raises her eyebrows. "More vodka?"

I'm getting tired of this. "It complements raw oysters."

Kate is getting tired of it, too, and comes to my defense. "Finnish standards concerning drinking are somewhat different than in the States, but Kari doesn't drink excessively. He's a good husband."

"I'm sure he is," Mary says.

She doesn't look sure.

John orders osetra caviar, menu price two hundred and eighty euros. Kate stiffens but says nothing. True, she's free to entertain here, but good relations with her employers dictate a modicum of restraint.

Mary notices Kate's reaction. "John, don't you think you're being a touch extravagant?"

He shrugs, giggles, looks at Kate. "It's all on the house, right, Sis?"

Kate forces a smile. "Yes, John. Enjoy yourself."

He orders vodka, too. "Also traditional with caviar. Isn't that right, Kari?"

He's correct. "Yep."

I check out Filippov. Bettie Page Linda nuzzles his neck. He sees me see him, gets up and comes toward our table. Just what I fucking need. He introduces himself. I don't want to, but in the interest of politeness in front of Kate's family, I make introductions all around.

"Inspector Vaara heads the investigation of my wife's murder," Filippov says in English, "and he has all of my confidence. May I assume Rein Saar is in custody and that his prosecution is imminent?"

"He's in custody," I say. "Make no assumptions about his guilt or innocence."

"I get the idea," Filippov says, "that you entertain some wild notion that I'm implicated in my wife's death. It's most hurtful."

He's fucking with me, playing games just to gauge my reaction. What's more, I'm sure he knows that I know he's having a good time at it. I say, "Your business associate, Linda, seems to be doing a good job of helping you through your time of grief."

Filippov switches to Finnish. "She and I are close, and yes, she is most sympathetic. Inspector, you might be more sympathetic yourself. You have a lovely wife. I see that you have a child soon to arrive. Can you imagine how it feels to have your wife beaten to death in the bed of another man? Perhaps if you could, you would be less judgmental."

I bristle. I'm not sure if he called up the image of my wife and child murdered as a taunt or a threat. Alcohol knocked my headache back to a dull roar, but now it thrums, almost seems to sing to me, *Kill this bastard.*

"I like you, Inspector," he says. "Do you know why?"

"Please enlighten."

"I sense something about you. There's a Russian saying. Comrade Wolf knows who to eat and isn't about to listen to anyone. In this world, there are sheep and wolves. Only a very few people are wolves. Wolves are

116

predators and don't bow to pressure. They see situations through to the end of the line, no matter the cost. You and I are wolves, and so you remind me of me. Because of it, I have no choice but to like you."

I get the impression that, with his flagrant disregard for his dead wife and cryptic talk, he's sending me a message, but I have no idea what it is or why he's doing it. He goes back to his table.

The tension between us was evident. The others look at me, waiting for an explanation. "Just some police business," I say.

Filippov makes a pretense of amends, sends a round of four vodkas to our table. I won't drink that bastard's booze and dump them in the champagne bucket. John's expression of longing says he mourns their loss. Our appetizers arrive. I eat oysters and listen as Kate, John and Mary retell family anecdotes, relive some humorous childhood memories. The mood lightens. They decide they're hungry enough for entrées, and we look at the menus again.

"Why does this first-class restaurant sell liver and onions?" John asks. "It strikes me as a bit low-rent."

"Because it's a Finnish classic," I say. "It's also one of my favorite foods."

His tone patronizes. "Oh."

We order dinner. Entrecôte for me. Duck confit for Kate. Sea-salted whitefish with leaf spinach and beurre blanc sauce for Mary. For John, roasted fillet of roe deer, of course the most expensive main course on the menu. And to go with it, a Château Gruaud-Larose 1966, Saint-Julien 2ème Grand Cru, Bordeaux, France. Price tag: three hundred and thirty euros.

I see Kate grimace. She's angry now and starts to object. I don't want her evening ruined. To exclude the others, I tell her in Finnish that I'll pay for it myself, and ask John if I can share it, so he won't drink the whole thing by himself. Kate accepts my gesture and lets it go. I see Filippov and Linda walk out, arm in arm.

Dinner arrives. We dig in.

Mary says, "Kari, since you're married to Kate, why do you want to live in Finland?"

"What do you mean?"

"America is the greatest country on earth. I can't imagine why anyone would want to live anywhere else."

The woman mystifies me. "By what standard do you measure countries to determine which is the greatest on earth?"

"In America, you can be anything you want. Have anything you want. Why live under socialism?"

I can't bring myself to engage in such an uninformed conversation. I turn to Kate. The look on my face says, *Help me.* She grins and shrugs.

"Finland isn't a socialist country," I say. "It's a social democracy, like most European countries."

"Wouldn't you like to live in a capitalist country, where you can become wealthy?"

"Are you wealthy?" I ask.

"Moderately. My husband's medical practice is quite successful."

The migraine hums. My patience with Mary is wearing thin. "In this regard, a vast cultural gulf separates us. Your capitalist country exists in a constant state of flux, and throughout its history has been in an almost constant state of war. We in Europe have learned over the centuries that change and transformation bring war, hardship and chaos. We fear it. By and large, we prefer a middle-class existence — with the knowledge that when we're sick, we can go to the doctor, that we won't go hungry or be homeless, that we can receive educations — to the excitement of the remote possibility that we might make a billion dollars, which we don't need anyway. So no, I feel no need to emigrate to your land of opportunity."

John snickers, then laughs. "Damn," he

says, "that was great. You should be a politician. Or a television preacher."

Mary's young eyes age twenty years in an instant, and they aren't dancing anymore. She folds her hands in front of her face and looks at Kate over her fingertips. "And how do you feel about the way your husband just denigrated our homeland?"

Kate takes a second before answering. "Mary, it wasn't a denigration, it was an explanation of differing political philosophies. Kari has spent time in the States, but you haven't been to Finland before, so if either of you has more right to an opinion, it's him. I've lived in both places, and Kari's viewpoint has some justification." She looks at me. "But that was a little harsh," she says.

"Well, Kari," Mary says. "I must say, you're quite well-spoken in English, considering that it's not your language."

"Thanks," I say. "Your English is good, too."

Under the table, Kate kicks my shin to get my attention. Her look asks me to stop.

My earlier feelings of goodwill toward John and Mary are gone. My fears about John and Mary being here for so long, during such a special time for Kate and me, are renewed. It's too late now, though, and I resolve to try and make the best of it.

"Anybody up for dessert, coffee and cognac?" John asks.

We manage to make it through the rest of the evening without further incident.

# 12

The four of us go home. Both John and Mary remove their shoes in the foyer without being asked. That they know we don't wear shoes in our houses speaks well of them. They made it a point to learn something about Finnish culture before coming here.

We make up the spare bed for Mary and the couch for John. His pick-me-up has worn off, and he and Mary are both exhausted from the long journey across the Atlantic. I'm dead in my tracks, too. I brush my teeth. John is waiting for me outside the bathroom.

"Hey, Kari," he says. "Got a joint?"

"Excuse me?"

"A little pot would help me sleep."

John just doesn't know when to quit. "No, I don't have a joint."

"Oh, come on, everybody knows cops have the best dope."

"Good night, John," I say, and push past him.

Kate is waiting for me in bed. I turn out the lights. She lays her head on my shoulder. "I don't know what to think about John and Mary," she says.

I stroke her round belly. "Me, neither. I guess so much time has passed that all three of you have changed. Maybe you have to get to know them again."

"You don't like them, do you?" she asks.

There's no point in lying. "I'm trying to like them, for your sake."

"Mary never laughs," she says. "And for John, everything is one big joke. When we were kids, it was the opposite. I don't know what happened."

She doesn't mention how much John drank. I don't mention his drug use.

"You were a little tough on them," she says.

"I had a hard day."

I tell Kate about Vesa Legion Korhonen, that I was a jerk to Torsten, that Filippov seems thrilled his wife was murdered. "My tolerance level for people is zero right now," I say, "and I'm overreacting to things."

She snuggles her face deeper into the crook of my neck. "I'm worried about you. Being short-tempered with people is something that happens, but making a boy drink a bottle of vodka is mean."

"I know."

"It's not like you. Is it because of the headaches?"

"That's part of it anyway. My nerves are bad."

"You're moodier than you used to be. You're always sweet to me, but with other people, you can be short-tempered. You're more unpredictable than before."

She pauses. I wait.

"I don't know why you wouldn't have the scar on your face fixed. Police department insurance would have paid for plastic surgery. It's not that it bothers me as far as your appearance goes, I just can't help but feel that all these things are related."

"It's just the headaches. I'll see Jari. Everything will be fine."

I wait for her to say more, but within a minute or two, her breathing goes deep and regular. She's asleep. My mind turns circles. I think about the skin sliding off Rauha Anttila's corpse. Baby wasps swarming out of her mouth. Blood spray from Iisa Filippov's riding-crop beating. But mostly about Ukki. About eating ice cream and sitting in his lap. He tickled me and made me laugh. He taught me children's rhymes. He taught me to dum-dum bullets. The last time I look at the clock, it's five thirty. It occurs to me that my behavior is unpredictable because I haven't really slept in months now.

# 13

After being awake for better than thirty hours, I manage some fitful slumber and wake up early. The others are still asleep, for which I'm grateful. At eight thirty, I wake Kate up enough to kiss her good-bye and head off for work. It's warmed up to around ten below. The snow has stopped. Helsinki is white. I couldn't ask for more.

I find Milo in his office. Forensics sent him the crime-scene photos and the report of initial findings. They're spread out on his desk. He peruses them, intent. Only a brief nod acknowledges my presence. I look over his shoulder.

"You see anything we didn't notice before?" I ask.

"No. These only confirm my previous conclusions. Cause of death was asphyxiation."

I note his choice of pronoun. *My.* He appears to think I play little part in the investigation. "Let's take this stuff and show it to Saska," I say.

He bridles. "You don't trust my assessment?"

I resist the urge to roll my eyes. This boy's ego is bigger than the planet Jupiter. "Blood spatter will play a key role when this case goes to trial," I say. "Saska is usually called upon as an expert witness in these situations. It makes sense to get his opinion now rather than later."

Milo shoves the papers and photos into a messy pile and scoops it up. "Fine," he says.

We find Saska in his office. Trophies and awards attest to his achievements, but unlike Milo, whose office bears none of these things, his ego seems in check. A radio plays low. He whistles along to *iskelmä* — Finnish tango — and types on his keyboard. "Hi, guys, what's up?"

I joke. "Murder most foul."

He chuckles. "As opposed to murder most virtuous?"

"It's a blood-spatter case," I say. "Mind looking at some evidence for us?"

"Sure."

Milo flops the documentation onto Saska's desk. I spell out the background. "A wealthy married woman had an affair with her riding instructor. He claims she waited for him in his apartment, that he arrived and was struck with a blunt instrument. A bloody iron skillet corroborates this. He never saw the attacker. The woman was restrained in his bed, also beaten with the pan, beaten with a riding crop, burned with cigarettes and suffocated. He says he woke up beside her and found her dead. The question is whether she hit him with the pan and then he killed her, or if he's telling the truth."

Saska skims the report and examines the photos. Milo stands near the door and glowers. I sit and wait.

Saska turns to me. "They haven't fed the blood-spatter patterns into a computer to determine flight paths, angles and velocities yet?"

"We're still waiting on it," I say.

"Offhand, I'd say this was a torture scene. The killer hit her more than a hundred times, whipped her in the same spots again and again to inflict maximum pain."

"Milo thought a hundred and twenty-six lashes. Anything you can add?"

He flips through the photos again and thinks about it. "This riding instructor had on a white shirt with a collar. If he did the whipping, when he swung the riding crop, the top of the swing arc was behind him, and blood droplets would have flown from the riding crop's tip in that direction. Check the shoulders and collar of the shirt at the back of the neck. You should find blood spatter there."

Milo forces out a curt thank-you and exits Saska's office.

"What's his problem?" Saska asks.

"He's a smart kid, but not as smart as he thinks he is. Whenever someone questions the greatness that is his, he gets a *vitutus*" — a dick grows out of his forehead.

Saska laughs.

"I have to work with him," I say. "How do you think I should handle him?"

"You're right, he overestimates himself. For instance, it's not possible to determine if the victim was struck exactly a hundred and twenty-six times. If I were you, I'd just wait. Sooner or later he'll make a king-sized fuckup. When he does, he'll feel his big big brain deflate. He might be a good cop after that."

"Good advice. Thanks."

I shuffle our documentation into a sheaf and go back to Milo's office. He folds his arms and stares at me. "Saska confirmed everything I said. Maybe now you won't treat me like a fucking punk."

The headache is creeping back. It makes

me caustic. "Milo, are you saying we're not friends? My feelings are hurt."

He pauses, uncertain if I'm teasing him or not.

I raise my voice. "Milo, you're right. We're not fucking friends. In fact, I don't have any fucking friends, I don't want any fucking friends, and if I had a fucking friend, it wouldn't be you."

He cringes, twitches, stares nervous at the floor. Then he smiles, then giggles, then looks at me and laughs. "Damn, you're a real fucking hard-ass. You know that?"

I ignore the commentary, don't clue him in to whether I was kidding or serious. "We needed Saska's opinion. You didn't find everything. In fact, we fucked up. We didn't check the back of Rein Saar's shirt for blood spatter. We have to get it done now."

He ignores the criticism, waits while I call forensics and ask them to look at the shirt.

I finish the call and Milo says, "Think about it. Rein Saar and Iisa Filippov had an affair going back a couple years. Ivan Filippov claims he knew nothing about it. He can't be that stupid. He lied."

"But consider the logistics," I say. "How would Filippov know for certain when his wife would be with Rein Saar, and when she would be in a location where he could have the opportunity to kill her?"

Milo's smile reflects glee. "I have an idea about the hows and whys."

"Please share."

"He's fucking his secretary Linda and wants his wife out of the way."

"I saw them together at Kämp last night," I say. "You're right about the fucking part."

"Iisa kept Saar's work schedule in her purse. Filippov knew it. He could monitor their possible tryst schedules, and it makes sense that he would check her cell phone for text messages, too. He sees the text asking Iisa to meet Saar and her message agreeing. She has a key to Saar's place. Filippov had a copy made and waited for his opportunity. He specializes in toxic waste disposal. He's got waterproof, disposable coated-paper suits, rubber and vinyl masks and gloves, all the gear necessary to cover him head to foot and keep DNA evidence off him. He puts the stuff on, hits Saar in the head and frames him, tortures his wife and kills her, then gets rid of the bloody gear. It's simple and practical."

Milo's theory begins to intrigue me. "It's possible."

"It's more than possible," Milo says, "it's what happened."

I think it through. "How about if we wait

to find out about the blood on Saar's shirt? If we don't find blood spatter to match the crime, we take a closer look at Filippov."

Milo nods.

"Did you look at Filippov Construction's security tape?" I ask.

"Yeah, they arrived at the times they stated."

"I expected that. Do you know when Iisa's autopsy is scheduled?"

"Eleven thirty this morning."

"I have another investigation going on," I say. "It's going to take up a big part of my day. Let's do it like this. Skip the autopsy. You go back to Saar's apartment. Now that forensics is done, you can really give it a thorough search."

"This other investigation of yours must have something to do with your late-night visit from the chief. Want to tell me about it?"

"No."

Now he's both impressed and slavering for details. "It's that top-secret?"

"I didn't say it was secret. I'm choosing not to discuss it with you."

He purses his lips. "You're a real prick today."

"Yep. When you search Saar's apartment, I mean search it. You look between the pages of every book, go through pockets of all his clothing. No stone goes unturned. Tear the place apart. Meet me back here at four thirty and we'll reinterview Saar. Can you work that fast?"

He scowls and salutes. "Yes, Drill Sergeant."

I leave him alone with his ego.

# 14

I stop at a fast-food place and intend to wolf down some lunch, think better of it and grab a coffee instead. While I sit and drink it, I get a text message from Jyri Ivalo: "I read the Filippov murder initial report. Charge Saar. Open and shut. Interview Arvid Lahtinen and report."

I ignore the text and call Jari.

"Hello, little brother," he says. "How are things?" I'm forty-one. Jari is four years older than me.

"They've been better. Can I see you?"

"You've been in Helsinki for the better part of a year. I wondered when you'd want to get together."

"Actually, I've got a headache problem, and I need to see a neurologist."

"Oh." I hear disappointment in his voice.

I don't know why I haven't seen him. I guess being around him makes me think about our childhoods, something I try to avoid. "I've been meaning to call, it's just . . . you know how things are. The new job. And I guess you heard Kate is pregnant. She's expecting soon, and I've been spending every free moment with her."

"I understand," he says.

He doesn't understand. "Tell me about your headaches," he says.

"It's not headaches. It's one long headache. I've had problems for about a year, but this particular migraine has lasted about three weeks now."

"Constantly?"

"Yeah, no breaks."

"Your nerves must be shot."

"They've been better."

"You shouldn't have waited so long to see me. Come to the polyclinic at Meilahti at nine a.m. tomorrow morning."

"Okay, I'll see you then."

He rings off without further chat. I guess I really hurt his feelings.

I've debated how to approach Winter War hero Arvid Lahtinen. The polite and respectful way would be to call, introduce myself and arrange an interview. This strikes me as a possible mistake. Whether he's a war criminal or not, I want Arvid to tell me the truth about Ukki, and I don't want to give him time to prepare fabrications. He lives in Porvoo, a town on the Porvoo River that dates from the fourteenth century. In this weather, it's about an hour's drive from Helsinki.

It's still minus ten degrees, but snowing a little harder now. The trip is pleasant, much of it through wooded areas. But my migraine gets worse. It's like a wolverine thrashing around in my head. I try to ignore it.

The old section of Porvoo is mostly made up of wooden houses. In the late eighteenth century, when Finland was a province of Sweden, the houses of the lower classes were painted red, and those of higher classes yellow, to impress the visiting Swedish king. Many of those houses still stand, and by tradition remain painted those colors.

I find Arvid's house. It's red and sits on the river among a group of similar buildings that were once warehouses. He has an old-fashioned door knocker. I bang it against its metal plate. He opens the door. He's ninety years old. I expected someone decrepit, but he's far from it. He's short and thin, his white hair thick. If I didn't know his age, I would think him a vigorous man in his seventies. I've broken a personal rule of police work. Never anticipate, it clouds judgment.

"Can I help you?" he asks.

I introduce myself, show my police card and ask for a few minutes of his time. He ushers me in. I look around while I take off my boots. The downstairs is one large room. A settee and three armchairs surround a coffee table. Against the wall to the left of it, an antique bookcase with deep shelves and glass doors serves as a well-stocked liquor cabinet. To the right is a fireplace with a crackling blaze. Deeper into the room, a dark oak dining-room table seats eight. Behind it, a soapstone stove stands floor-to-ceiling. It breaks my view of the kitchen, but the part I see, a big stove and hanging pots and pans, tells me that the people who live here like to cook, and the smell wafting out confirms it.

Four cats lounge at various points around the room. The house carries the faint scent of cat piss. Somehow, it makes the place even more homey. I once had a cat, named Katt. He felt compelled to mark his territory on occasion, and my house smelled the same.

"Forgive me for coming unannounced," I say.

He folds his arms and looks up at me. "I'll consider forgiving you once you explain why you did it."

His presence is commanding. It's clear that he considers himself a man not to be fucked with. I start to make up a lie, but the headache roars, and I can't speak for a moment.

"Well?" Arvid says.

I pull it together and half lie. "I was asked to speak to you about something and had other business in Porvoo. If I'm imposing, we can talk another time."

"Asked by whom?"

I walk over to the fireplace and warm my hands. "Indirectly, by the interior minister."

On the mantel above the fireplace, among mementos, war medals and photos, sits one of Ukki's guns. I blink, think the headache has induced some kind of weird déjà vu. It's a little Sauer Model 1913, 7.65mm automatic pocket pistol. A low-power peashooter sometimes called a suicide gun.

I pick it up, turn it over in my hand. "Where did you get this?" I ask.

"Why? You want to see my license? I haven't got one."

"No, it's not that."

He cuts me off. "Put it back where you got it, or I'm going to take it away and shoot you with it."

Our conversation is off to a bad start. My fault for touching his things. The headaches make me lose my manners and common sense. I lay it back on the mantel. "My grandpa had one just like it."

"Boy," he says, "you don't look well."

"Just a headache," I say.

He softens. "My father carried that pistol in the Civil War, and I carried it when I was a Valpo detective during the Second World War. It's the only belonging of his that I have left." He pauses, I think deciding how to deal with me. "Let's sit down," he says.

We take easy chairs on opposite sides of the coffee table. He raises his voice. "Ritva, we have a guest. Make coffee."

A voice calls back from upstairs. "Make it yourself!"

He laughs. "I'll make it in a minute," he says to me. "You were saying about the interior minister."

He sits with his back straight, at a sort of relaxed attention. Ukki did that, too. Must be a generational thing. "This is a simple formality," I say.

Matter-of-fact, I explain the accusations leveled against him and give him the background: about Tervomaa's book, Valpo collaboration with Einsatzkommando Finnland in Stalag 309, about the Simon Wiesenthal Center's request for investigation, about Germany's request for extradition. "They want to charge you with accessory to murder," I say.

I see anger well up in him. "Boy, who the fuck do you think you are to come here and talk to me like this? Accessory to murder my fucking ass. How many girls have you kissed?"

Off the top of my head, I don't know. "What difference does it make?"

"Because if you take that number and multiply it by a hundred, that's about the number of goddamned Communist Bolshevik Russian fucking bastards I've killed. And I wish I killed a hundred times more than that. You fucking pissant, you go back to the interior minister, that fucking cocksucker, and tell him to take his charges and accusations and stick them up his fucking ass."

I realize I won't get the opportunity to ask him about Ukki. Arvid leans forward in his chair and stares at me. I take in his starched white dress shirt, his tailored pants. Ukki dressed well every day, too. At home, I wear sweatpants and T-shirts. Arvid is a man with a great deal of pride. He has earned and demands respect.

The migraine thunders. My vision blurs.

"You look like shit," he says.

"My head is killing me," I say.

I stand and the world sways under me. I

feel myself falling and realize I'm blacking out.

I start to regain consciousness. I'm fuzzy and confused. I look up at Arvid. "Ukki?"

Arvid slaps my face to focus me. I shake my head to clear it. He slaps me again. He packs a wallop for an old man. "You can stop now," I say and sit up. "What happened?"

He hands me a glass. "Apparently, your headache made you pass out. Drink this."

"What is it?"

"An opiated painkiller dissolved in water."

I drink it down. "Thank you."

He helps me to my feet and back into the armchair. He goes to his bookcase bar, comes back with a half balloon of cognac and hands it to me. "You need this," he says.

I shake my head. "The painkiller was dope. I shouldn't mix it with alcohol."

"I'm ninety fucking years old. Don't lecture me about health practices. Just drink it."

I set it on the coffee table.

He sighs. To him, I'm a hopeless child. "You're not going anywhere for a while. You're going to stay here and eat lunch with us. When you feel better, you can leave."

He's ordering, not asking. I take a drink.

The rush of opiates and booze is immediate. It helps.

A woman walks in from the kitchen. "I'm Ritva," she says. "I suffer the misfortune of being Arvid's wife. While you were passed out, I told him to stop being mean to you."

She's tiny and frail, maybe fifteen years younger than Arvid. Her face is kind, her long gray hair pulled back and rolled into a bun. Arvid's smile exudes love for her.

"What happened to you?" Ritva asked.

"I don't know," I say. "I had a bad headache and passed out. It's never happened before."

"Finish your drink and come to the table. Some food will do you good."

Ritva starts setting the table. Arvid and I sit in silence. He studies me. I drink the cognac. Dope and booze kill the headache, and its absence leaves me ravenous. Ritva calls us to eat. We take our places.

"It's simple fare," Ritva says.

"I'm grateful," I say. "Thank you for having me."

It's some of my favorite food from childhood. Moose meatballs and brown gravy over boiled potatoes. Lingonberry jam to accompany the moose. Homemade *perunapiirakka* — little pies with potato filling — smoked whitefish, dark rye bread and *pi-*

*imä* — buttermilk — to drink.

We pass dishes around and start filling our plates. I look at Arvid. "I didn't mean to offend you earlier."

"I blamed the messenger," he says. "You didn't do anything wrong. I still have so much shrapnel in me that I set off airport metal detectors. No one has the right to question me about anything that happened during the war."

We dig in. Everything tastes just the same way that my grandma made it. I tell Ritva this. She looks gratified. I need to know about Ukki, and I work up my courage. "The truth is," I say, "I couldn't care less about what the interior minister wants or doesn't want. I was told you served in Stalag 309 with my grandpa, and I came here to find out if it's true."

I neglect to mention that said work in Stalag 309 implies Holocaust participation, and I want to know if Ukki was a war criminal.

Arvid is a hearty eater. He swallows and chases moose with buttermilk. He points at the whitefish. "You like the eyes?" he asks me.

"Yeah."

"They're the best part," he says and scoops them out, one for him and one for me. We chomp them. They have an initial pop and crunch, then a little juice. I think he's stalling, preparing his answer.

"Son," he says, "I never served in Stalag 309. During the time that camp was open, I was stationed in Rovaniemi, not Salla. What was your grandpa's name?"

"Toivo Kivipuro."

"Sounds familiar, but I can't picture him. It was almost seventy years ago, after all."

"How do you think they made the mix-up?" I ask.

"Maybe a paperwork error. Valpo was a big organization, and a few men from the Rovaniemi station went to 309. Maybe there was another Valpo detective by the same name."

I can't put my finger on why, but I'm not quite believing him. "I'm sure they'll figure out their mistake and this will come to nothing," I say.

I'm lying. I think he's banking on his hero status to pull through this, but it won't go away. The German government won't let it.

We finish our meals. "Want some ice cream?" Arvid asks.

Aside from his ferocious temper, he reminds me so much of Ukki that it's uncanny. Maybe Ukki had a temper, too, but I never saw it.

We have dessert and coffee, chat about nothing. I thank them and get up to go.

"Are you feeling well enough to drive?" Ritva asks.

I'm pain-free and well-fed. Relaxed. I haven't felt this good in a long time. "I'll be fine," I say.

Arvid walks me to the door. He's one of the few people I've met over the past year who have neither stared at nor inquired about the scar on my face. He's sharp, seen a lot of scars like it and didn't need to ask. He knows I got shot in the face. He offers his hand. We shake. I thank him for his hospitality. He says it was good to meet me. I have the feeling we'll meet again.

## 15

I drive back to Helsinki. My next stop is the library. I take out *Einsatzkommando Finnland and Stalag 309,* the book that Jyri told me implicates Arvid Lahtinen as a collaborator in Nazi war crimes. I don't have much time before meeting Milo, but I want to check on Kate. Besides, I need to look at the book and want a few minutes of peace and quiet.

Kate sits at the dining-room table with Mary. Kate is wearing a T-shirt that reads PROPERTY OF JESUS.

When we decided to move to Helsinki, we also decided to get all new furnishings. The things in our house in Kittilä were acquired by me and predated our relationship, had the traditional Nordic blond-wood look, which Kate doesn't care for, and so we made a clean start in that way as well. Our new apartment has a big living room, decorated with dark leather couches and chairs, a walnut coffee table and a big entertainment center with a flat-screen TV. The interior wall is lined with built-in shelves that hold hundreds of books and CDs.

It's a corner flat, and two sides of the room are lined with windows looking out onto Harjukatu and Vaasankatu. At the corner, where those two sides meet, a door opens onto a small balcony. I don't smoke inside our home, so I insisted that we find a place with one, so I can have a cigarette without leaving the apartment.

At the rear of the living room, a low dais next to the kitchen serves as a dining area. We bought a big table for it that can seat ten, so we can have dinner parties. The kitchen has brushed-stainless-steel fixtures. The refrigerator and induction oven are the ultimate in functionality and look like something designed in a space program. The bathroom is on the small side, but like maybe half the apartments in Helsinki, has a sauna in it, which I also insisted on. It's electric instead of wood-burning, and because of it, the heat it throws off is too dry for my taste, but it serves its purpose. We have two bedrooms, one for us and one for the child on the way.

I kiss Kate hello, exchange pleasantries with Mary. They seem to be having a serious conversation, so I leave them in peace. John has gone out to explore the city. I'm tired and want to rest and read for a while. I take *Einsatzkommando Finnland and Stalag 309* and lie down on the sofa.

I open the book and go to the index, look up Ukki, and, to my disappointment, find his name. There's only one listing. I turn to the appropriate page. Toivo Kivipuro is mentioned as one of seven Valpo detectives working in Stalag 309, along with five Finnish interpreters fluent in Russian and German. I find no account of Ukki's actions there. Details concerning Arvid are more extensive. A prisoner in the camp recounts that Arvid and other detectives took part in executions. Only one particular instance is cited in explicit detail, but the implication is that where there's smoke, there's fire.

I skim through the book and learn a few things. The Finnish security police, Valpo, was founded in 1919 to protect the new Finnish Republic from Communists in both Finland and Soviet Russia. Professional links to German secret police were established during the 1920s and maintained after the Nazi rise to power. Finland and Germany cooperated in the fight against both domestic and international Communism, an acute concern in Finland because of her shared border with the Soviet Union. Their common enemy unified Valpo and the Gestapo.

Valpo and Gestapo leaders developed personal friendships and cemented the relationship. Racial hatred seeped out of Germany into the Valpo consciousness, and into the Finnish mind-set at large. Racial slurs for Jews began to appear in Valpo documents. Valpo sniffed out ideological enemies on Finnish soil. They surveilled and detained them. They traded information with the SS leadership. The SS had a say in the fate of detainees.

I skip around the book and hit the high points.

Stalag 309 opened in July 1941. It was a normal German prisoner-of-war camp. In other words, an abattoir. Twelve Finns and between fifteen and thirty members of Einsatzkommando Finnland worked together there. It was huge, held several thousand inmates, had special sections for "dangerous prisoners." Bolsheviks, both military and civilian. Jews. Commissars. Russian officers and maybe also noncoms. Details remain fuzzy. The German army destroyed most of its records when it dismantled the camp in 1944.

Germans looked for informers in the

camp and used them to collect data. Valpo assisted in setting up these networks. On page 218, I find a set of eleven criteria used to determine eligibility for execution. The rules were written in such a way that the Gestapo could execute anyone they chose at their discretion: political organizers, administrators, Red Army officers, intelligentsia. And, of course, all Jews.

Each day, individuals were selected, their names called out. They were driven outside the camp. Their clothes were taken away. They were dressed in sacks and forced to climb down into bomb craters. A bomb crater could hold a hundred and fifty, maybe two hundred people. They were machine-gunned to death. When the craters were full, the victims were covered over with dirt.

I read enough to get a good sense of what happened there. Pure evil. A little piece of the Holocaust. I also see that, while not much is written about Arvid, it's enough to get him extradited, maybe convicted. I need to find out if he lied to me. If he told the truth, I want to help him. Even if he lied, I consider whether I want to help him wriggle out of this mess. I don't know yet. If Ukki were alive, I would still love him. I wouldn't condemn him for past sins and ancient history, so how can I do it to Arvid? I check my watch. It's time to go back to work.

## 16

I drive to Pasila. Two detectives, Ilari and Inka, are sitting in the common room. They glance up at me. Ilari nods. Inka ignores me. Ilari is in early middle age, has a bad haircut — he parts it too far over on the side and rakes thinning hair over his scalp to cover his bald spot — a mild dandruff problem, and a paunch. He does, however, wear expensive suits to work. Inka is middle-aged, has a short, shapeless haircut that renders her sexless, as do her frumpy clothes. She also has a paunch. Our two other team members, Tuomas and Ilpo, are working a kidnap murder and are seldom seen lately.

Ilari and Inka are reading today's *Helsingin Sanomat,* the nation's largest-circulation newspaper. They quarrel over who gets the sports section. I pick up the local news section. Murders rarely make the front page of *Sanomat.* The Filippov murder gets an eighth of a page, says nothing of interest. The press has left me alone about it. Arto and the PR folks are fielding the calls, an advantage of working for a major metropolitan police force.

One pastry sits in a box on the table. Ilari takes it.

"I wanted that," Inka says.

Ilari shrugs. "You snooze, you lose."

She calls him a bastard. He tells her to go fuck herself. I go to my office.

I log on to my computer and check e-mails. Without knocking, Milo jerks my door open and shouts, "Boo!"

It makes me jump in my chair.

"See," he says, "you don't like it, either."

Milo is strange and antagonistic. It makes me laugh. "At least I wasn't building weapons of mass destruction in secret," I say. "Did you turn up anything at Saar's apartment?"

"The only thing of interest was in his laptop. He has a collection of photos and videos of himself having sex with Iisa and other women in his bedroom. Judging by the camera angle, that's the purpose of the hole in his closet door."

"Doesn't make him a murderer. Have a seat. The Filippov autopsy results are here."

Normally, autopsy transcriptions aren't

delivered until months after the event, but I asked nicely, so the coroner sent me a summary.

Milo pulls up a chair next to mine so he can see my monitor screen. The autopsy painted a portrait of the crime much as we imagined it: Iisa's broken bones, torture with a riding crop, cigarette burns, and cause of death — suffocation. But it turns up a major surprise. Several of the burns were inflicted not with a cigarette but are consistent with wounds caused by a drive-stun taser. This suggests that the killer first used the taser to incapacitate Iisa, then enlisted it as a pain compliance tool by inflicting multiple and prolonged shocks.

Time of death was somewhere between six and eight a.m.

"If Iisa was tased," Milo asks, "then what was the point of hitting her with the frying pan?"

"Maybe to cover up the tasing," I say, "to make it seem like a crime of passion rather than premeditated. The murderer might have thought the taser burns would go unnoticed because of the multiple cigarette burns."

Milo looks thoughtful.

Forensics has e-mailed the results from Rein Saar's shirt. I open up the file. The collar and shoulders were soaked in his own blood, from the blow to his head. His blood makes blood-spatter patterns from the riding-crop beating of Iisa Filippov hard to analyze, in terms of angle and velocity. It will have to be sorted out through DNA analysis and will take at least a few days. His right collar and shoulders bear some spatter, but it could be the result of his lying beside her while the beating took place. The results are inconclusive. Most interesting, though, is that the lower back of the shirt bears a scorch mark that, once again, is consistent with taser burn.

Milo stretches, folds his hands behind his head, and sits back in his chair. "Told you Filippov did it," he says. "He tased them to knock them out, tortured Iisa and framed Rein Saar."

I have to admit that, as Saar claims, it seems possible he was left alive in order to frame him. If Saar was convicted of Iisa's murder, it would close the case and allow the true killer to avoid investigation and walk free. "Let's go down to the lockup and talk to Saar," I say.

We go downstairs, walk along the long white corridor and stop at cell S408. Out of politeness, I knock before entering.

"Might be nice if you showed your colleagues the same courtesy as you do your prisoners," Milo says.

Saar shouts for us to enter and I open the door.

As jail accommodations go, ours are pretty good. The cell has a decent bed, a bench and a small writing table fixed to a wall decorated with creative inmate graffiti. Every cell has a few books in it for entertainment. The prisoners have a gym to work out in, and a canteen where they can buy snacks and smokes. They eat the same food as the staff.

Saar is sitting on the edge of his bed. Washing the shower of blood off has done wonders for his appearance. "Mind if we have a little chat?" I ask.

"Will it help me get out of here?"

"Possibly."

"Then by all means, let's chat."

"I'm going to ask you some personal questions. Would you rather talk here, off the record, or in the interrogation room and have your statement recorded?"

"If we're going to talk about my sex life," he says, "let's keep it between us for now."

I sit on the bed beside Saar. Milo sits on the bench. "Would you lift your shirt and let me see your back?"

He does it, shows me a nasty burn just above his waist.

"How did you get that?"

"I don't know."

"Why didn't you mention it before?"

"To be honest, when we talked before, my head hurt so bad and I was so drunk that I didn't even notice it. Hurts now, though."

He pulls his shirt down, sits forward with his elbows on his knees.

"Mind if I smoke?" I ask.

"Not if you give me one."

"You don't have any?"

"I don't have any money on me to buy them."

I take a twenty out of my wallet and give it to him. "You can pay me back. Tell me about you and Iisa — in more detail than before — and about your affair."

He folds up the bill, unfolds it, puts it in his pocket, thinks how he's going to spin this. "Iisa was wild," he says, "loved to party. I wasn't the only guy she fucked behind Filippov's back. Just the only steady one. And I had other lovers, too. Like I told you, we had fun. We were comfortable together. Enough so that I gave her a key to my place."

"Did Iisa use drugs?"

"Sometimes. Coke. Ecstasy. GHB."

"You think Ivan Filippov killed his wife and framed you. Lots of women fuck around on their husbands. Their husbands don't usually turn murderous. Why him?"

He ponders, stares at the wall. "Iisa didn't like fucking her husband. Didn't do it, in fact. She liked fucking me. I guess his bruised ego could have driven him to it."

Yes, it could have. "What did you give Iisa that Filippov didn't?"

"Iisa liked to play games." He hesitates. "Maybe I shouldn't have played them."

"Describe these games."

"Iisa liked to watch me fuck other women."

This explains the source of the videos in his computer. "She hid in your closet and shot videos through the hole in your closet door."

He nods. "I would fuck a girl, she would film it. I would get the girl out of my house, then fuck Iisa while we watched it on my laptop. It got her off."

This explains the stool in the closet and the camcorder in Iisa's purse. His story rings true. "How did these games begin?"

"I made a mistake giving her the key. She made a game out of coming to my house when I wasn't home. She would hide under the bed or in the closet or in the shower. I might be there an hour or two before she jumped out and surprised me."

I give Saar another smoke and we light up. "Seems like that would piss you off."

"It did the first time, but it was hard to be mad at Iisa. She was like a little kid, just playing games and having fun. One day I brought a girl home and fucked her. Iisa came in the front door while we fucked. She did it quiet, so I didn't hear her. She peeked through the door from the living room and masturbated while she watched. That's how it started. Actually, the game was fun. Got us both excited."

I stop interrogating him for a minute, take a break, smoke and think, try to sort all this out. Milo jumps in. "Do you know Ivan Filippov's secretary, a woman named Linda Pohjola?"

"Yeah. She was a friend of Iisa's."

"They looked a hell of a lot alike. Was that a coincidence?"

"No. They'd known each other since they were teenagers and worked at the look-alike thing. Sometimes they would go to parties dressed in identical clothes. It was another one of Iisa's games. They tag-teamed me once. They even looked the same naked. That was fun, too."

"What else do you know about Linda?"

Milo asks.

"Not much. Iisa didn't talk a lot about her personal life. Really, our relationship just revolved around fucking."

"Tell me more about Iisa's games and other lovers," Milo says.

"I don't know much more. She kept a diary, though. She kept it in her purse sometimes. Maybe you could find out something from there."

"You texted Iisa and asked her to meet you at seven thirty in the morning. Why?"

"I hooked up with a girl. She was going to come home with me, but she got too drunk and tired and took a rain check. Iisa was going to watch us fuck."

"You lead an exciting life," Milo says.

Saar manages a wan grin. "I try."

He looks at me. "Are you going to charge me with murder?"

I remember Jyri's demand to that effect. "Not today," I say.

I set my pack of cigarettes on his table. We leave him in peace.

Back in my office, given the interview, I ask Milo what he thinks.

"Same as I have since the beginning. That motherfucker Filippov killed his wife and framed Saar. I turned that apartment inside out, and there's no taser in it. The killer took it with him."

"Exactly," I say. "The taser burn lends veracity to his story, and the taser is conspicuous by its absence. It's possible that Iisa tased him, he recovered enough to fight and was angry enough to torture her to death, then dumped the taser and called the police himself. But given his head wound, it's too much of a stretch. A third party took the taser out of the apartment."

Milo starts to shake his head and laugh.

"What?" I ask.

"I just can't picture one guy getting so much pussy. The only dates I've had lately are with Rosy Palm and Five Fingers."

This makes me laugh, too.

Our boss, Arto, walks in behind Milo. "It always pleases me to see detectives enjoy their work," Arto says. "Want to let me in on the joke?"

"Sure," Milo says. "What do you call epileptic lettuce?"

"What?"

"Seizure salad."

Milo howls at his own joke, which makes me laugh more than the joke. Arto giggles and says, "Jesus, that was awful."

When Milo stops cackling, Arto asks, "You two have time to investigate a death?"

"No," I say, "but we can make time."

"Head over to the Silver Dollar nightclub. The bouncers there killed some guy."

"Sounds good," Milo says.

The problem is that when Milo says it sounds good, I think he means it.

## 17

Milo and I sign a car out of the police garage at seven thirty p.m. Today we get a 2007 Toyota Yaris. It's dark out now. Snow still falls, and our headlights illuminate it. Helsinki is a lovely city in winter when it's not hammered by sleet and covered in filthy slush.

I drive. Milo jabbers. "So you have an American wife," he says.

"Yeah."

"What language do you speak at home?"

"Mostly English. Kate has been here for going on three years. She's learning, tries to at least use some Finnish words and phrases."

"Well," he says, "Finnish is a tough language. It takes time."

"Yeah."

"English is a moronic language."

This seems to be my week to have strong and unsupported opinions thrust upon me.

"And why might that be?"

"The letter C is unnecessary. It makes the same sounds as K and S. That's a lot of waste. They should get rid of it. They don't need B either. P is almost the same, does just as well."

I make conversation, since I was so hard on him earlier. "Kate thinks A and O with the dots over them are pointless. English gets on just fine without them."

Milo takes a pack of unfiltered North State cigarettes out of his coat pocket, cracks the window and lights one. My dad smokes the same brand. Tough-guy cigarettes. "So during this car ride," he says, "we've managed to take two letters out of the English language, and two out of Finnish. We changed the world."

Inane chatter. He's trying to kiss and make up because he pissed me off earlier. "So you started smoking again," I say.

He takes a drag and nods. "You really are a good detective."

"How long did you stay off them?"

"Four years."

His new job in *murharyhmä* must be getting to him. We sit in silence for a few moments.

"Did you know Ilari and Inka are fucking?" he asks.

164

"Is this deduction another product of your people-person skills and extreme powers of empathy?"

"It's the product of hearing them fuck in the bathroom after everybody got drunk at my 'welcome to the new guy' party."

They both have spouses and children, and even though they're partners, act as if they hate each other. I thought their vicious invective toward each other seemed forced.

At seven forty-five p.m., we pull up in front of the Silver Dollar and park next to an ambulance. To call the place a nightclub is a bit of a misnomer. It's multifunctional, soaks up money in different ways. It opens at four p.m. to accommodate after-work drinkers. A couple nights a week, it offers line dancing. Finnish country-music fans don cowboy boots, hats, bolos and collar tips, and giddy-up, pardner. Its biggest cash cow, though, is its four a.m. liquor license. Every other bar in the neighborhood closes at two, so when shit-drunk people get kicked out at closing time, they come here to this shithole to get shit-drunker for another couple hours. The place is packed most nights.

Milo and I walk inside. Two uniform cops are here. I introduce myself. They explain the situation. I tell them Milo and I will take it from here.

Music blares. People slurp beer. I look around. Plastic cups sit on beat-up dirty tables. The floor is filthy, the bar grimy. Dim blue-and-red pseudo-nightclub lighting is intended to mask these things, but it doesn't work. A prostrate body lies face-up in a corner. Two crime-scene techs and a pathologist crouch around it.

The dead man isn't fat, but maybe two hundred and sixty pounds, well over six feet tall. He's a baby-faced corpse, not much more than a kid, and appears as if he's sleeping. Two bouncers and two rent-a-cops in police-style coveralls and boots stand around the massive corpse, hands in their pockets, shift their weight back and forth on their feet like they're guilty of something.

I flash my police card. Milo pushes past the bouncers and rent-a-cops, bends down and talks to the pathologist.

A bouncer starts to shout in my ear, over the sound system. I yell, too, and cut him off. "Shut down the music. Turn up the houselights. Close the bar. Lock the door. Nobody leaves. The club is closed for the night."

He tries to argue. The law doesn't require that an establishment that serves alcohol be closed in the event of a death. His boss will be pissed off.

I shake my head. "We're operating under my law. Do it now."

Bouncer number one scurries off to follow instructions. Milo comes over. "Dead as a bag of hammers. Most likely because his hyoid bone is broken."

The music dies and the house goes quiet, except for a lone sobbing. A heavyset young guy, another giant, sits on a barstool, holds his face in his hands and cries. I ask Milo to take photos and witness statements from customers while I question the bouncers and rent-a-cops. Milo uses the camera in his cell phone to snap pics of the corpse and the club. Apparently, he doesn't mind deferring to me in matters that don't require his overwhelming intellectual prowess.

Bouncer number two stands near me. He has big muscles encased in a layer of fat. He wears jeans and a tight black T-shirt.

I take out a notepad and pen. "What's your name?" I ask.

"Timo Sipilä."

"Address, telephone and social security numbers."

He gives them to me.

"What happened?"

"This guy and his brother," he points at the boy giant in tears, "got into an argument. They started shoving each other. First we called Securitas — the rent-a-cops — then me and my partner, Joni Korjus, went over to calm them down."

Korjus is also huge. I'm in a bar full of mastodons.

"The dead guy had an attitude, so we told him to leave," Timo says. "He refused and started yelling at us to mind our own business. Securitas got here about the time we started to carry him out. They can back up my story."

The rent-a-cops nod agreement.

I get to the meat of the issue. "Why is he dead?"

"I got him in a headlock, and Joni grabbed his legs. We carried him outside like that and then dropped him outside the front door. He wasn't breathing anymore."

"You held him suspended by the neck," I say. "How long was he in that position?"

"Ninety seconds, two minutes tops."

More than enough time to kill him. "You broke his hyoid and caused him to choke to death."

The bouncer says nothing.

"Why so long, why was it necessary to remove him in that manner, and did his brother interfere?"

Timo ignores the first two parts of the

question. "No, his brother just followed us and screamed for us to stop."

Now I have a sense of the situation. Two brothers have a spat. Two bored bouncers overreact because they have nothing else to do. They have a bit of fun at the victim's expense while they eject him. He dies.

The rent-a-cops are a man and a woman. The man is in his late twenties. The woman, just out of her teens. He's a skinhead, has an Iron Cross tattooed on the meat between his right thumb and forefinger. A tribal tattoo runs up his neck and curls around his ear. She looks like a mean-spirited, gum-chewing cow with bad acne.

I take their personal information. "Did anyone try to revive him?" I ask.

The skinhead says, "I did. I tried mouth-to-mouth and chest compression. They didn't work."

"That much is apparent," I say, and turn back to Timo. "You dropped him outside. Why is he inside?"

"We carried him back in."

"Why?"

"It's warmer in here."

"He wasn't breathing. I don't think he cared."

Timo goes quiet, and I get it. It had nothing to do with the victim. He and his buddy were cold, since they just have on T-shirts. Bouncer number one comes back. I tell him to stand behind the bar and await further instructions. I don't want him and his buddy to talk and mesh their stories together any more than they already have. I call for cruisers to take them and the rent-a-cops to the lockup. They'll remain in custody while we sort this out.

I go over to the victim's brother and introduce myself. He's sniffling. He has a big baby face, too. It's glazed from shock.

"What's your name?" I ask.

"Sulo Polvinen. My brother's name was Taisto."

Using the past tense makes him sob. The brothers' names are old-fashioned, were popular during the Second World War. Sulo means "sweet." Taisto means "battle." Their family is patriotic.

"Those bastards killed him," he says.

"Tell me why."

He blinks, shakes his head. "It didn't make any sense. We were just squabbling, we argue all the time. It's a brother thing. We pushed each other a little, just playing, and those guys started to manhandle us. I stopped moving so they wouldn't hurt me, but Taisto struggled a little and yelled at them. They bent him over and the fat one got him by the head. The other got his knees and picked him up. I followed them and begged them to leave him alone, but they just laughed. And then they took him outside, tossed him up in the air, and when he hit the ground he wasn't breathing."

"How much did you and Taisto have to drink?" I ask.

"Four beers."

"Tell me the truth. Toxicology will measure the alcohol in your brother's system."

"We weren't drunk. I swear. We were drinking our fourth beer when it happened. Why did they kill my brother?" He starts to cry again.

"I wish I knew. I'm sorry. Is there anything else you want to tell me?"

"The *securitas,* the one who tried CPR. When we were outside and he couldn't bring Taisto back, he looked up at the bouncers and said, 'Why did you have to kill one of us instead of one of those goddamned foreigners?' "

I sigh. This situation makes me sad. The Silver Dollar has a reputation for foreigners showing up at last call. They try to score with blasted Finnish girls. A last-ditch end of the night effort to fuck some random drunk girl. When Finns witness this, especially if the foreigners are black, xenophobia often wells up. *Goddamned foreigners come here and take our jobs. They steal our women. Run the cocksuckers out of the country.*

Securitas has become more prominent in the Helsinki law enforcement apparatus over time. The police department has no room for additional officers in its budget. As a result, many businesses, especially bars, and even the public sector, like our transportation system, use rent-a-cops. Some of them are pretty good, military-trained, have even studied to be cops but couldn't get jobs.

However, many *securitas* are poorly trained, and worse, have psychological profiles that make them unfit as guardians of the community. The pay is bad, the work thankless. Bullies, racists, the kind of people who like authority so they can use it to push others around, tend to gravitate toward the rent-a-cop business. Often, they're the kind of people our citizens need protection *from,* and have no business enforcing the law. What pisses me off most is that the city has the money for things like heated sidewalks in the shopping district, so tourists won't get snow on their shoes, but not enough to provide its citizens with adequate protection.

"Those bastards killed my brother," Sulo

says. "What are you going to do to them?"

I see no point in lying and causing him disappointment later. "I'm going to investigate, but I doubt much will come of it. This kind of thing happens on a regular basis. Very few bouncers are even charged, let alone convicted."

"But they murdered him."

"I'm sorry to tell you this, but at most, they'll be charged with involuntary manslaughter. You can file a civil suit if you want. They'll counter and have you charged with disorderly conduct. Most likely, they'll walk and you'll end up paying a fine."

"That's insane."

Sulo is right, it's insane. Finnish drinking culture is a hypocrisy. Men are expected to drink. If they don't, they're considered untrustworthy. Both social and business life revolve around booze. Deals are often made at night, drunk. The good ole boy system comes into play. Since a lot of those drunken meetings take place in saunas segregated by sex, women are often shut out from the decision-making process.

If something goes wrong in a bar and somebody gets killed, most of the time it's just too fucking bad. Witnesses are discredited. They can't prove they weren't drunk. The courts lay blame on the victim and refuse to convict. Alcohol abuse is a cultural requirement, but once people are drunk, they in effect lose all legal rights.

"I feel for you," I say, "and I'll do the best I can. I just don't want you to expect too much."

Shock combines with anger. His face turns scarlet. Veins in his neck and forehead pulse. He's unable to speak.

I get his address, telephone and social security numbers, and tell him I'll have him taken home.

My cell phone rings. I answer.

"Hi. My name is Arska Kuivala. I'm Securitas. Are you related to an American named John Hodges?"

"He's my wife's brother. Why?"

"He's in trouble, and this is a courtesy call. I'm with him in Roskapankki. He ran up a bar tab close to three hundred euros, doesn't have money to pay it, and he's fucked up. Do you want to come here and fix this? If not, he goes to jail."

Kate will be devastated if he gets locked up. "I'll be there," I say, "and I owe you a favor."

"Yeah," he says, "you do. Your brother-in-law is an asshole." He hangs up.

I've got the Filippov murder, the Arvid Lahtinen situation, and various and sundry other deaths to investigate at the same time. My qualification to be in *murharyhmä* is already under question by my colleagues, and now I have to walk out on an investigation because my brother-in-law is a lush. It's more than just an inconvenience, it's fucking humiliating.

I tell Milo I've got an emergency and have to leave. He says he can clean this up. I give him the car keys and take a taxi to Roska-pankki.

# 18

Roskapankki — the Garbage Bank — is one of Helsinki's most notorious dives. It opened during the financial crisis of the early nineties. Banks went under left and right, and the government instituted a state-guaranteed bank to absorb their toxic assets, hence the bar's name. It offered some of the cheapest beer in the city to help medicate personal depression caused by the economic depression. The place has become synonymous with a low-priced buzz, and enjoys tremendous popularity with a certain clientele. It must have sold close to a couple million beers by now.

I check my watch. It's nine p.m. John sits at a wooden table, his hands cuffed behind him. A rent-a-cop sits across from him. He drums his fingers and stares at the wall, bored.

I walk over and ignore John. "Are you Arska?" I ask.

He nods.

"What did you cuff him for?"

"I would have duct-taped his mouth shut, too, if I had any. He's an annoying fuck. You gonna take care of this? I have things to do."

"I'll pay his tab and make things right."

Arska uncuffs John, shoots him a dirty look and leaves.

John starts in. "Those fucking dickheads —"

I cut him off. "Just explain yourself."

I watch him concoct a lie. It takes a while. He's sloppy, drunk as hell, but propped up by speed or coke. I wonder how it's possible to run up a three-hundred-euro tab when a pint of beer only costs two and a half euros. "Never mind," I say, and go to the bar.

The bartender tells the story. John came in early, started drinking hard, got drunk and loud. He bought people drinks to make friends. He dropped a credit card. In the late afternoon, he asked if he could take a hundred euros in cash on his card. The bartender didn't run the card, just made a note to add it to the final tab. John annoyed the shit out of everyone, but they put up with him since he kept the beer flowing. The bill got high, the bartender got suspicious.

He ran the card. The card was dead. He asked John if he had another card. John gave him two more. Both dead. John got haughty. John started name-calling. John feigned indignation and tried to leave. A bouncer stopped him. Securitas was called in.

"I'll pay the bill," I say, and hand over my MasterCard. John has been in Helsinki for two days. Between champagne last night and his drinking binge today — and the hundred he took from the bartender, which I'm sure he used to buy drugs — he's become an expensive annoyance. I'm not happy.

I go back to the table and sit across from him. My headache isn't monster-from-*Alien* bad, but it's getting worse again. "What the fuck is the matter with you?" I ask.

"Kari, it wasn't my fault. Listen, Kari, there's something wrong with their credit card machine, and they made out like it's my mistake. Kari, you're a cop. Do something. Kari, I swear to God I'm going to sue these bastards."

I hate the American habit of using a person's name over and over to create a fake sense of intimacy. "John," I say, "here's what I'm going to do, and here's what you're going to do. John, you're a lying whore. John, you're drunk and stoned. John, you're going to sober up. John, you dumb mother-fucker, you and I are going to cover this up because if Kate finds out, it's going to upset her. John, when someone upsets my wife, I get upset. John, do you want me to be upset?"

He shakes his head no.

"Good. I should be finishing a death investigation right now and going home to Kate, where I want to be. Instead, I'm going to call Kate and tell her we're having a little boys' night out, to do some bonding." I hate that term, but think he'll relate to it. "My plan is this. I'm going to take you to a sauna, then to get something to eat. When we get back to my house, you're going to act like a choirboy."

He starts to speak. I press a finger to my lips. "I don't want to hear your voice for a while. We clear?"

He nods yes. I call Kate. He stands, puts on his coat, weaves. I help him toward the door.

Kotiharjun sauna is within walking distance of both our apartment and Roskapankki. John never intended to go sightseeing today. He just wandered out and got smashed in the first place that looked inviting to him. He stumbles through the snow. The cold air and exercise will do him good. The sauna will be good for both of us, and also serve as a small punishment for his bad behavior. I'm going to use the opportunity to fuck with him, just a little.

Kotiharjun sauna opened its doors in 1928. It's a Helsinki institution and one of my favorite places. The only public sauna left that's both wood-fired and keeps to the old traditions. We approach it. A line of men are outside in the snow, sitting on a low wall, wrapped in towels, smoking cigarettes and drinking beer.

"What the fuck are naked guys doing in the snow?" John asks.

"The same thing you're going to do, *sans* beer."

We go inside to the front desk. They know me here. I'm a regular, like to come here after lifting weights in the gym. Our little electric sauna at home does its job, but their big wood-fired sauna is a special experience. It generates a wonderful soft heat.

I pay our admission, get us towels and a *vihta* — a bundle of leaf-covered birch branches tied together at one end. "My brother-in-law, John, needs the full treatment, a wash and a *kuppaus*," I say. "Is there somebody still here to give it to him?"

The cashier is a friendly young guy. "Ellu

was about to go home," he says. "John looks like he should go home, too."

"That's the point, I don't want him there yet. Tell her I'll tip her an extra fifty if she stays."

He checks it out, Ellu agrees. We go to a room that looks like a little operating theater. I tell John to take his clothes off. He protests. I stare at him. He peels down to his underwear and stops. I keep staring. He takes off his briefs and stands there embarrassed and naked. Ellu waits, impatient. I tell him to lie down on the table. He does it. Ellu proceeds to give him a good scrubbing while I watch. Usually, *kuppaus* is done after spending some time in sauna, because the raised body temperature enhances bleeding. But I figure what the hell, John can bleed slow.

After a few minutes, John relaxes. "Thanks Kari," he says, "this is nice."

Ellu finishes washing him and starts taking out the plastic bubbles used for sucking blood in *kuppaus.* "You sure about this?" she asks me.

I answer, "I've never been more certain of anything in my life."

She brings over to the table the clear suction bottles with short hypodermic needles extending from them.

John gets suspicious. "What are those? They look like they hurt."

"It's an old Finnish folk remedy," I say. "It gets the poisons out of your system."

"I don't want it." He starts to sit up.

I shove him back down. "Sure you do. Don't be a pussy."

He understands I won't take no for an answer. Ellu attaches the first bottle to his back. He grunts, but doesn't complain. Ellu attaches six bubbles. John looks over his shoulder and watches them fill with blood. "It doesn't hurt much," he says, "but what the hell is the point."

"They're like plastic leeches," I say. "Now you can tell your buddies that you're a true-blue Finn and got your blood sucked."

He manages a laugh. "Most of their stories are about getting their dicks sucked. I think this story is better."

I thought John would piss and moan. He's impressed me, if only slightly. I get undressed in the locker room. We rinse off in the shower room and I take him into the sauna. It's a Tuesday, so the crowd is small, maybe fifteen men. On weekends, the place gets packed and rowdy. Friends come here to drink and sweat together.

The iron stove is massive. Logs heat it. The sauna is hotter or cooler, depending on where you sit in relation to the stove. John and I take a spot almost behind it, on the third and top seating tier. John has sobered up somewhat, his humiliation from Roska-pankki faded, his courage bolstered by a successful engagement with *kuppaus.*

"This feels great," he says. "You know Kari, I had my doubts about you, but you're all right."

"Wow," I say. "Thanks. I was worried you didn't like me."

I wet the *vihta* and start smacking my back with it. It occurs to me that I'm employing much the same motion that Iisa Filippov's murderer used while torturing her with a riding crop.

"What's that for?" John asks.

"Being hit with the branches makes you sweat more, and the birch leaves are cura-tives, help get the toxins out of you."

"Finns must be chock-full of poisons," he says. "You go to a lot of work to get them out of you."

"Believe me," I say, "we are. Try it. I'll help you, teach you the technique."

He smiles. "Okay."

There's no technique. I take the op-portunity to whack the hell out of him. It doesn't hurt, just stings a little. The guys in the sauna heard us speaking English and realize I'm teasing a foreigner. They chuckle. John gets it, takes it in stride and laughs with them. He has problems, that's apparent, but he also has a good side. I want to like him, but he's done his best to make it hard for me.

We sit for a while until he gets too hot, then go outside and sit in the snow and cold air for a bit, go back to the sauna, repeat the process. An old man I know offers me a beer and asks me to play a game of speed chess at the table in the dressing room. He and I pass a Koskenkorva bottle back and forth a couple times. The sauna and vodka dull my headache. John looks at the bottle but knows better than to ask for a drink. Despite John, I'm enjoying myself.

We go back to the sauna a third time. John says he would like to try it hotter and asks how to do it. I say the valve on the stove releases water and creates more steam. Before I can instruct him further, John hops up and moves toward it.

This sauna is holy ground, a place for aficionados. Many are older men who've practiced the art of sauna for a lifetime. The rules of Kotiharjun sauna are as sacrosanct as those of a church service. A major rule is that only men sitting in the hottest area of the sauna may throw water without asking permission. Too much steam turns the hot corner into an oven.

Exuberant John yanks the valve open and lets water fly. Way too much. Even in our cool corner, the steam burns my lungs and the inside of my nose. The guys in the hot seats get scalded and turn furious, start screaming at John and calling him names. He doesn't know what he's done wrong. They come out of their corner after him. The floor is slick. He can't move fast enough to get away from them. Plus he's naked and has nowhere to escape to. Four men grab him and force him across the room.

"Kari!" he yells. "Help me!"

I might if I could, for Kate's sake, but I can't. I consider that John has come halfway around the world and, within a day, has managed to almost get himself thrown in jail, and now finds himself attacked by four naked men. I can't help but laugh. Welcome to Finland. Three men force him to sit down. Another comes back and throws the valve open. He yells at John, "Let's see how you like it, you stupid cunt."

"Just sit still for a minute," I say. "You won't die. Try not to breathe too deep."

The four men stand in the middle of the room with their arms folded and stare at John while he cooks. They don't want to hurt him, just teach him a lesson. They go outside to cool off. He creeps out of the hot seat over to me. "Can we go now?" he asks.

"Yeah," I say, "let's get something to eat."

I get a taxi and take John to Juttutupa, a favorite restaurant. I figure if I have to babysit Kate's brother, I might as well enjoy myself as best I can. The building sits opposite the water and resembles a small castle constructed from granite blocks. It's been around for better than a century. Juttutupa is next door to the offices of SDP, the Social Democratic Party, and has a reputation for politicos hanging out and making deals over food and drink.

A couple of nights a week, Juttutupa offers live jazz. I like good jazz, and Kate has picked up my appreciation of it, so we sometimes come here together. I reflect that I've offered John an ultimate introduction to classic Helsinki culture this evening, even if only for my own benefit.

A waitress comes to our table. I ask her to speak English, for John's sake. She asks what we want to drink. I order *kossu* and beer. John looks sad, like a little kid, asks if he can have a beer. I feel sorry for him, revert to Finnish and order an *ykkösolut* — a weak beer — for him. He won't be able to taste the difference. John was shit-drunk when I rescued him earlier. He's better now, but no way he can pass for sober. If I have a few drinks, too, to make it seem like we were drinking together, it will help maintain the pretense for Kate that he's not a fucked-up drunk doper. I'm drinking to spare my wife's feelings. A strange day.

The waitress brings our drinks and menus. I say we don't need them and order for both of us. Snails in garlic butter as an appetizer to share. Liver and onions with mashed potatoes for him and a big horse steak for me. Bloody rare.

Still drunk, John protests. "What the hell is wrong with you? I hate liver, and no one should eat slimy things or horses. You're blackmailing me because the credit card machine at a bar was broken."

He won't eat snails, but has no problem with caviar. I guess the price of caviar makes its texture more appealing to him. "No, John, you're wrong. I'm doing what it takes to hide whatever is wrong with you from Kate. When we go home, you're going to be in presentable condition. You're going to tell Kate what a wonderful time we had, and starting tomorrow, you're going to behave yourself. Don't eat the snails if you don't like them, but you're going to eat the liver, because it's the best sobering-up food I know."

The speed or coke he ingested is wearing off, only booze is left in his system. He starts to slur. "Kari, you're wrong about me. You think I'm some kind of loser. It's not my fault if a credit card machine in a goddamn bar doesn't work with American cards."

We stare at each other for a minute.

"If you'll excuse me," he says, "I'm going to the bathroom."

I take a sip of Koskenkorva, see the longing in his face. "If you come back high," I say, "I'm going to be more than pissed off."

"So now you're accusing me of taking drugs."

"Yes, I am."

"Screw you."

"I covered your bar tab. You forgot to thank me."

He huffs and gets up. When he comes back, he's not stoned. I eat the snails by myself. Our main courses come. He looks at the liver with distaste but digs in. He must be hungry. His indignation disappears. "It's good," he says.

"I know."

"What's the red jelly for?"

"It's lingonberry jam. Take tastes of it with the liver. It's traditional."

We eat in silence. He cleans his plate. I pay our bill and order a taxi to take us home. On the way, he stares straight ahead. After a few minutes, he says, "Thanks for paying my bar tab."

"You're welcome."

"I won't upset Kate."

"Good." I take out a notepad, scribble my number on it and give it to him. "Stay out of trouble, but if you don't, call me, not Kate."

He nods.

As an afterthought, I take his number and put it in my cell phone, in case he disappears and I need to find him.

My impression is that John is a decent person when he's sober, but those moments are few and far between. He needs help, and because he's Kate's brother, I'd like to get it for him, but our baby is on the way. John frightens me. I'm scared he'll upset Kate and cause her to lose our child. I can't let that happen. I want him to go back where he came from.

# 19

John and I get home around two a.m. Mary is in bed asleep. Kate wanders out into the living room in a nightgown. "So what have you two been up to?" She sniffs. Her voice is testy. "Never mind, I can smell what you've been up to."

"Just a Finnish boys' night out," I say. "A couple drinks, sauna, some good food."

John smiles and nods. "I ate liver for the first time since Mom was alive. I even liked it. I got my blood sucked. I haven't decided if I liked it or not."

She looks at me. "Blood sucked?"

*"Kuppaus,"* I say.

Her vexation fades. She laughs. "You really did have a Finnish night out. John, what did you do all day?"

"I'm pretty tired. I'll tell you about it tomorrow."

"Kate, let's go to bed," I say, "so John can have peace and quiet on the sofa."

She hugs her brother good-night. I wash my face and brush my teeth. On the way back, I tell John to invent a lie about what he did today.

He's already half asleep. He nods. I go to our room and get into bed with Kate. She snuggles up beside me. I wrap an arm around her.

"Did you really have fun?" she asks. "I was afraid you two wouldn't hit it off."

"Let's just say we're getting to know each other. But yeah, we had a good time. He learned a little about Finnish culture this evening."

"The baby is kicking," she says. She takes my hand and rests it on her belly so I can feel it, too. "How is your head?" she asks.

It hurts. I lie. "It's okay."

"Our day got off to a strange start," Kate says. "After you left this morning, John and Mary and I were having breakfast, talking about things that happened when we were kids. After Mom died, and Dad started drinking, we didn't have much money and moved into a run-down little house. We had a neighbor who was just a regular guy, a nice guy. He lived by himself. Another neighbor drove home drunk and crashed his car through the wall of the nice guy's house into his living room while he was watching TV. The car went over top of him and crippled him for life. The three of us kids ran over and saw him pinned under this big Buick. The strange thing is that we all have different memories of what Dad did. John remembers that Dad ran into the house to help. Mary remembers that he stood on the porch and watched. I remember that he was drunk, sitting in the kitchen alone, and didn't even get out of his chair to see what happened. It was an awful thing to see, traumatizing for us."

"Trauma affects people in strange ways," I say.

"I was the oldest and I'm sure Dad was dead drunk. Maybe the trauma hurt John and Mary so badly that they invented better memories so they wouldn't have to think of Dad like that."

I think of John's behavior today, and wonder if reliving the ugly memory set him off. "Could be."

"After cancer got Mom," Kate says, "I became their mother. I was supposed to protect them. When I went off to college, I thought Mary was old enough to look after John, but they've changed. I feel like something is my fault, but I don't know what it is."

Kate is a grown woman. I don't want to

treat her like a child, but the miscarriage hurt her in deep places. It can't happen again. I think of preeclampsia, hypertension, placental abruption — the placental lining separating from her uterus — the child's death, her death. I want to protect her for just a little while, until our daughter is born. The idea of this visit from her siblings seems worse and worse to me.

"Kate, you were thirteen when your mother passed on, still a child yourself. Your father was the grown-up. He was responsible for all of you. He failed you. Don't take that failure onto yourself."

"I can't help my feelings," she says.

It's hard to blame the dead for anything, easier to shoulder their guilt. "But you can try to rationalize them, to maintain perspective." Pot calling kettle black. I can't do it, either.

"Enough about that," she says. "Tell me about your day."

I tell her about the Filippov murder, the Silver Dollar death, about Arvid Lahtinen, about the accusations against him, and about his connection to Ukki. Again, I lie by omission, and don't tell her about passing out on Arvid's floor.

Kate rolls toward me and lays her head on

my chest. "You haven't told me much about Ukki."

"He was a good man. I loved him. And my grandma, too. They were kind to me."

"You shouldn't worry about it then. Mass murderers aren't kind to children."

Couldn't they be? "I just want to know the truth about him, for good or ill."

"Why? If he was a good grandpa, what difference does it make what he did in wartime?"

A good question. I haven't asked it of myself. The answer is apparent. "It's my nature. If he took part in the Holocaust, I won't love the memory of him less. I just need to know."

"Yes," she says, "you're like that. Life would be easier for you if you weren't."

She's more right than she knows.

"Do you have to get up early tomorrow?" she asks.

"Yeah, to see Jari."

"Let's get some sleep then," she says, and snaps off the light.

# 20

Rescuing John meant I had to leave my car in the police garage overnight. I get up and leave early to fetch it, then drive to the hospital. In the waiting room of the neurology polyclinic, I browse household cleaning tips in a women's magazine. The reading selection here leaves much to be desired. The polyclinic radiates sterility, but I stand instead of sit. The last time I took a seat in a public medical facility, when I left, my clothes smelled like piss.

Jari calls me into an examination room. He sees the gunshot scar on my face and flinches, but doesn't comment on it. The last time we saw each other was three Christmases ago. He's aged since then. His hair is grayer, he's thinner. We share a quick brotherly hug, he tells me to sit down. I describe my headaches. He types the symptoms into a computer.

"On a scale of one to ten — one being

mild discomfort and ten being the worst screaming pain you can imagine — how would you rate your headache at the moment?" he asks.

The pain is dull but nagging. "About a three."

"You say that the problem started about a year ago, but that you've had a constant headache for three weeks."

"Yeah."

"Would you describe the headaches as increasing in severity as well as duration?"

"They've gotten a lot worse over time," I say.

"On that one-to-ten scale, how would you rate the worst episodes?"

I picture all my teeth being drilled through to the roots without anesthetic as ten. "Eight."

"You've always been laconic," he says. "I think you've been through some intense suffering. Why did you wait so long to have this taken care of?"

"I saw a general practitioner six months ago. She gave me extra-strength Tylenol and something she called a pain diffuser. She said they give it to people with chronic problems, for instance, who've lost limbs but still feel pain in the missing parts. I took it for three days, and it helped the headaches but made me so stupid that it was hard to speak. I threw it in the trash."

"Does the Tylenol help?"

"It used to. Not anymore."

"Are your nerves so bad that you can't eat or sleep?"

"I'm a little off my feed, but I eat. I can't sleep."

Jari has me track his finger back and forth with my eyes, checks my balance and reflexes, a few other things. He runs his fingers over the scar on my face, tells me to open my mouth. He looks inside with a medical penlight. "The bullet took out two back teeth," he says.

"Yeah."

"Do you have chronic pain or any paralysis as a result of the wound?"

"Just some stiffness in my jaw and minimal paralysis. My smile is a little crooked."

He grins. "That's no big deal, you don't smile much anyway." He sits, ponders the situation. "There's a bundle of facial nerves in the vicinity of the bullet wound. Damage to them could cause your headaches, but your lack of other symptoms makes me think that's not the case here. There's nothing readily visible wrong with you," he says. "We need to run tests."

"What do you think the problem is?" I ask.

"This is largely a process of elimination from the most to least likely causes. Let's see if you have a brain tumor, then we'll check for nervous system disorders."

This alarms me. "Those are the most likely causes?"

"Little brother, you don't seem to understand the gravity of the situation or how very fucking stupid you've been. You need an MRI. The waiting time for an MRI in the public health system in Helsinki is nine months. You could die while you wait. It happens all the time."

"The police have private medical coverage," I say.

"Screw the system, both public and private," Jari says. "I'll twist some arms and get you as far up the line as I can. You'll get the MRI in at most a couple weeks, and a blood test as soon as you leave this office."

"Okay," I say. Something occurs to me. "I thought you were getting rich in private practice. What are you doing here in a hospital?"

"The pay for public doctors is so abysmal that most of the good doctors have fled to private practice. So what you have left is recent graduates from medical school, some bad doctors, some older doctors, and lately an influx of foreign medical workers. There's nothing inherently wrong with that, but many of the foreigners speak poor Finnish and often depend on English."

"But foreign doctors have to pass a language test in order to practice."

"That doesn't guarantee spoken fluency. Two parents brought a child with an ear infection in to see me last week for a second consultation. They'd seen a foreign doctor and his language skills were so poor that all he could tell them was, 'It's not cancer.' And when, for instance, elderly people come in and don't speak English, they sometimes feel that they can't relate their problems. They feel neglected by the system. I come here two mornings a week to help out. I think of it as my civic duty."

Jari always was a good guy.

"How's your bum knee?" he asks.

"Worse every year. There's not enough cartilage left to hold it together. I have to sleep with a pillow between my knees to keep the pressure off, or it starts to go out of joint in my sleep and the pain wakes me up. At least it used to, back in the days when I slept."

"Getting kneecapped with a bullet has a tendency to do that. Have an orthopedist examine it again. Reconstructive surgery probably won't fix it, but might improve it."

"I've got a baby coming. Better to limp than not walk at all."

We share an uncomfortable silence. I wait for him to ask the inevitable.

"Why have you been avoiding me?" Jari asks. "You don't return my phone calls."

I've been asking myself the same question. I discovered the answer but can't share it with him. It's about old hurt and anger. Dad used to beat the hell out of me. Jari is older than me, but never did anything to stop it. Maybe he couldn't.

When Jari got out of high school, he told Dad he wanted to be a doctor. Dad asked him who the hell did he think he was, told him he thought he was better than his upbringing, to come down off his high horse and get a job. They argued. Dad punched him in the face. Jari left that night, and I didn't hear from him for almost two years. He had moved to Helsinki and gotten into the university. He abandoned me.

"I don't know why," I say. "I didn't realize I was doing it until Kate and I had been here for a few months and I hadn't gotten in touch with you."

He nods. "I get that, but I'm still your brother."

"I know. For whatever reason, I've been distant, but it has nothing to do with you and I'll make myself get over it. Kate's brother and sister from the States are here visiting us. Why don't you bring your wife and kids over on Thursday. I'll cook us a big family dinner."

"Sounds good," he says. "You have to go now. Patients are backing up." He hands me some papers. "These are the order for your blood test, which I expect you to take now, and prescriptions for some new meds."

"What kinds of meds?"

"Opiated painkillers, tranquilizers and sleeping pills. I want you to use them freely. You need rest and relief from pain."

I grab my coat and start to protest. He pushes me out the door. "See you Thursday," he says.

# 21

I go to another waiting room, stand and read until my turn comes up. I have a busy workday ahead and waiting frustrates me. A nurse draws some blood. I exit the hospital and look at the prescriptions in my hand. I dislike taking medication in general, but Jari was right. Passing out at Arvid's house taught me that I need relief. I go to a pharmacy and get them filled.

It's minus ten degrees, crisp and pleasant, a little after ten a.m. A darkened sky looms over a snow-white city. I lean against my Saab, smoke cigarettes and make phone calls. First in line is Milo. His voice is hushed, uncharacteristic of him. I ask him if he can run background checks on Iisa Filippov and Linda Pohjola. He says he's working the case from a different angle at the moment and can't talk right now. He asks if we can meet later, outside the police station. He has things to tell me. I suggest

Hilpeä Hauki at two thirty. He says perfect, he lives in the neighborhood. My interest is piqued.

Next I call Jaakko Pahkala. I've know him for years, since I was a uniform cop in Helsinki, before I moved back to my hometown of Kittilä and took over the police department there. He's a freelance writer for the Helsinki daily newspaper *Ilta-Sanomat,* for the gossip magazine *Seitsemän Päivää,* and the true-crime rag *Alibi.* Jaakko loves filth, specializes in scandal.

"Hello, Inspector," he says. "This is a pleasant surprise. I thought you would never speak to me again after the Sufia Elmi case."

Jaakko committed obstruction of justice by releasing details of the murder that I wanted suppressed, published morgue photos that demeaned the victim and did his best to discredit me and have me fired because I refused to grant him an interview.

"I didn't, either," I say, "but you have your uses."

He laughs. His high-pitched voice grates on me. "Who do you want dirt on?"

"Iisa Filippov."

"I'm interested in her murder myself. What do I get?"

Jyri wants Rein Saar hung out to dry. I'll make it hard for him. "A good scoop, provided I stay anonymous."

"Give."

I light another cigarette, exhale smoke and frozen breath in a long plume. "Iisa Filippov and Rein Saar were both stunned with a taser. He would have had a hard time giving her a prolonged torture session after that. And the taser is missing, wasn't at the crime scene."

"Damn," he says, "that's good."

"Your turn," I say.

"Iisa Filippov was a party girl, fuck monster and trophy dick collector. Notches on her bedpost include Tomi Herlin, Jarmo Pvolakka, Pekka Kuutio, and Peter Mänttäri."

Herlin: a heavyweight boxing champion and hero-of-the-people-turned-politician and then finally drug-addled sad case. He committed gun suicide eleven days ago and lay dead for two days before his body was discovered. Pvolakka: the only ski jumper in the world to have won gold medals in Olympic Games, World Championships and Ski Flying World Championships, and to have finished first in the overall World Cup and Four Hills Tournament. Also hero-of-the-people-turned-nutcase and finally loser with a penchant for stabbing others. Kuutio: former minister of foreign affairs. Forced to resign because of a scandal involving hundreds of harassing text messages he sent to a stripper. Mänttäri: aka Peter the Great. Washed-up porn star.

"Drugs?" I ask.

"Of the recreational variety."

"Her husband?"

"Straitlaced cuckold."

I was once made a cuckold and was hell-bent on murder for months, even though I never committed it. I can imagine Filippov feeling the same. I picture my unfaithful ex-wife, Heli, sociopath and killer, burned to death on a frozen lake. I remember some of her last words to me. "Deserve," she said. "Nobody gets what they deserve. If we did, we'd all burn in hell. We're all fucking guilty."

"Friend Linda Pohjola?" I ask.

"Party girl but not fuck monster. Iisa and Linda liked to get high and dress up alike to titillate. They even learned to speak and act alike. Iisa usually followed through after aforementioned titillation, Linda generally didn't."

"Anything else I should know?"

"Maybe. I'll think about it. More will cost you more, too."

I ring off and go to work.

# 22

I take the elevator from the parking garage in Helsinki's central police station in West Pasila and head up to my office. My head throbs from the migraine again and it makes me stupid. I get off the elevator and walk ten paces before I realize I'm on the fifth floor, home to sex crimes and arson. I walk down the stairs to the fourth floor, which houses our three homicide teams and two robbery units.

I ask our unit secretary, Tia, to run background checks on the bouncers and *securitas* from the Silver Dollar through the computer system. I don't see much of Tia, or the other team members for that matter, because I'm so often on evening and weekend shifts. She and I communicate mostly through notes and e-mails. Tia keeps the *murharyhmä* ball rolling: takes care of paperwork, requests search warrants, does all the little things that make life easier for us detectives.

Milo typed up eyewitness statements last night and e-mailed them to me. They're inconclusive. The bar was dark and noisy. Only a handful of patrons noticed the incident, and of those that did, most were too drunk to make credible witnesses. None state the belief that the bouncers caused intentional harm to Taisto Polvinen. The rent-a-cops' version of events rings true. Milo also formally interviewed the bouncers and *securitas.* I read their statements. They stuck to their earlier version of events.

One by one, I take the bouncers and rent-a-cops from their cells to the interrogation room. They got their stories straight before Milo and I arrived. They keep their narratives vague enough so that it's hard to punch holes in them. The bouncers portray Taisto as on the edge of a rampage. They're sorry he's dead, but they acted in self-defense. The rent-a-cops confirm that Taisto struggled as the bouncers ejected him. No doubt he did. I would have, too.

When I'm done with them, I go back to Tia's office. She has their crime sheets waiting. I take them to my office. The bouncers have each had a couple previous complaints filed against them, but no charges brought. Gum-chewing cow has a clean sheet. Skinhead has had two assault charges filed against him, one conviction. But he tried to revive Taisto. I have no reason to suspect him of wrongdoing. Milo and I will pass this on to the prosecutor, but much as I told Taisto's brother, nothing will come of it. It's Milo's case, too, so I'll ask his opinion first, but we have no reason to hold any of them, will have to release them. It's dispiriting to me.

I give the Internet versions of Helsinki's three major daily newspapers a quick skim. They all contain thin stories about both the Filippov murder and the Silver Dollar death. I brought *Einsatzkommando Finnland and Stalag 309* to work with me. I flip through it, consider what to do about Arvid, ask myself what I can do to help him. The interior minister wants me to file a report stating that the charges against him are fabrications. I question whether, if I do it, the matter will be dropped.

Jyri said that Germany recently extradited an accused war criminal from the United States. I Web-search the case. The man's name is John Demjanjuk. Israel, Germany and the Wiesenthal Center started bulldogging him twenty-four years ago, in 1986. They've managed to have him stripped of his U.S. citizenship twice. They've charged him with murder under two different identities. They'll stop at nothing. Arvid's guilt or innocence may have no bearing on whether he's forced to stand trial. Filing a false report will accomplish little more than buying Arvid time. At age ninety, with enough delays, he might die before he's arrested, but he looks too healthy to be that lucky.

Pasi Tervomaa's book doesn't contain enough information about either Arvid or Ukki for me to draw conclusions about their guilt or innocence or the degrees thereof. I need to talk to the author. I Google his name and find contact info for him at the National Archives. I call and identify myself. He's no longer employed there. He's working from his home, writing books. They give me his cell phone number.

I call Tervomaa and explain the situation. "If they extradite a Winter War hero," he says, "the nation will be up in arms. Finland might declare war on Germany again."

His joke is poignant. The consequences would be dire. "Do you know anything about Arvid Lahtinen that's not in your book? Something that might help me out?"

"No. Of course I looked into him while doing research, but he wasn't the focus of my book. He played rather a small part in the events I described."

"Why didn't you call him and ask him for an interview?"

"I did. Several times. He kept hanging up the phone on me."

"What about another Valpo detective at Stalag 309? Toivo Kivipuro."

"Why him?"

"He was my grandpa."

"So you have a vested personal interest in your investigation."

"Yes."

"I don't know more about Toivo Kivipuro either, but I think what you're really asking me is if the Finns stationed in Stalag 309 took part in the Holocaust. The answer is yes. In terms of scale, Finland's participation was minuscule. In my opinion, though, any part in the Holocaust is unacceptable and punishable. Whether the detectives there killed men themselves or not, they colluded in the decision-making process of who would die."

Not what I wanted to hear. The truth of it unsettles me. "Where can I research this myself?"

"Many of the Valpo records are where they've always been, in Ratakatu 12. It was then and is now security police headquarters, but historians are allowed to search records up through the year 1948. I'm going there this afternoon to do research for a new book. You're welcome to join me. Get permission to visit and have them pull the files for you."

We agree to meet in an hour.

"Bring a pen and notepad," Pasi says. "They don't allow cameras or photocopying." He hangs up.

I call Jyri and tell him to get permission for me. I need to see the Valpo files, but I don't want to. The Bible tells us that the truth will set us free. I reflect that Jesus must have been unclear about certain of life's realities.

## 23

I find Pasi Tervomaa waiting for me in front of SUPO headquarters. We recognize each other but haven't met. He's a regular at Kotiharjun sauna. He's fortyish, thin and gaunt, but his smile reflects warmth. He waits while I finish a cigarette. The building is fortresslike granite block, gray and yellow, reminds me of pictures I've seen of the Lubyanka — KGB headquarters, former Soviet prison and charnel house — only smaller and less ornate. In fact, SUPO, as was Valpo before it, is Finland's version of the KGB. They deal in counterespionage, counterterrorism, prevention of threats to internal security and related matters.

"Your inquiry is an interesting confluence," Pasi says. "I'm also researching a so-called war criminal. Lauri Törni."

I know about Törni. He fought for Finland, then for Germany in the Waffen-SS, and finally for the Americans. He changed

212

his name to Larry A. Thorn, joined the Green Berets and died in a helicopter crash in Laos in 1965, while on a covert mission.

We go inside. A custodian type meets us and checks our IDs. He has the files Pasi requested ready for us and escorts us to a jail cell in the basement. It only contains a wooden table with a reading lamp on it, and a couple of chairs. The custodian sets our files on the table and leaves.

I think of the Lubyanka again. "Did Valpo torture enemies of the state in this cell?" I ask.

"No," Pasi says, "they did that in the interrogation rooms."

"I was only half serious. I can't picture Finnish police torturing anyone."

"Don't be naïve. Of course they did. In general, not as brutally as the Nazis or Soviets, but interrogations sometimes employed physical coercion. Beatings. Hitting the soles of the feet with nightsticks. Things like that."

We sit. He hands me files on Arvid and Ukki. "Let's take a look," he says.

The dossiers are thin. I open Arvid's first. Pasi and I read it together. The photo clipped to it is nearly seventy years old, but it's Arvid. The top sheet gives vital stats.

DOB: January 3, 1920. Arvid enters Valpo

service in 1938, at age eighteen, is stationed in Helsinki. I wonder how he got into the security police at such a young age. By 1940, he receives two citations for distinction in service. Reasons not stated.

He's fluent in German and Russian. He leaves Valpo service for a time to go to the front during the Winter War. He's wounded in action. After recovery, he goes back to work for Valpo, this time up north, in the Rovaniemi station. In 1941, he's attached to Einsatzkommando Finnland. The sheet states only Salla. No mention of a stalag. In January 1943, he's again stationed in Helsinki. He's fired by Valpo in June 1945. I ask Pasi why this might have been.

"Anti-Communist White Valpo was replaced by Red Valpo, Communists and leftist radicals. The new security police were by and large men that the old security police once investigated. Out with the old and in with the new."

Arvid's sheet details his commendations and medals. The Mannerheim Cross — the medal of honor. The Commemorative Medal of the Winter War. The Badge for Wounded Veterans. A German-awarded Iron Cross. The Order of the Cross of Liberty. The Order of the White Rose of Finland. The Order of the Lion of Finland. The list goes on.

The last page of the dossier is a letter of recommendation dated August 12, 1938. The writer is Bruno Aaltonen, deputy director of Valpo. He requests that Arvid be accepted into Valpo service forthwith.

"Arvid Lahtinen was connected to people high up in the intelligence community," Pasi says. "Aaltonen took such matters seriously and wouldn't have taken Lahtinen into Valpo unless he had the highest confidence that he was detective material."

I open Ukki's dossier. In his photo, he's nineteen years old. Ukki was a year older, but other than that, their files are nearly identical. Ukki and Arvid entered Valpo service at the same time, worked in the same duty stations during the same time frames, won almost all the same medals. Everything. The last page is a recommendation from Bruno Aaltonen that Toivo Kivipuro be taken into the security police as a detective. The date: August 12, 1938. It's like reading about twin brothers.

"Arvid lied," I say. "He told me he didn't know my grandpa."

"Given that they were so young, and Aaltonen wrote the letters on the same day, there must be a connection between your family and Arvid's. My guess is that Aaltonen knew their fathers, and together, they asked Aaltonen for their appointments. That also might explain their assignment to Einsatzkommando Finnland."

"How so?"

"Aaltonen was acquainted with the Gestapo hierarchy, all the way up to Reinhard Heydrich, chief of the Reich Security Office, who formed Einsatzkommando. Aaltonen was also a friend of Heinrich Müller, the head of the Gestapo. They engaged in extensive correspondence. Dozens of their letters have been preserved. The letters discuss family and work issues as well as politics. These kinds of personal ties became the basis for collaboration between German and Finnish officials. Arvid Lahtinen and Toivo Kivipuro were likely given their positions at Stalag 309 because their families were highly regarded and trusted."

I know nothing about my great-grandfather, not even his name. "You're certain Arvid and my grandpa were at the stalag? Without a doubt?"

"I'm a historian, an academic. I seldom state that anything is without doubt unless I've seen it with my own eyes, and I wasn't there. But let's call it a ninety-nine percent certainty that Arvid Lahtinen lied to you."

"Can you make a reasonable guess about

what Arvid and Grandpa did there?"

"Well, Einsatzkommando Finnland was mandated to liquidate Jews and Soviet political commissars. These are the people Arvid and Toivo worked with. Let's just say that I think the verve and enthusiasm of Einsatzkommando might have been infectious. I gather the Finnish detectives and interpreters there often drank heavily. It's easy to picture them getting drunk and doing things they never would have dreamed themselves capable of."

"You're saying Finns lined people up and shot them."

"I can't say that. I can say that, given the atmosphere, it seems likely."

He's saying in that prevaricating way, typical of academics, that Arvid and Ukki were stone-cold killers. I've barely started this investigation, and I'm already discovering things that, four days ago, would have been beyond my comprehension. "How in the hell could this have remained secret for so long?"

"Einsatzkommando destroyed records. Valpo destroyed records. But mostly, I think, nobody wanted to know about it. Those that did know wanted to forget."

"But all those deaths. Where are the bodies? Haven't families looked for their relatives' remains?"

"I assume the bodies are still in mass graves in Salla. I estimate around a thousand of them. The Salla area was close to the western border of the Soviet Union after the war, a border that the Soviets eventually came to seal off with three parallel ditch-and-barbed-wire-fence installations, with checkpoints in between, to prevent their own citizens from escaping abroad, less so to prevent anyone getting in. So, if you were a Soviet citizen, you didn't even consider digging somewhere close to the border area, no matter how strong a hunch you might have had about your vanished loved ones' whereabouts. You were wary of even making public inquiries about such matters, because Soviet law forbade surrendering to the enemy, and so by Soviet policy, their prisoners of war were considered traitors. If the USSR had deemed it important to discover the fate of their nonreturning POWs, something probably would have been done. But the Soviet state didn't, and such initiatives by private citizens weren't options."

I shake my head. "It doesn't make sense. Finns don't hate Jews enough to round them up and kill them."

"Maybe not. At most, something like eighty Jews were murdered in 309, and they were suspected Communists. Think of it this way, Einsatzkommando's meat and potatoes in 309 were Communists. If they were Jews, too, it was an added bonus."

This is more than I can take in. "You're telling me Arvid and Ukki are war criminals."

"I don't condone their actions, but I understand the mind-set. I told you I'm researching Lauri Törni, one of Finland's greatest heroes. Do you realize that he was a traitor?"

"No."

"He fought the Soviets as a Finnish soldier, but when Finland signed a peace treaty with Soviet Russia, he was dissatisfied with the terms. Finland declared war on Germany, their former ally, but Törni joined the Waffen-SS in 1945, so that he could continue to fight Communists. He undertook saboteur training in Germany in 1945, so he could organize resistance if Finland were overrun by the Soviet Union. He surrendered to British troops near the end of the war, escaped from a British POW camp and returned to Finland. When he arrived, Red Valpo arrested him. He was sentenced to six years in prison for having joined the German army, with which Finland was at war. An act of treason. President Paasikivi pardoned Törni in December 1948."

"I've read about Törni, but never thought of him as a traitor."

"Few of us have. He was a hero. He went on to fight for the U.S. in Vietnam. He fought under three flags. Can you think why he might have done that?"

"Because he was a warrior."

"Perhaps. But I think also because each conflict he participated in gave him the opportunity to kill Communists. He was a professional Communist hunter. You might consider Arvid Lahtinen, your grandpa and all White Valpo detectives in the same way, as Communist hunters. If you think of them in that light, perhaps you won't judge them so harshly."

My head starts to pound. "I need time to absorb this."

"If I can be of more help," Pasi says, "don't hesitate to call."

I thank him, and leave him to work in his scholar's jail cell.

# 24

I step out onto Ratakatu. The temperature has dipped to near minus twenty again. A little snow is falling. My phone rings and I answer.

"It's John." His voice quavers.

"Hi, John. How's my new best buddy?"

"I'm in trouble. Please help me."

The disclosure comes as less than a bombshell. "Anything for you. You know that."

"I've been robbed."

This strikes me as suspicious in the extreme. I test him. "I'm near a police station. Get in a taxi, then call me back. I'll give the driver the address and pay him when you get there."

"That's not a good idea."

I thought not. "And why might that be?"

"Please come and get me. I'll explain then. I can't go far. I'm outside and don't have any shoes, and my socks are wet. I'm freezing."

No shoes? I have him walk to the nearest corner and spell out the names of the cross streets. "I'll be there in ten minutes," I say.

John isn't far from Juttutupa. I make the short drive and pull over to the curb. John hops in. He's the picture of misery, takes off his socks and pulls his legs up so he can warm his bare feet with the car heater. I park the car in a space next to the water. "Let's have it," I say.

"I went for a walk and was headed toward downtown. A guy mugged me. He took my boots." He sniffs. "I loved those boots."

"He didn't take your wallet?"

Head shake. "No. But he took the money in it."

"The truth, John."

He wants to concoct a better lie. He reads my face, knows I won't buy it. He averts his eyes, stares at the floor of the Saab.

I roll down the window and light a cigarette. Frigid air turns the car into an icebox, and barefoot John shivers in misery. I don't care. "You promised me you wouldn't upset Kate," I say.

He sighs. "I wasn't trying to. It's a long story."

I check my watch, have an hour until I meet Milo. "I'll make time for it."

"I'm not a teacher anymore. I lost my job a few weeks ago."

Big shock. "And?"

"It wasn't all a lie. I was a Ph.D. candidate with a doctoral fellowship. I was a graduate teaching assistant and a good one, but I showed up drunk to teach a couple times and got warnings. Then I got tanked at a party and let a freshman seduce me. Word got around. I got fired."

"You should have taught at a Finnish university. You can fuck your students."

"You can?"

"Yep. Two consenting adults. And?"

"I turned into my dad. I got depressed and started drinking from the time I get out of bed in the morning and using drugs. The truth is, I didn't come here just to be with Kate. My life is shit. I came here to get away from it for a while."

But instead, he brought his life and its attendant shit here with him and dumped them in our laps. "I'm curious," I say. "The expensive clothes and boots, your — shall we say discriminating — palate for food and wine. How did you develop such expensive tastes on a grad student's budget?"

He smirks. "I had a girlfriend with a rich daddy. We lived high on the hog on his money. When I fucked the freshman, I lost

223

my cash cow along with my position."

"Bummer. And how did you come to lose your fancy boots?"

"When I was in that bar — the one where you bailed me out of trouble — I hung out with a couple guys. We did some lines of speed. One of them told me how much he liked my boots."

John pauses.

I light another cigarette. "And?"

"I really didn't know all my cards were maxed out. I thought I had a little credit left. I told you I wouldn't upset Kate."

"You're a considerate human being, but you digress. And?"

"I still had a hundred-euro bill in my wallet. He told me to call him today, said he had more speed and we'd party all day."

I resist the urge to slap him. "After what happened to you yesterday, are you so incredibly stupid that you were going to do the exact same thing again today?"

He nods.

"And this speed freak set a trap for you. He thought you're a dumbass drunk druggie foreigner, unable to do anything about it, so he ripped you off for a few euros and your boots."

He nods again.

My headache begs me to smack his head

off the windshield. "You fucked up bad."

The muscles in his face twitch. "I'm broke. It's twenty below and snowing. I don't have any shoes or money to buy them. I don't know what to do."

"Let me think for a minute." I light Marlboro number three and shut my eyes. The migraine issues an earsplitting shriek. I open my eyes again, look out the driver's-side window and see a cash machine across the street. "Wait here," I say.

I take two hundred and forty euros from the machine and give it to John. "Now you have money, you can maintain your pretense for Kate. Make it last. How bad are your drug and alcohol problems?"

His face goes sheepish. He massages his pale feet. "I can make it without the speed. I mostly use it to keep from getting sloppy when I binge-drink. I found a bottle of *kookoo* or whatever that vodka is called in your house this morning and took a couple hits to get rid of the shakes."

"Did you do what I told you and lie to Kate about your outing yesterday?"

He holds his soaking socks up in front of the heater. It blows wet dog smell around the car. "I went to the National Museum. The prehistory of Finland archeological exhibit was incredible."

"Today you went shopping," I say. "You wanted some warmer boots and got some just like mine."

"What happened to my Sedona Wests?"

"You're a humanitarian. You gave them to UFF, our version of Goodwill. I'm going to fix this. What did the guy who ripped you off look like?"

"Tall. Thin. Stringy shoulder-length black hair. He wears a worn-out black leather biker jacket."

I check received calls in my cell phone and their times, and find the number that must belong to Securitas Arska. I call him and tell him I'm looking for a speed-head that hangs out in Roskapankki and repeat John's description of him. Arska knows who he is. I offer Arska a hundred euros if, when he sees the speed-head again, he'll detain him and call me. Arska agrees.

I pull the car out into traffic and give John instructions. "I want you out of the country as soon as you can do it without rousing Kate's suspicion about why you're leaving earlier than planned. Until then, I'll keep booze in the house for you. Hide your drinking from Mary and Kate. And no drugs. I want you on your best behavior."

"Okay," he says. "Thank you."

Migraine screams deafening loud. I light

cigarette number four.

"Kari, I'm grateful for what you've done for me," he says, "and I'm sorry that I've put you in such an awkward position."

He's sincere. It makes it hard for me to hate him.

I wear army combat boots in the winter, and have since I was in the service. They're warm, comfortable and durable. I take John to an Army-Navy store near our house, so he can get a pair for himself, give him directions to the nearest liquor store, tell him to get semi-tanked and go home.

## 25

I park on Vaasankatu, in front of a shut-down Thai massage parlor. It's snowing hard now. My knee throbs along with my head, and I limp toward Hilpeä Hauki. I hear a dull creak over my head and look up. Heavy snow on a slanted rooftop breaks free and avalanches toward me. I press up against a building. The avalanche passes in front of my face, lands with a thud and forms a three-foot-high snow dump at my feet. I wade through it and go on to Hilpeä Hauki.

Milo got here before me. He's sitting on a couch in a rear corner nook, away from other customers, a cup of coffee in front of him. The bar is almost empty. "I'd rather have beer," he says, "but I've been up for more than thirty hours. It's hard to stay awake."

I get coffee, too, and sit in an armchair at a right angle to him. "Why haven't you slept?" I ask.

"I'll get to it."

"So what's this secret information you can't tell me at work?"

His eyes are red slits. The black circles around them have that excited dull shine. "I said I'll get to it."

He's going to start with the story of creation and work his way forward through the history of the world before he gets to the point. He's having fun and he's exhausted. I give him latitude, sink back in my chair and wait.

"What do you want to do with the Silver Dollar case?" he asks.

"I want to send the bouncers to jail for involuntary manslaughter, but it won't happen. Securitas isn't guilty of anything. We should turn them loose."

"They could have tried to stop it, to make the bouncers put Taisto Polvinen down."

"Not stopping isn't the same as doing."

He shifts in his seat. His movements are jerky from exhaustion. "That rent-a-cop girl is a fucking cunt," he says.

"For a man of your intelligence," I say, "you have a limited vocabulary."

Then I get it. His tough talk is a facade. "I think of her as 'gum-chewing bitch cow,' " I say. "She speaks with this annoying

Helsinki teenager accent. When I interrogated her, she repeated the questions back at me and made fun of my northern accent. I don't care for being mocked. I asked her where she's from and she said Helsinki, which was a sham. I called her a liar and told her I could tell she's from the Kotka area. She called me a cocksucker."

"It's funny how so many people in Helsinki are from somewhere else," Milo says, "but pretend they're from here."

"They want everyone to think they're big-city sophisticates, instead of small-town rednecks. It's the Finnish innate sense of shame. I think some of us feel guilty just for having been born."

"Yeah, we can be like that," he says. "We can hold the bouncers until Friday without charging them. Let's leave them in the tank for a couple more days just to fuck with them. Maybe the prosecutor can make a case out of it later."

"Agreed."

Milo finishes his coffee, goes to the bar and comes back with a refill, takes on a furtive smile. "I went back to Filippov Construction last night, then to Filippov's house," he says.

"Why?"

"To search trash cans," Milo says. "I

230

hoped he was stupid and threw out the gear he wore while he killed his wife. He wasn't."

"Filippov is an asshole, but missing taser or no, there isn't any evidence to hang the murder on him. Not yet, anyway."

My lack of confidence irks Milo. "And that's why I'm trash-diving, to find evidence and hang him."

I switch gears. "This thing I'm investigating for the national chief of police is taking more time than I thought. Can you do the legwork, background checks and basic stuff on the Filippov case for a day or two?"

"Sure. If you tell me about your top-secret mission."

"No."

"Why not?"

Because explaining about Arvid would lead to a question about the reason behind my involvement, and the answer is Ukki. I'm not prepared to go there with Milo. "It's just not your business."

"You're an annoying fuck," he says.

"Funny," I say, "I've had the same thought about you."

This gives him pause. "I've been doing the Filippov case legwork," he says, "which is why I was up all night."

At long last, he approaches the reason for our clandestine liaison.

"Iisa Filippov's life insurance policy makes her worth eight hundred and fifty thousand, dead," he says.

"It's not a pittance, but not exactly a fortune either these days."

"This afternoon, I spent some time going through her phone, making calls, finding out who her friends are. Everyone spoke well of her."

He must think his detailed account of routine police work builds my anticipation. It only makes me miss the days when you could smoke in bars. "Glad to hear it."

"And neither her husband's nor her own personal bank accounts show signs of abnormal transactions."

I sip coffee, work on my tolerance management skills.

"Last night," Milo says, "while I was trash-diving at Filippov's house, I looked in the windows and saw Linda there with him. They left together and I decided to tail them. They went to Linda's apartment. I stayed and surveiled them."

"Hoping to discover what?"

"I got an idea that if they collaborated in the murder and he used protective clothing while he committed it, they could have stowed it in her place."

"Why wouldn't he have disposed of it immediately after the killing?"

He shrugs. "You never know with people. I trash-dived Linda's dumpsters and came up empty."

He's boring me shitless. My mind drifts to Ukki. I picture him executing a Communist with his little suicide pistol.

"Something the matter?" Milo asks.

"Nope. Please continue."

"So I sit outside her building all night, in case they try to sneak out to dump the stuff. Nothing happens. Early this morning, they left together — I guess to work — so I broke in and black-bagged her apartment."

My attention snaps into focus. "What?"

His coat is beside him. He takes a nylon wallet out of a pocket, unfolds it, sets it on the low table in front of us to show me a lock-pick set. Seven picks and two torsion wrenches. "I busted a burglar once," Milo says. "In return for letting him walk, he gave me his picks and showed me how to use them. It's pretty easy."

I shake my head, disgusted. "So you committed breaking and entering."

"It's a hobby with me. I don't steal anything, I just like to see how other people live, take a peek into the lives of strangers."

More sharing of personal details I don't

233

want to know. "Why are you telling me this?"

"Because I like to see the look on your face when I tell you about my hobbies."

I didn't know I had a look on my face. "Do you tell other people this shit?"

"No. Just you."

"I'm honored."

"You should be." He changes the subject. "Linda Pohjola is fucking hot."

I nod. "She looks like Bettie Page."

"Who?"

"Doesn't matter."

"She collects 1950s pinup magazines and movies. A lot of it is S&M and bondage, fetish-type stuff. She also has an excellent lingerie collection, which she scents with perfume."

I take this to mean she consciously impersonates Bettie Page. "So you break into apartments and sniff women's undergarments."

"Not necessarily, but in this case, I had to search her underwear drawer. You know the old joke that goes, 'What's a Russian ass-shaker?'"

It's a classic. "Yeah. It doesn't shake and it doesn't fit in your ass."

He grins. "That's the one. Well, lovely Linda has a non-Russian ass-shaker. A big green double-donged dildo. Big end for pussy and small end for ass." Milo starts to sing a Beach Boys' tune. "I'm pickin' up good vibrations. She's giving me excitations."

I want to see if anything causes him shame. "How did Linda's dildo smell?"

"Like soap," he says. "She washes it."

My tolerance level just maxed. "You didn't ask me to come here so you can tell me about your proclivity for voyeurism and Linda's underwear and dildo."

He's having the time of his life. His eyes sparkle, their dark circles have a liquid sheen. He folds up his lock-picker's wallet, puts it back in his pocket, and puts a digital audio player in its place on the table. "I found her MP3 and bumped this over to my iPod. Listen to the second-to-last track," he says.

I put the earbuds in and listen. I hear smacks, followed by high-pitched grunts and squeals. Slurping sounds, like a blow job. Muted low moans at intervals, some of which are from a male voice. I'm nearly certain it belongs to Filippov. It goes on for eight minutes. Milo has a recording of Iisa being whipped to pieces. I stop the machine.

"No, keep listening," Milo says.

A Nine Inch Nails song, "Closer," from

*The Downward Spiral* album, starts. It's a dirgey anthem to self-hatred and sadomasochistic sex.

This isn't the studio version. It's a home mix. The sound track from Iisa Filippov's torture session has been dubbed over the song. Her blunted cries syncopate with the song's rhythm. It's sickening, makes my stomach churn.

"Pretty cool, huh?" Milo says, "and ingenious. Linda and Filippov have sex while they murder Iisa and make a recording, so that later they can fuck along to the sound of Iisa dying. I'm picturing them killing her, that dildo in Linda's cunt and ass. Filippov's dick in her gorgeous mouth. If you listen close, it sounds like they come together when Iisa dies and goes quiet."

I listen again. He's right. The idea is so appalling that for a moment I sit stunned.

" 'Closer' may be the best fucking song of all time," Milo says, "paralleled only by Led Zeppelin's 'Kashmir.' You ever fuck to the rhythm of 'Kashmir'?" He hums the bass line, makes little grinding motions with his crotch.

In fact, I've fucked to both songs, but that's not his business. "To your credit," I say, "you were right. Filippov and Linda colluded in Iisa's murder, but you fucked everything up. Now we have the evidence, but it's inadmissible in court. What, Sherlock, are we going to do with it?"

I don't wait for his answer. Something hits me. Milo is unpredictable in the extreme. "Give me your pistol."

It's in a quick-release holster in the small of his back. He grins, hands his Glock 19 over to me. I look around to make sure no one sees, pop the clip and rack the slide. A round flies out. He's ready for anything, carries it with one in the chamber, cocked and locked. I pick the ejected bullet up off the floor. It's crosshatched, as is the one at the top of the clip. He's loaded up with dumdum rounds. Teaching him how to make them was a serious mistake. I turn the pistol over in my hands. It has a selector switch at the rear left of the slide that my Glock lacks.

I want to scream at him but keep my voice down. "You maladroit imp. You mental fucking pygmy. You installed a three-round-burst selector."

His smile is smug. "No I didn't. It's a fullauto switch. Making the three-round-burst selector was harder than I thought. I got the schematics to the Glock 18, which has full auto-fire capability. The models aren't too different. I had to do some hand tooling on the slide and barrel, but made it work."

"I told you not to fuck with your service pistol. What did you do that for?"

He sticks his chin out, defiant. "Maybe because you're not my fucking boss."

"Take it out."

"No."

"I'd like to turn you in for breaking into Linda's apartment and jeopardizing this case, but that would botch everything, and she and Filippov would walk."

Milo says nothing, just stares at me.

"I've had just about fucking enough of you," I say. "I've treated you as a professional, and in return you've been arrogant, conceited and childish. I outrank you, and whether you like it or not, I'm going to be the boss of you. We can change the nature of our relationship. I can call you detective sergeant, and you can call me inspector. I have twenty years more than you as a cop, and you're going to treat me with the respect I've earned."

He sneers, grits his teeth. We stare at each other. He clears his throat and holds out his hand. "My pistol."

I give it back. He does some minor disassembly, removes the switch and puts a little screw in its place to cover the hole it left. He puts the loose round back in the clip, racks the slide to re-chamber it and re-holsters the pistol.

I hold out my hand. "Give me the switch."

He hesitates, frowns, does it. I hear a series of distant popping sounds. The door to the bar opens. A woman yells, "Someone's shooting on Helsinginkatu!"

Milo and I grab our coats, get up and put them on as we run.

## 26

We follow the sounds of sporadic gunfire. Big booms that I'm pretty sure are from a high-caliber, short-barreled pistol. The noise takes us to Ebeneser School. A small crowd on the sidewalk peeks into the schoolyard from behind the ivy-covered fence that I smashed a man's face off of two days ago. Helsinki residents aren't used to Arctic cold. They shiver and stamp their feet in the snow. We show our police cards. A woman tells me the shooting is coming from inside the school. I call it in, request backup.

This is a nightmare scenario. Finland has suffered three school shootings. The first in 1989, in Rauma. A fourteen-year-old shot two fellow students. The second in November 2007, at Jokela High School, near Tuusula. A sixteen-year-old gunman killed eight and wounded twelve before turning the gun on himself. It rocked the nation. Then, not long after, in September 2008, it happened again in Kauhajoki. Ten people murdered before the shooter blew his own head off. Finland seems to be following the U.S. school-shooting trend. Parents are terrorized. And now, here we are again.

Not long ago, such situations fell under the province of Karhuryhmä — the Bear Team — or, as they're nicknamed, the Beagle Boys. They have SWAT units, handle riots, special ops and counterterrorism. In the past, in a case such as this, normal police would have waited on the Beagle Boys to bring in snipers and hostage negotiators. The Finnish National Police, however, made a recent decision — because schoolkids can't wait while they're being shot to pieces — that the first officers on the scene must respond in the event of a school shooting. The responsibility falls to me and Milo.

We enter the gate and scurry to the front door. My heart pounds and blood roars in my ears.

Milo looks calm enough. His face doesn't betray how he feels inside. "How do you want to handle it?" he asks.

"Have you tried out your modified pistol?" I ask.

"Not yet."

"Then don't. If it misfires, you or someone

else could die."

"It works."

Adrenaline makes my hands shake. I draw my Glock. "You haven't talked down anyone with a gun. I have. If possible, let me handle it."

I don't say, but I'm certain he knows, that I tried such a thing once, not long ago. I failed, and my friend blew his brains out before I could stop him.

I open the front door. Milo crouches and darts through it. I don't crouch. My bad knee won't allow it. There's no point anyway. Thirty feet down a hall decorated with crayon artwork by students sits Vesa Legion Korhonen with a boy of about eight clutched in one arm. He has a chrome snub-nosed .357 Magnum pressed to the child's head. A bottle of Finlandia vodka rests on the floor beside him.

I level my Glock at his head and walk forward.

"You," he says. "Dis is pwovidenthial."

"Vesa," I ask, "what are you doing, and why are you doing it?"

"I am saving souws," he says. "Da childwen's and my own. And now youahs."

With peripheral vision, I see Milo to my right and behind me. He circles farther to the right, close to the wall of the hall, trying to keep Legion's attention on me and away from him.

"You made me dwink da whoe bottle. You hewt me," Legion says.

"I'm sorry," I say. "I shouldn't have done that."

The boy is motionless and quiet. A dark stain spreads around his crotch. My own bladder wants to let go. I tell the child to stay calm and not to move.

"Put yooah gun down," Legion says.

"No."

"I wiah shoot dis boy."

I lower the Glock to my side, but inch closer. With my bad knee, I can't move fast. I have to get within arm's reach of Legion if I'm to have any chance of restraining him. Given his .357, though, I can't imagine how I might accomplish that.

"Have you hurt anyone?" I ask.

"Oh, yeth. Many." He chugs vodka.

Milo continues to slink along the wall. He's almost at a right angle to Legion now.

"What would it take to get you to let the boy go?" I ask.

"Hmm," he says. "Wet me think. I know. Shoot youahthelf."

"Why?"

"You toad me, 'Bottaw to wips and dwink.'

I'm tewing you, gun to head and puu twig-ger."

Fuck. I don't know what to do. I put the Glock to my temple. It pounds from the migraine. I'm still inching forward, just a little more than three feet away from him now.

Legion jams the Magnum harder against the boy's head. The child whimpers. "Shoot youahthelf," Legion says again.

I'm at a loss. I might consider shooting myself, if it would save the boy's life, but there's no reason to think my suicide would change anything. I wait, terrified.

"Do it," Legion says and drinks again.

The boy squirms. Legion holds him tighter. Legion turns his face toward him. The back of Legion's head faces Milo.

A piercing sharp crack. For a brief instant, I think I accidentally shot myself, or Legion shot the child. But Legion's head jerks and slumps. His gun arm drops, his hold on the boy releases. I kneel down and gesture to the boy. He gets up and falls into my arms.

Legion slumps to the floor. Blood from his head trickles onto the tiles, much as it trickled onto the ice after I gave him a beat-ing. I look at Milo. He smiles at me and winks, then blows imaginary smoke from the barrel of his Glock.

"Jesus, Milo." It's all I can say.

"You're welcome," he says.

I still shake, but now from relief. I still feel like I might piss myself. "I guess you had to."

"Well," he says, "it's like this. One of us had to shoot him. First: you weren't in much of a position to do it. Second: a shot that will paralyze and render a killer incapable of pulling a trigger must be placed at the junction of the brain and the brain stem. A target about the size of an apricot. I didn't know if you knew that. Third: if you did know it, I didn't know if you were capable of doing it. So I did it myself."

I realize the bullet didn't exit Legion's head because the cross-hatched round split into four chunks and didn't have much punch left. "Hurry," I say, "other cops will be here in a second. Swap clips with me and get that dum-dum out of the chamber."

We make the switch fast. Beagle Boys come through the front door. They run past us to clear rooms and search for victims.

"Congratulations," I say to Milo. "I guess your hobbies and weapons enthusiasm paid off. You're the first Finnish cop in modern history to gun down a suspect without being fired upon first."

"You criticizing me?"

"No. You did the right thing. You enjoyed it though. That, I am criticizing."

He spins his Glock on his index finger, gunfighter-style, re-holsters it fast. "We're the only partners in the Finnish police to have both killed perps. We're going to be famous, like Wyatt Earp and Doc Holliday."

The Beagle Boys lead teachers and children into the hall and out of the building. They found no murdered children, no casualties at all. Legion just walked around, screamed weird religious gibberish, swilled vodka and shot holes in the walls and ceiling. Commander Beagle asks Milo and me for our accounts. I explain that Milo had no choice, killing Legion was warranted. Commander Beagle shakes our hands, thanks and congratulates us for saving the boy. He doesn't request Milo's weapon.

Legion didn't come here to hurt anyone, probably wouldn't even have let me shoot myself. He came here to die. Torsten was right. He sought punishment, but for what crimes I can't imagine.

Milo finds the idea glamorous and I loathe it, but he's also right. I killed an armed robber in self-defense many years ago. Because I was with Milo today, that old bad business will be resurrected. We're going to be famous as killer partners, particularly among our colleagues, stuck with the label for the rest of our lives. Worse, because the children in the school lived, we'll be celebrated in the media. Legion dies. We live. Legion vilified. Milo and me lauded for bravery. Some fucking heroes.

## 27

Milo and I exit the school together. A large crowd has formed, despite the freezing cold. Police cars and officers ring the building. The press got here fast. Their camera lights and flashes break the darkness. Reporters beg for statements.

I point at a cruiser and turn to Milo. "Fuck this, let's get out of here."

We push through the crowd. People shout at us. We hop in the back of the squad car. Two uniforms are in the front keeping warm. They congratulate us. I ask them to take us to the Pasila police station. The car pulls out.

"I know that guy I shot," Milo says.

I'm more than a little surprised. "From where?"

"He's in Mensa. I've run into him at meetings. He's a freelance software engineer."

This floors me, I'm not sure why. Maniacs

are all around us, but we usually don't recognize them for what they are. "What kind of person was he?" I ask.

"Timid. Soft-spoken. Like he was ashamed of his speech impediment. I got the idea that he attended the meetings so he could be around people who wouldn't make fun of him."

"Then why didn't you talk to him before you shot him?"

Milo shrugs. "Seemed pointless. Better to get it over with."

I'm not much of a talker. Maybe because Dad beat me for any show of emotion, I tend to regard anything less than total self-containment as a weakness. I like people, but from a distance. I feel that most other people just don't have much to offer me, and I don't have anything to offer them either, and so I prefer to observe more than interact with others.

I have a low bullshit threshold, and, since for me, most chat is mind-numbing drivel, I don't often engage in it. I can count the people I enjoy talking to on my fingers, including Kate. She's not just my wife, she's my best friend. Before I met her, I had only ever really opened up to one person in my life, my ex-wife, Heli, and she betrayed me. For the better part of the next dozen years, my best friend was a cat named Katt. And even that dumb bastard died on me.

At this moment, though, I feel an urge for some mind-numbing drivel. "So what do you geniuses do at Mensa meetings?"

Milo shifts in his seat to face me. "They're fun. We get together maybe once a month, get drunk and have dinner. We might have a speaker, or we might play poker or Go or maybe just hang around and yack. High-IQ geeks have more interesting hobbies than you might think. Scuba diving. UFOs. Witchcraft."

The requirement for entrance into Mensa is a measured IQ in the top two percentile of the population. As such, I could join, too. I'll pass on it.

"Later," Milo says, "I need to tell you the rest of the story about Linda's apartment."

"There's more?"

He grins. "Much more. But I don't want to talk about it in the station."

Apparently, Milo enjoys nothing more than dragging his stories out forever. They go something like: God made the heavens and the earth. God gave Adam and Eve the boot out of Eden. God said to Abraham, kill me a son. Moses parted the Red Sea. Now let's talk about the Filippov murder.

We arrive at the station and step out of

the cruiser into a media frenzy. More lights and flashes blind us. We push our way up the stairs. Journalists scream for interviews. I start to open the front door. Milo asks me to wait. He puts an arm around my shoulder and raises his other hand to hush the crowd. They go silent, expectant.

Milo wipes away an imaginary tear. "I have little to say on this sorrowful day," his voice fake-cracks, "but I'll make a brief statement. Praise God the children were saved. Let's all pray for the soul of the poor man who had to die as a result of his sad mental illness. I wish that the burden of taking his life hadn't fallen upon Kari and myself."

We go through the door. Once inside, we look at each other and burst into simultaneous laughter. It's just a stress reaction, but we laugh harder, can't stop, and soon we're howling. We find ourselves hugging each other. Two hours ago, I could never have imagined such a thing. "You're too fucking much," I say.

"Aren't I, though," he says, and we laugh even more.

Cops stare at us, bewildered. We calm down, and a parade of cops congratulate us, shake our hands. We make our way to my office. Our boss, Arto, greets us. "Detectives, well done."

We thank him. He tells us the background info for Vesa Korhonen is already in. He attended Ebeneser School as a child, has no priors, has dysphasia but no history of mental illness, lived a quiet life with his parents, ran his own business out of their home. Where he got the pistol remains unknown. Legion just came out of nowhere. It happens.

Milo and I sit in my office. To avoid departmental conflict of interest, Arto brings in a detective from Vantaa to interview us and write the report. Our phones keep ringing, interrupting us and slowing us down. Most are media, and we don't answer unless our phones display the names of callers we know. Mom calls. Then my brother Jari. Then Timo, another brother. I don't hear from my oldest brother, Juha, but he's working in the Norwegian oil fields and probably hasn't heard about the shooting. Kate might see me on TV and worry. I call her, tell her a brief and edited version of what happened, let her know everything is fine. Her voice shakes. She asks me to come home as soon as I can.

Jyri Ivalo calls. "Nice work," he says. "I got you a slot in Helsinki homicide, and you make me look better and better all the time.

Keep it up."

"I'll kill as many school shooters as possible," I say.

"Good. You haven't filed a murder charge against Rein Saar. Why?"

"It's complicated, and I'm a little too busy to explain right now."

"Just get it done." He rings off.

The Vantaa cop gets the report written and leaves. I check my e-mail. Pasi Tervomaa has e-mailed me scans of documents containing testimony stating that Arvid was an executioner at Stalag 309. I forward them to Jyri and the interior minister.

I stretch out in my chair and turn to Milo. "I need to get home to Kate."

"You need to hear the rest of my story," he says.

"Just fucking tell it."

He shakes his head. "No way. Not here."

Moses led his people to the Promised Land. The Jews were exiled to Babylon. I sigh. "Where, then? Anywhere we go, we'll be mobbed."

"My house," he says. "It's on Flemari, just a ten-minute walk from your place."

Legion's death brings back bad memories of other people I've watched die. I want to go home. "Okay, but let's make it quick."

Two cops give us a ride to Milo's apartment in a patrol car. We step inside a one-room dump, kneel and take off our boots. I look around. Newspapers, books and mail are scattered everywhere. A sink full of dirty dishes is in a dirtier kitchen. Dirty laundry is in a pile beside an unmade bed. The place smells of must and mildew. Milo shoves a pile of papers off a chair by a big computer table onto the floor. "Make yourself at home," he says.

He goes to the fridge, brings two beers and a bottle of *kossu*. He sits on the edge of the table, unscrews the cap from the bottle and hands it to me. "Sorry, I don't have any clean glasses."

I take a deep swig and pass it back. "The bottle will do."

He drinks, shuts his eyes for a moment. He's been up for almost two days and looks like shit. Between fatigue and adrenaline, it's a miracle he made the kill shot, put the bullet in the right spot in Legion's brain. "You need to go to sleep," I say.

He drinks again, hands the bottle back. "Soon."

He stares at me.

"What?" I ask.

"The scar on your face is cool."

Trauma is making him strange. "I'd give it to you if I could."

"Your wife's name is Kate Vaara. Right?"

"Yeah."

"*Katevaara*, in English, means, for example, highway asphalt erosion. You should tell her that."

He's spewing hogwash to release tension. I indulge him and I swill *kossu*. "I'll make a point of it."

Vintage posters from the Second World War hang on the walls. A gun cabinet stands in the corner. A long and narrow glass case with daggers and bayonets from the war — Finnish, German and Russian — rests on the rear edge of the table. I look closer at them.

He points at one of them. "That's a Nazi Hitler Youth dagger. The inscription reads BLUT UND EHRE — Blood and Honor. There's a good story behind it."

I don't want to hear any of his long-winded stories at the moment. However, I'm becoming somewhat interested in him as a person. An ammo-reloading setup is on the other edge of the table. Empty shotgun shells and lead shot I don't recognize are piled around it.

"What's the fascination with war and guns?" I ask.

"It's a hobby I picked up from my father. I inherited his collection of militaria."

He waits for me to inquire further about his father and said "militaria." I don't. "And these shotgun loads. What are they?"

He sips beer. "Beehive rounds. Shells loaded with razor-sharp darts instead of normal shot. They'll take a man's whole leg off."

"I see." I change the subject. "Nice computer."

"It's an Apple MacBook Pro notebook with a seventeen-inch monitor. Expensive as hell."

"You seem to have top-notch computer skills. With your big big brain, you could be earning a lot of money. Instead, you became a cop. You spend your time building toys that inflict death. Why?"

"I want to help people."

He doesn't smile when he says it. Strange, but I think he's being honest. The worst lies are the ones we tell ourselves.

My phone rings. It's Kate. "Kari, why aren't you home?"

She sounds near tears. I check my watch. Nine thirty p.m. "I'm sorry, Kate. I'm still working. I'm just around the corner and I'll be home soon."

"The school shooting is a headline on *BBC World.* The report said a maniac forced you to put a gun to your head and tried to make you commit suicide. I'm upset. Please come home now."

"Kate, I'm fine, and I'll be home soon. I promise."

"I love you," she says.

"Me too," I say and hang up.

I think of preeclampsia, hypertension, obstetric catastrophe. Fear runs through me. "Okay, Milo, spill it. I have to go home. No drawn-out stories. I appreciate the drinks, and after today, I think we deserve them, but keep it short."

He puts on his hurt look, doesn't say anything. He starts his computer and plugs a memory stick into it. We drink beer in silence while the computer boots up. I watch him. He's pissed off because we went through a life-altering experience today — he needs friendship and offered his hospitality — and I'm declining it. I would give him what he needs if I could, but my first responsibility is to Kate.

He opens a video file. "I found this in Linda's computer," he says. "It was shot in her bedroom."

Even though Linda and Iisa impersonated

each other, Filippov is — I presume — with Linda, because the video was shot in her bedroom and was in her computer. They strip. He dons an industrial toxic-cleanup respirator and long black vinyl protective gloves. She kneels in front of him beside the bed. He grabs her by the hair and ears. She sucks his cock, sticks the big green double-donged vibrating dildo in her cunt and ass and masturbates with it. He's rough with her. She's not giving him a blow job as much as he's holding her head like a bowling ball and fucking it. She tremors and orgasms. He spreads his legs. She sticks the dildo up his ass and deep-throats his dick. He grunts and comes, collapses onto the bed, dildo still in place. She swallows, looks up at him with profound satisfaction, with gratitude and bliss. End video.

From within their black holes, Milo's eyes reflect triumph. "They like weird S&M. I think she was at the crime scene, and while Iisa died, they enacted the sex game we just watched."

"Given the audio recording," I say, "it must have gone down that way. Get some rest. We need to figure out how to use your illegally obtained evidence to build a case against them. Let's meet in the morning and talk about it."

I stand to go and put on my boots. He stays quiet. "You did a good job today," I say. "I'd like to stay here and drink with you, but my wife needs me."

He just stares at me, expression flat.

"If you stay up for a while, I'd like you to Web-search a 1950s pinup and soft-core fetish porn star named Bettie Page. The reason will be self-explanatory."

He slurps out of the *kossu* bottle. "Okay."

"And we need to run background checks on Iisa Filippov and Linda Pohjola. I want to know who these women were and are. Whichever one of us has time first should do it."

He quaffs again. "Yeah."

"See you in the morning," I say.

"Yep. See you in the morning."

I think he's waiting for me to leave so he can cry. I don't look at him as I walk out.

# 28

Our bedroom is dark, but I know the sound of Kate's breathing when she's sleeping, and I can tell she's not. I don't bother to take my clothes off, crawl in bed beside her and put an arm around her.

"I thought you were working?" she says.

"I was."

"Then why do you smell like booze?"

"I went to Milo's place to talk about the Filippov murder. He had something to tell me in private. We had a hard day. A couple drinks was good for us. I didn't want to leave you alone any longer than necessary and made it home as fast as I could."

She turns toward me, wraps her arms around me, buries her head in my shoulder. "You could have died today." She sobs, then bursts into tears.

I wish I could deny it. "But I didn't."

"The news said a man tried to make you commit suicide, but Milo killed him."

"That's what happened, but the man was emotionally disturbed. It was the guy I made drink a bottle of vodka outside the school a couple days ago. He didn't shoot anyone and he just wanted to scare me, to punish me for hurting him. I'm pretty sure he just went to the school to die. He got what he wanted."

"Kari, I saw the news and it reminded me of Kittilä and the Sufia Elmi case and you getting shot. I started to shake and my heart started to pound. I'm scared, and I'm afraid I'll lose this baby, too. I can't fail as a mother again."

I hold her tighter, confused. "What are you talking about? You didn't fail as a mother. Miscarriages happen all the time."

She sobs, pauses, collects herself. "I went skiing when I shouldn't have and I fell. The doctors said it didn't, but I think that fall caused us to lose our babies."

I had no idea she felt this way. She bursts into big sobs and blurts out, "I failed you and them and I feel so guilty all the time."

I pull her tight while she sobs, and wait until she quiets down before speaking. "Kate, that's not true. If anything, the stress I caused you by pursuing the Sufia Elmi case to the ends of sanity caused you to miscarry."

She tries to keep her voice down and whisper-shouts. "No. No no no no no. It was my fault. My failure. That's why I wanted to start trying to get pregnant again as soon as I could, so I could give you a baby to replace the ones I took away from you with my selfishness and stupidity."

She cries so hard that she shakes. I feel awful because I didn't recognize that she was carrying all this around inside her. "No, Kate. It was my selfishness and stupidity. And I'm terrified I'll do something selfish and stupid again. I worry myself sick. I thought you were upset with me tonight because I got myself into another danger-ous situation that could make you stress and miscarry."

She wipes her eyes. "Kari, these notions of yours are just silly. I'm upset because I saw you on TV and I realized I've been ly-ing to myself. We came here and I've been happy in Helsinki, but I've ignored the fact that you haven't been. I've made English-speaking friends in the international com-munity, and I thought we had built a safe and cozy life. I believed we had left mad-ness, depression and senseless violence behind us in the Arctic Circle. I realized tonight that Helsinki is the same, and it scares the hell out of me. Your job is dangerous and I'm frightened of losing you. I'm afraid for our little girl growing up surrounded by crazy people. You've been different since the Sufia Elmi case, and I'm worried about you, too. Right now, everything scares me."

I brought Kate to Helsinki to quell her fears about life in Finland for nothing. Once again, I've failed her. I have no consoling words, her fears are justified. "Kate, there are no safe places in the world. It's something all of us have to live with. But your belief that you caused the loss of the twins is unfounded. It's just silly and you have to let it go."

"You never let anything go," she says.

She's right. "I won't lie and say the Elmi case didn't hurt me, but I'll get past it. I just need time, and I need time to adjust to Helsinki."

"Will you ever?" she asks.

"For you," I say, "there are no limits to what I can do."

"And my brother and sister," she says. "There's something wrong with both of them. I raised them and I failed them."

I don't like to talk about my childhood, but I want to prove to her that she's wrong, that she didn't fail them. "Do you think there's something wrong with me?" I ask.

She props herself up on her elbow and looks into my eyes. "I think you have a mild case of posttraumatic shock from what happened last year, but given the circumstances, no, I think you must be solid as a rock to have survived all you've been through as well as you have."

"Did I ever tell you why I wear my hair cut short?"

"No."

"When I was a little kid, back in the seventies when it was in style, I had longer hair. When my dad flew into drunken rages, he used to snatch me up by the hair, pick me up off the ground, swing me in a circle or jerk me around like a rag doll. Once, I tried to get away, and Dad chased me in a circle around the kitchen table. We stopped for a moment. He gave me a tiny smile and made me feel safe. I thought he was proud of me for sticking up for myself and all was forgiven. Instead, he used that smile to make me let my guard down, then caught me and swung me around by the hair like usual, then beat me for running. I never felt safe around him again. That's why I wear my hair short to this day."

Kate's eyes water up again. "Kari, I'm so sorry."

"That's just one example of how I was

sometimes treated. You don't need to feel sorry for me. The point is, you treated your brother and sister well, but they came out a little weird. Dad treated me like garbage, and I came out solid. People survive their childhoods, but even the best childhood doesn't guarantee a stable adult."

My head hurts. I take a sleeping pill.

"Did you see Jari?" Kate asks.

"Yeah. I need some tests. He and his family are coming over for dinner on Thursday evening."

"That's nice."

She's lost in thought for a moment. "I still feel like a guilty failure," she says.

"Me too," I say.

Me and Kate. Two of a perfect pair.

## 29

Once again, I wake before the others. It's eight a.m. The couch is empty. John didn't come home last night. I enjoy quiet mornings alone and don't miss his company. I doubt Kate will feel the same. I make coffee. While it brews, my cell phone rings. "Inspector. This is Ivan Filippov. I trust you're enjoying a pleasant morning."

"Well," I say, "I was."

"I told you at our last meeting that if I came upon something of interest, I would deliver it to you. Could you meet with me this morning, perhaps around ten o'clock? I could come to your office."

"Might this thing of interest be your wife's diary? I'd very much like to see it."

"Iisa kept no diary."

"I've been informed otherwise. Bring it to me, or I'll get a subpoena and seize it."

"We've had this discussion. You can try. I'll get the subpoena quashed. Will you meet with me or not?"

"Sure, Ivan, because you're such good company. See you then."

I can't imagine what Filippov wants to show me, but I doubt I'll like it.

I go outside to the balcony. We got fresh snow overnight. I kick some to the sidewalk below to clear myself a dry place to stand, and smoke my first cigarette of the day. The sky is ash-gray. A fierce wind almost jerks the cigarette out of my hand. The cold hurts my face. I check the thermometer. Minus twenty-five. It turned even more frigid overnight. The wind burns down my cigarette so fast that I only get three drags off it before it self-extinguishes.

I sit on the couch, sip coffee and think about Arvid. I could follow his instructions, relay his message to the interior minister and tell him, as Arvid put it, "to stick his charges up his fucking ass." But that won't help Arvid. I feel certain he'll end up on trial in a German court. I like Arvid and don't want that to happen. I call him.

"I saw you on the news," Arvid says. "Well done."

"I'd rather not discuss it," I say.

The image of standing in front of Legion, holding a gun to my own head, the boy whimpering in his clutches, is so vivid I forget for a moment that I'm talking to Arvid.

"Boy," he says, "what do you want? I expressed my thoughts on this horseshit in a most clear manner. Our business is concluded."

I snap back to reality. "I respect both you and your wishes, but you have a problem. I'd like to assist you with it, if you'll let me."

"What problem?"

"I've done some minor investigating. You've been disingenuous. You were at Stalag 309. If I can find the truth in a day, anyone else can, too. If I handle this situation in the way you told me to, it won't go away. You'll find yourself in a jail cell. We need to clear you of the charges leveled against you."

The pause is long. I hear him sigh, then swear under his breath. "You're a good eater. I like that. Come here today for lunch at twelve and we'll talk about it."

I thank him for his indulgence and hang up.

I get to the Pasila station about nine a.m. I check Milo's office. He's already at his computer. "What are you working on?" I ask.

"Getting bio material on Linda and Iisa."

Dark circles render his eyes almost invisible red slits. Looking at his face is like staring into an abyss. "Get any sleep last night?"

The abyss stares back at me. "Some."

"Ivan Filippov called and wants to meet with me at ten. I expect some kind of antagonistic confrontation. I'll do some digging, too. Finish getting whatever info you can in the next little while, then come to my office and let's compare notes. It might help me prep for my discussion with him."

He nods, turns back to his computer.

I go to my office and give the main newspaper Internet pages a quick scan. Vesa Korhonen, Milo and I are splattered all over them. I don't read the articles. Jaakko wrote a piece in *Ilta-Sanomat* stating that Iisa Filippov and Rein Saar were tased before being brutalized. He implies cover-up. I call him.

"Hi, Kari," he says. "Congratulations for yesterday."

"We're not friends. Call me Inspector Vaara."

"All right Inspector Vaara. What do you want?"

"More dirt on Iisa Filippov and Linda Pohjola."

"I anticipated your wishes. Gotta give to get."

"I want to know more about Ivan and Iisa Filippov's relationship, and about Linda's relationship to both of them."

"That will cost you dear," he says.

Rein Saar won't enjoy seeing this in the newspapers, but it will help him in the long run, and like the rest of us, he also has to give to get. "Iisa Filippov had an affair going on with Rein Saar for about two years. It was based on voyeuristic sex games. He was supposed to arrive home that morning with another woman. Iisa intended to hide in the closet and watch them fuck."

"Inspector, that's exactly the kind of thing I'm looking for. You're a man after my own heart."

"Give."

"Iisa's father died in 1998 and she inherited a decent sum of money. She set about spending it dilettante-style. She went on a party trip to St. Petersburg and met Ivan there . . ."

I cut him off. "Year?"

"Two thousand two. They had a whirlwind romance and marriage soon followed. They moved to Helsinki, and she used much of the remainder of her daddy's money to finance Filippov Construction. Ivan proved himself a good businessman and has done well."

"How did Iisa go from happily married woman to trophy dick–collecting fuck monster?"

"Her boundless affection soon waned. Ivan was twenty-four years older than her. I guess she wanted a replacement for Daddy, then decided romance with the new daddy was dull."

"And Daddy number one. Where did he get his money?"

"This is where it gets interesting. Her first daddy was one Jonne Kultti. He had his fingers in a lot of pies, but made the bulk of his money with an escort service."

I take the ashtray out of my desk drawer, crack the window and light up. "Escort services come in a lot of flavors and varieties. What kind was his?"

"The soft kind, as such things go. Expensive. Gorgeous women mostly catering to foreign businessmen. Kultti's escorts didn't necessarily provide sex including orgasm, but some of his girls offered S&M, bondage and other fetishes."

"And Iisa knew Linda how?"

"Linda, as you may have noticed, looks much like Bettie Page. She went to work for Kultti in 1997, in the midst of a worldwide Bettie Page revival. She turned tricks as a Bettie Page impersonator. I would assume

271

that Iisa met Linda while she worked for her father."

"And the Linda–Iisa–Bettie Page look-alike game?"

"I don't know how that came about, or anything else about their early friendship."

"Keep digging, I'll keep giving. Anything else of interest?"

"Jonne Kultti didn't insist that all his escorts actually engage in sex with customers, but he did make them all audition for the job by blowing him. Apparently, he took quite a shine to Linda. I think Linda was sucking Iisa's daddy's dick on a regular basis."

"More?"

"Jonne Kultti committed suicide by putting a hunting rifle under his chin and pulling the trigger with his toe."

Good stuff. I thank him and hang up. The phone rings with my hand still on the receiver.

A receptionist says Filippov is in the lobby. I request that he be escorted up to my office.

Milo walks in and sits, puts a sheet of printer paper down on my desk. "I went through some databases and made some follow-up phone calls," he says, "and put this together."

I read it:

LINDA POHJOLA:
SSN# 090980-3828
DOB September 9, 1980.
Mother: Marjut Pohjola.
Father: not listed on birth certificate.

Marjut Pohjola deceased November 13, 2000. Marjut died of a cerebral brain hemorrhage after spending ten years in Oulun Palvelukoti, a rest home for people with mental disabilities near Oulu.

IISA FILIPPOV:
SSN# 030280-7246
DOB February 3, 1980.
Mother: Noora Kultti.
Father: Jonne Kultti.

Noora Kultti deceased February 3, 1980. Complications during childbirth. Jonne Kultti deceased September 16, 1998. Suicide death.

Milo isn't speaking much today. He's still hurt about last night. He killed a man less than twenty-four hours ago and is still an emotional wreck, still looks like shit. I bring him up to speed on Iisa's and Linda's backgrounds, as per my chat with Jaakko.

He grimaces. "Where did you get all that from?"

I guess he spent a lot of time getting basic info, and my having learned so much so quick has injured his self-esteem. I grin and joke. "You're not the only detective in the room."

The joke fails to lighten the situation. Milo can't stand to be bested in anything. He grips the arms of the chair and his knuckles turn white. He doesn't speak. His ego is on the ropes.

"Filippov will be here soon," I say. "I got the impression he wanted to talk to me alone. I think you should get some sleep. You've been through a lot. Take a day or two for yourself."

He glares at me. "You're saying I'm not competent to do my job because I did some street-cleaning?"

More put-on tough talk. "I've experienced what you're going through and I sympathize. Some time will help."

He's near to throwing a fit from rage. "If you think I'm going to step aside, let you break this case and take all the credit, when I'm the one who figured it out, you're out of your fucking mind."

Filippov knocks on the frame of my open door. Milo storms out.

"Are you two having a lovers' quarrel?" Filippov asks. "I sense trouble in paradise."

I don't stand or offer to shake hands, gesture for Filippov to take a seat. He doesn't sit or speak, just hands me a memory stick and stands waiting with his arms folded.

I plug the stick into my computer. It has one file on it, called "Breaking and Entering." It's a video file shot with a zoom lens, and Milo passes in and out of view in an apartment window.

"Your partner's prowess with computers got him a position as a detective," Filippov says, "and apparently he's able to shoot mental defectives, but his stealth skills need serious improvement."

"It appears so," I say.

"I saw him watching my home, then he followed me and my secretary to her apartment. He climbed into her dumpster and rooted around in it, then he watched her building all night. We pretended to leave for work in the morning, but circled around and came back to watch our watcher. He stayed inside her apartment for a considerable length of time. His search must have been quite thorough."

I won't apologize for Milo. "Why bring

this to me? I'm not responsible for his actions."

"Perhaps not, but I assumed you would find them interesting. Failure to report his actions would constitute collaboration in them. Did you know about his illegal search of Linda's premises?"

I debate how much to reveal and how much to hold back. Whether to try to humiliate him with knowledge about his sexual fetish. Whether to let him know that Milo's illegally obtained evidence goes a long way toward placing Filippov at the crime scene. He's playing a game with me. I decide to give him nothing. He wouldn't be intimidated. Knowing what I know would only give him ammunition, better cards to play. Linda, however, might make a better target for interrogation.

I hand his memory stick back to him. "You're entitled to press charges against Milo if you like. It might be good for him, teach him a lesson. Give this to the national chief of police. It seems you and he are well acquainted."

He lays the stick on my desk. "You may decide you want to give it to him yourself."

As he did in the restaurant, he's sending me a message. I still don't have a clue what it is. "You tortured and murdered your wife," I say, "and you don't even pretend otherwise. You make no attempt to hide your affair with Linda. You're a sadistic cunt."

"If you ever had a chance of making a case against me," he says, "your moron partner destroyed it with his bungled illegal search." He stands and walks out.

I recall Milo's theory about the murder and protective clothing. I picture how it might have been. Filippov and Linda engage in their sexual fetish. As seen on video, Ivan is naked except for the mask and black vinyl gloves. Linda wears black lingerie. A bra that exposes her nipples for easy torture, crotchless panties, garters, stockings and pumps.

During the murder though, they have on toxic-waste gear to keep blood and attendant DNA off of them. She has on a white paper suit with a hood and foot covering, and probably industrial vinyl gloves, as in the video. Only her mouth is exposed. She would have had to tear a hole in the crotch of the suit in order to insert her dildo. Filippov also wears a hooded paper suit and gloves, plus respirator. He also needs a rip in the crotch for his penis to extend through, in order to get it into Linda's mouth, and for Linda to be able to jam the dildo up his ass.

It comes to me. Filippov and Linda didn't just make an audio recording of the murder, they made a video. Making the video, so they could watch it again and again during ritualized sadomasochistic sex, may have been as much of a motivation for killing Iisa as committing the murder itself. Because of this, I believe that somewhere, that video exists.

I ask myself — if they got rid of the toxic-waste protection garments after the murder — what might they not have disposed of that could have picked up blood spatter? Answer: Linda's dildo and the camcorder used in filming. Milo says the dildo was recently washed, but it's hard to give a camcorder a scrubbing thorough enough to remove all DNA. I think Filippov filmed Milo's illegal entry of Linda's apartment with the same camera. We no longer need Milo's illegally obtained evidence. One way or another, I'll find the camera and video, and Iisa's diary, if it still exists. And I'll convict them.

I go down the hall to Milo's office and knock on his door. No answer. I open the door anyway. He's sitting at his desk, staring at a black computer monitor, brooding. I toss him the memory stick. He makes no effort to catch it, lets it land at his feet.

"You got caught," I say.

No response.

"Iisa's time of death was in the neighbor-hood of eight a.m.," I say. "The security tape proves they got to Filippov Construction around nine. If Filippov and Linda wore protective clothing while they murdered Iisa, they must have dressed for work there in Saar's apartment, then got rid of the bloody gear somewhere along the drive from Helsinki to Vantaa. Make yourself useful. Figure out their most likely route, drive it, and look for places they might have dumped the gear."

A waste of time. Useless busywork. Milo is unpredictable at his best, has already come near to destroying this investigation. Killing Legion made him an incompetent emotional wreck, a liability. I picture Legion slumped on the floor, blood trickling out of his head. The experience didn't do a lot for me, either. Still, as much as possible, it's time to cut Milo out of the investigation so I can finish it.

# 30

I make the journey through a snowstorm, along icy highways, back to Porvoo. The faint smell of cat piss and the strong gamey scent of roasting moose and turnips fill Arvid's house. He invites me in, cordial but wary. I'm not sure if he regards me as friend or enemy. Maybe a bit of both. Ritva greets me with warmth, asks me if I'm feeling better. Arvid and I sit at the dinner table. Ritva serves us coffee and bustles in the kitchen.

I lay Pasi Tervomaa's book, *Einsatzkommando Finnland and Stalag 309,* on the table between us. "Maybe you should read what's been written about you," I say.

He sits straight up in his chair with his hands flat on the armrests. His clothes are again starched and pressed. He's the most military civilian I've ever met. He doesn't even glance at the book. "I've read it," he says. "I make it a point to read everything about historical events in which I've played a part."

"I went to SUPO headquarters and found your file. Your version of events doesn't hold water, because you and my grandpa, Toivo Kivipuro, had parallel careers. You entered Valpo service together. Bruno Aaltonen wrote letters of recommendation for both of you, and you and Ukki worked in the same duty stations at the same time. You even won the same medals. The odds of you and him being separated in 1941 and 1942 are almost nil. You said you didn't know Ukki, but in fact, your families were associated before the war, and you were paired up for the duration of your careers."

"Okay," he says. "You got me. I was at 309 with Toivo. You say you want to make the Germans fuck off and leave me alone. How?"

"A statement from you admitting your presence at Stalag 309 but denying any participation in murder might do it. If it's the truth."

He smirks. "Nobody gives a damn about the truth. This is about payback. The story really started in 1999, when Martti Ahtisaari was president. He decided to honor Finland's Nazi Waffen-SS volunteers during the Second World War by erecting a monument in the Ukraine, where the bodies of about a hundred and fifty Finnish SS volunteers are buried."

Ahtisaari, president, diplomat and Nobel Prize winner, commemorates Finnish SS war dead and, by association, endorses our part in the Holocaust. Fucking amazing.

"Finland's Jewish groups protested," Arvid says. "The European Jewish Congress said that Ahtisaari undermined efforts to combat anti-Semitism. The Simon Wiesenthal Center said that by suggesting equality between its perpetrators and victims, Ahtisaari denigrated the memory of the Holocaust dead."

"What does all this have to do with you?" I ask.

"Ahtisaari fucked up. The commotion resurrected nearly forgotten history. Suddenly the world remembered that Finland had around fifteen hundred volunteers in the SS. The Nuremberg War Crimes Tribunals held that all Waffen-SS troops were guilty of war crimes and crimes against humanity. This would include Finns. Heinrich Himmler formed a Finnish Waffen-SS Volunteer Battalion called Nordost. It was attached to the Nordland Waffen-SS Regiment of the Fifth SS Viking Division, a most vicious and fanatical bunch. Then Jewish groups recalled that rather than punish our SS volunteers, in 1958, the government exonerated them and then gave them full veterans' rights. All this gave the Wiesenthal Center a hard-on for Finland. They want a scapegoat. It took them ten years to find the right one. A Finnish icon. Me."

Arvid Lahtinen. National hero. Political football. I tap Pasi's book. "There's only one eyewitness account accusing you of murder," I say, "and the accuser is dead. Say he made a mistake. Deny everything."

"It won't work," Arvid says. "If they dig a little, they'll find other witnesses."

The implication gives me a start. "The allegations against you are true?"

"Actually, the account in the book is mistaken. I didn't shoot that particular Commie, it was your grandpa, Toivo."

It jars me like a punch to the head. I didn't realize that, if I found out Ukki was a murderer, it would affect me so. I'm crushed. "Ukki was an executioner?"

"Not exactly. He and I and some of the others shot people, though."

"Why?"

"We drank a lot in those days. Sometimes we got carried away in the spirit of things. Whacking the occasional political commissar didn't seem like a big deal at the time.

Still doesn't, really. He and I both killed hundreds of Bolsheviks. That was our job. Whether they were combatants or prisoners didn't make any difference to us. We just wanted them dead. Toivo had a vicious streak, by the way, a lot worse than mine."

I need to hear this. "Tell me about him."

"Our fathers were friends. We saw each other sometimes growing up and got to be friends, too. As you thought, our fathers had some political influence and got us into Valpo. Toivo and I were close during the war, but it affected him in different ways than it did me. He could be less than reasonable. He used to make saps out of sections of fire hose filled with shotgun pellets. They save your hands when you hit people. He beat men so often and so hard that he went through a sap almost every week. They would wear out and burst and lead would go flying all over the room."

This hurts. "How many people did Valpo detectives kill in Stalag 309?"

"Some dozens, maybe a hundred. Toivo and I killed maybe half of them. The SS guards found it soothing to see us take part in their cause and show solidarity, but not too often, because if we did the shooting instead of them, it ruined their fun."

I was wrong. I didn't need to hear this. "I

don't want to know any more."

He nods understanding. "Don't judge Toivo. Or me. You don't have the right. Those were different times. Strange times. I don't feel guilty about them. On the contrary, I'm proud of what we did for our country. Our patriotic duty. Toivo was a good man and a good friend. I still miss him."

My temples pulse migraine, but the evil creatures in my head lie dormant. "I miss Ukki, too," I say. "You remind me so much of him, in a way it's hard to be around you."

Arvid smiles. "I always wanted to be a grandpa. Ritva and I had two boys. Cancer took one. The other died in a car wreck. Neither one made it out of his teens. You're a good boy and a detective to boot. You can call me Ukki if you want. Maybe it will make you feel better."

The idea seems silly. I question his motivation for suggesting it, and it makes me suspicious, so I play along. "Okay, Ukki. Why did my grandpa move to Kittilä?"

Despite my mistrust, calling him Ukki feels good, makes me feel like I'm a kid again.

"He was braver than me. I was afraid of persecution by the new Red Valpo. I thought they would execute me or at least put me in prison. I fled the country and moved to Sweden for a while, then to Venezuela. I had a farm there and didn't return until the late 1950s, after the amnesty. I met Ritva and settled down. Toivo was furious about the settlement with the USSR, called it a betrayal. The Kittilä area had a lot of Red partisans. Toivo moved there and joined an underground network of White partisans. They stockpiled weapons and hoped the tide would turn. They wanted to overthrow the government and slaughter the Reds. It never happened, so he lived out his life as a blacksmith. We exchanged letters, I visited a couple times. His disappointment over the war was bitter, but in general he was happy enough."

Sixty-five years later, Arvid's fears of persecution are renewed. It disturbs me.

Ritva sets the table. Arvid carves the roast. "A friend of mine killed a big moose and gave me a lot of it. Take some home with you if you want."

I find myself liking Arvid more and more, and I'm less and less certain I care about what he did in the Second World War. A lifetime ago. "Listen," I say. "After what you told me, I don't know what to do. I'm afraid you're in real trouble."

"I'm afraid, too," Ritva says. She's been

quiet today, looks like she's not feeling well.

Arvid ladles gravy on baked potatoes, carrots and turnips. "Here's what we do. You go back to the interior minister, and tell him to fucking fix this or I start telling state secrets."

He's ninety years old, and his secrets must be from the war. I can't imagine that they carry much weight anymore. "Can you give me some examples?"

"Things contrary to Finland's perception of its own history. Unpleasant things. Most of it has been written about in one place or another by historians, but often disputed or discredited, called surmise or conjecture, because no one wants to know the truth. I'm a national hero. I'll write a book and give this unpleasantness the official stamp of veracity."

I'm still doubting. Arvid and I compliment Ritva on the moose roast.

"What do you think of Finland's great Lord and Savior, picture of moral rectitude and man of supreme honor?" Arvid asks.

"You mean Mannerheim?"

"The one and only."

Baron Carl Gustaf Emil Mannerheim. Descended of Swedish royalty. Imperial Russian army officer. Commander in chief of Finland's defense forces in the Second

World War, and later the nation's sixth president.

"He was a great man," I say, "a great leader. Finland might not exist today without him. The Russians or the Germans or both would have destroyed us."

"That's correct. Much recent historical research has taken up the question of the extent to which Finland protected Jews during the war. Mannerheim is lauded for his efforts."

"You're the one they're going to accuse of being a Jew killer, not Mannerheim," I say.

"I killed Communists. I didn't give a flying fuck if they were Jews or not. Jewish prisoners of war were concentrated in the middle of Finland, near the Second Central POW camp in Naarajärvi. Can you think why that might be?"

"History books say they were placed there for their own protection."

"Wrong. They were placed there in case it was necessary to sell them off to the Gestapo."

"Sorry," I say, "but how could you possibly know that?"

"Bruno Aaltonen was friends with the head of the Gestapo, and they discussed it at length. My father was friends with Aaltonen. He told Dad about it. Dad told me.

And besides, it was a common topic of discussion among Valpo detectives."

"You're telling me Mannerheim was an anti-Semite and prepared to take part in the Holocaust."

"No, I'm telling you he was a pragmatist, faced with weighing the lives of a few hundred Jews against the liberty of Finland, a country he protected at all costs, and the lives of its citizens, which at that time numbered about four million. I'm telling you great men don't become great without getting their hands dirty."

"It's hard to believe," I say.

"You believe fabrications in history books. You're brainwashed. Our relationship with Germany was rooted in ideology as well as shared military goals. The Continuation War was about expansionism. Through Valpo, we only handed over about a hundred and thirty people to the Gestapo through extradition. But the military turned over about three thousand, mostly Red Army. You know why?"

"Why?"

"Because we wanted slave labor. Germany had an enormous number of prisoners of war. We were trading our Red Army prisoners for their Finnic and especially Finnish-speaking prisoners so we could settle them in Karelia, which we had captured from the Soviet Union and which we intended to ethnically cleanse of Russians. It would have eased the labor shortage on the home front. It was an ideological decision. Nationalists had dreamed about the opportunity to occupy Eastern Karelia since before I was born. Mannerheim signed off on this. He refused to send our troops to attack St. Petersburg with the Germans. Giving the Gestapo three thousand POWs was a way of smoothing that over."

"What about Jews?" I ask.

"We gave the Gestapo latitude. If they requested extradition of a particular person, like as not, we wouldn't inquire about the basis for the request. We knew goddamned good and well though, that an extradition was a death sentence."

"This is powerful stuff. How could it have been kept secret for so long?"

"Near the end of the war, Valpo saw trouble coming. We destroyed as much documentation as we could."

I'm in over my head. I'm a detective, have no business in the political realm. "You're asking me to relay a threat to blackmail the Finnish government into protecting you."

"It's not a threat. I *am* blackmailing them. Tell the interior minister that I'll also discuss our treatment of POWs."

"The death rate in our POW camps was high," I say, "but be fair. We didn't have food to adequately feed ourselves, let alone them."

"We held sixty-five thousand POWs. About thirty percent died. That rate was surpassed in Europe only by Nazi Germany, with its death camps, and by the USSR. Stalin was just as bad as Hitler. The death rate here wasn't so high until we decided to use already sick and starving POWs for forced labor. Then they started dropping like flies. And we could have made sacrifices, fed them better if we wanted to. We just didn't want to."

"I'm sorry, but I don't think anyone will believe all of this, even from you."

"Boy, you're naïve beyond words. We shared the Nazi vision. Expansionism and room for the nation to grow. An agrarian paradise populated by ethnic Finns. That dream lives on. Don't you watch TV?"

"A bit."

"Think about, for example, the Elovena ads. They're not selling porridge, they're selling Aryan propaganda. If Leni Riefenstahl had made those commercials, Hitler would have come in his pants. A hardworking beautiful blond mother in the countryside, surrounded by her adoring, content, and even blonder oatmeal-glomming children. Fields of grain ripple in the breeze. Like it or not, boy, that idyllic Nazi vision is alive and well in this country today."

His cultural view is extreme, but his point is well taken. I think about Christmas Eve, and the beginning of the twenty-four hours of official Christmas Peace. At noon, in front of the town hall in Turku, a band plays *Porilaisten marssi* — *March of the People from Pori* — and the Christmas Peace song reminisces about covering the land in the blood of our enemies.

"You still haven't told me how my great-grandpa and your father knew each other," I say.

He gets up and brings me a package of meat out of his freezer. "As I said, you're a good boy. I've decided I enjoy your company, so I'll save that story. Come back tomorrow, we'll eat and I'll tell it to you. You'll like it, it's a good one. Ritva is tired. You better go now."

I have a murder to solve, don't have time to lounge around and listen to war stories, but I realize, to my surprise, that I don't care. Somehow I need it, and I'm already looking forward to it. "Okay," I say. "I'll see you tomorrow."

# 31

It's time to pick up where Milo left off. I'll tail Linda, maybe have a chat with her if the opportunity arises. I head southwest, from Porvoo toward Vantaa. Powerful winds gust and make the car shimmy. Snow drifts in fat flakes. The air currents shift, and for a couple minutes, the snow flies up toward the sky instead of down toward the ground. It amuses me, doesn't happen often.

I ponder Arvid's revelations. Part of me wants to believe him, because I feel some affection for him and Ritva. As a Finn, though, I want to dismiss all of it as a cheap scam designed to weasel out of trouble. The detective in me is skeptical. First, because he lied to me in the beginning and claimed he was never at Stalag 309. Second, because he may be jerking my emotions, using the grandpa angle, telling me to call him Ukki to make me let my guard down and use me as a patsy. I need to be wary of Arvid. I wonder, too, if he would really write a book intended to destroy the self-image of a country he worked so hard to protect.

The ring of my cell phone breaks my thoughts. Securitas Arska calls. He's at Roskapankki. The guy who stole John's boots is there. "Give me half an hour," I say.

I change direction and start toward Helsinki, drive fast despite the snow. I call John and tell him to meet me at Roskapankki. He says he's busy right now. I hear a squeal and giggle in the background. I'm interrupting a fuck session. Good for John. "Too bad," I say. "Go there now. I'm going to get your boots back for you."

He brightens. "I can be there in twenty minutes."

Headache Alien screeches. I find myself furious. John is a decent guy, problems or no, didn't deserve to have a speed freak steal his boots and leave him barefoot in the snow in minus twenty degrees. Then I realize the real reason for my anger is that said speed freak was mean to someone Kate loves. Same difference, I'm enraged.

I enter Roskapankki. John skulks near the bar, ashamed. Arska sits on a bouncer stool near the door, says he didn't have to detain the guy I'm looking for, he isn't going

294

anywhere. He points at a table with four losers sitting at it, half-full pints of beer in front of them. I slide Arska two fifties. I order six beers at the bar, tell John to bring them to the table. I pull up two chairs and sit with four derelicts in their mid-twenties. Their eyes tell me they're flying. They look at me, amused and curious. John sets beers in front of all of us and takes a seat beside me, huddles close for protection. I note, to my surprise and pleasure, that he's sober.

"Hi, guys," I say. "My name is Kari. Let's be friends."

They check out the gunshot scar on my face. Their laughs are bemused. They're thinking, what the hell, free beer. We clink glasses. John doesn't have to tell me who stole his boots. The lank-haired greaseball fuckwad beside me is wearing them. I don't have to tell him I've come for the boots. My presence here with John announces it.

"Nope," Fuckwad says.

I smile. "Nope what?"

*"Haista vittu."* Sniff cunt. His friends tense up, smell violence brewing and start working themselves up to beat the shit out of me, en masse.

My dad says that to me when he's drunk and angry. I don't like it. "I'm a cop," I say, "and I'm prepared to overlook your stealing

295

John's boots if you kindly and quietly return them. I also won't shake you down for drugs."

He shakes his head. "I'm not holding, and I'm keeping the boots. Fuck off and run along now."

He wants to be tough in front of his friends. They chuckle. I sigh. "I'd rather not go to the trouble of arresting you."

One of his buddies says, "I recognize you. You're one of the cops that killed that retard down the street yesterday."

"Yep," I say.

Fuckwad laughs, has no respect for anyone or anything. "Please, arrest me. It will make a great story. Retard killer arrests boot thief." He points at John. "You should have seen the look on that guy's face when I told him to take his boots off and give them to me. He didn't even put up a fight, just sat down in the snow and did it."

He cackles at the memory. He's serious, he'd rather go to jail than return the boots. I suppose he's arrested on a regular basis and it makes no difference to him. John stares down at the floor, humiliated. Fuckwad's friends howl and knee-slap.

Of course, humiliating John was the point of stealing the boots in the first place. Disgracing others is Fuckwad's idea of a good time. Both my headache and temper flare. I won't arrest Fuckwad. At least not today.

When I was a young guy and first moved to Helsinki, I bartended in *räkälät* like this on occasion to make ends meet. The beer glasses are cheap and thick — hard to break — but the surface tension of the glass is so great that when they shatter, they explode.

I laugh along with them, good-natured. With my left hand, I hold up my pint in front of Fuckwad's face and squeeze. He looks at me, smirking and quizzical. I squeeze harder, the glass goes off like a bomb, shatters into a thousand pieces. Beer and glass fly away from me toward Fuckwad, into his face and across the room. He recoils in his chair and gawks disbelief, face beer-soaked and covered with tiny bleeding cuts.

His friends shoot upright to their feet and back away. John and I remain seated. I glance around. Arska still lounges on the bouncer's stool. He winks at me, amused. The bartender gapes, says nothing.

Fuckwad's eyes brim with tears. "You fucking asshole," he says, "you could have blinded me."

I pick little glass shards out of my left hand and flick them at him with my right.

"That was the idea," I say. "Didn't work." I pick up another pint. "I could try again."

He trembles and raises his hands to his face. "Please no."

"I asked you nicely. Give me the boots."

He tries to jerk them off as fast as he can. He turns his chair over and pitches to the floor. He keeps tugging at the boots.

I get up, stand over him and wait. I let blood drip from my hand onto his head. He offers me the boots.

I take them. "Get out," I say.

His eyes dart, looking to his friends for backup, but they're chuckling again, this time at *his* humiliation. He rights his chair and pulls himself back into it. He gives me a pitiful look of appeal.

"I said out."

He whimpers. "It's minus fucking twenty-five degrees."

I nod toward John. "If it's good enough for him, it's good enough for you. I'm going to stand outside and watch. You're going to walk until I can't see you anymore."

He gathers his courage and little remaining dignity, and starts to take his coat from the back of his chair.

I shake my head. "No coat."

He lurches toward the door. I give John his boots and follow, and John tags along

298

behind me. I thank Arska, step outside, ball up some snow in my cut hand and watch Fuckwad hurry along the ice.

John stands beside me. "I didn't know it was possible to crush a beer glass in your hand," he says.

"Me neither," I say.

He puts an arm around my shoulders. "I'll never forget this."

"Me neither."

"I don't know how I can ever repay you."

"Be a brother your sister can be proud of. Be her friend."

"I'll do my best," he says.

"Tell her you missed your Sedona Wests and bought them back from UFF," I say.

"I haven't been around much. Nobody noticed they were gone."

I check my watch. We're near the house. Jari and his family are coming over for dinner tonight. I have just enough time to grocery-shop, go home and check on Kate, and still make it to Filippov Construction and tail Linda when she gets off work.

## 32

It starts snowing hard again. John tags along while I grocery-shop. We go to Alko. I buy a couple bottles of wine and two bottles of Koskenkorva. I tell John to hide one in his suitcase and sneak drinks to stay level, warn him not to let Kate catch him boozing alcoholic-style, especially in the daytime.

We go home. Kate and Mary are watching Dr. Phil. A bad sign. Kate hates Dr. Phil. It tells me Kate prefers listening to the good doctor to conversation with her sister.

I say hi to Mary, kiss Kate hello and touch her belly. "Learning anything from Phil?" I ask.

She mimics him. "Haaaney, what yoo got yourself is a drankin' problem. Watcha need to dooo to cure yoor problem, haaney, is quit yer goddamned drankin'."

She does a good imitation. It makes me laugh. John sits down to watch TV with them.

"What's for dinner?" Kate asks.

*"Karjalanpaisti."*

She smiles. "Dee-yummy."

"I better get it started. Kate, I have to go out to work again. If I prep it now, can you pop it in the oven at five, so it will be done when Jari and his family get here?"

"Sure," she says. "What happened to your hand?"

"I slipped on the ice, and rock salt in the snow cut it. No big deal."

"What is *karjalanpaisti?*" Mary asks me.

"Something good. You'll see."

"How's your headache?" Kate asks.

"Not bad."

My head is splitting. I go to the bedroom and get a painkiller, so I can make it through the evening without my migraine singing songs that tell me to do bad things, and put dinner together. When I'm done, I go to the living room, sit down next to Kate and read the newspaper. I come across an article about the harsh treatment of Jews in Finland, and Helsinki in particular, during the nineteenth century. I think of the word Pasi Tervomaa used. Confluence. The persecution of Jews is suddenly everywhere I look.

The article says Jews were confined to living in designated areas. Jews were denied passports. Jews were forbidden to conduct many types of business, including, of course, moneylending. The list of citizens' rights denied Jews is long. Because of these oppressive laws, a quarter of Finnish Jews either left Finland on their own or were deported.

This runs contrary to my perception of the Finnish treatment of Jews. Our country takes pride in its wartime record in that regard. Common wisdom holds that we protected Jews. During the war, they fought alongside other Finnish troops. Strangely enough, this means that Jews also fought alongside Germans. Finnish soldiers even operated a field synagogue.

Heinrich Himmler pushed for the deportation of our Jews to concentration camps. Our legendary general Gustaf Mannerheim replied, "While Jews serve in my army, I will not allow their deportation."

Mannerheim's hero status is such that he's viewed as Finland's Messiah. His military prowess and adroit political abilities allowed him to play the Soviet Union and Nazi Germany off one another, and ensured that neither overran us. On Independence Day in 1944, Mannerheim visited the Jewish synagogue in Helsinki and took part in a commemorative service for the Jewish soldiers who had died in the Winter and

Continuation Wars, and presented the Jewish community with a medal. These things are common knowledge.

An SS stalag, manned in part by Finns, where Jews were sent by the Finnish government with full knowledge that they would be murdered, is antithetical to history as written. We love Jews. We hate Jews. Which is it? I call Pasi Tervomaa and explain my confusion and misgivings. "Did Mannerheim know about the slaughter in 309?" I ask.

"Let me put it this way. Mannerheim had the means to know if he chose to, and as such, he bore responsibility. If the Stalag 309 case had been brought before a tribunal at the end of the war, under the Nuremberg principles, Mannerheim would have been prosecuted as accessory to murder. That said, a lot of papers hit his desk, and he was an old man. He could have overlooked something. And the responsibility wasn't his alone. The president and the interior minister at the time, Risto Ryti and Toivo Horelli, probably also gave their indirect blessings to Finnish collusion in 309 and the events that occurred there."

"I remember that President Ryti and some ministers were convicted in war responsibility trials. Is there any connection?"

"No. Ryti and the others were sentenced in a show trial as a sop to the Soviets. They were charged with influencing Finland to wage war against the Soviet Union and United Kingdom in 1941, and for preventing peace during the Continuation War. By the way, it's rumored that Mannerheim wasn't charged because Stalin intervened. He liked Mannerheim. Or maybe Stalin didn't actually *like* anyone, but found Mannerheim useful."

"This is all demoralizing," I say.

"I was disappointed when I learned these things, too," Pasi says. "There's a lot more information out there if you care to look for it. A lot of it in the public domain on the Internet. Most people just don't want to hear it."

When I get off the phone, I hear Kate, John and Mary chatting. Mary isn't lecturing. John isn't drunk. Their voices are cheerful. They're smiling. This heartens me. I say good-bye to them and set out to find Bettie Page Linda.

## 33

I drive to Vantaa. Road conditions are bad. Helsinki is experiencing a near-record snowfall. Snowplows run twenty-four/seven but can't keep up. Towers of snow line the streets. Usually, snow is carted away in trucks and dumped, but the city has run out of places to put it. Some roads are impassable.

I get to Filippov Construction at four forty-five p.m. and park about fifty yards from the front door. Because of the falling snow, my car is almost invisible from this distance. Filippov and Linda exit the building at five and leave in separate cars. She drives a 2003 Ford Mustang. He drives a new Dodge Journey. They go in different directions. I suspect he's going home and she's going to Helsinki.

Following Linda is easy. She doesn't drive too fast, road traffic is light, and I'm difficult to spot because of weather conditions.

I was right, she goes straight to downtown Helsinki and enters a parking garage. I park in the same garage. She walks toward Stockmann Department Store. I close the gap between us and catch her under the big clock at the main entrance. I touch her arm, and she turns.

"Ms. Pohjola," I say, "I'd like a word, if I may."

She bats her dark eyes at me and her red lips turn up into a charming smile. "Tell me, Inspector, what would you like to talk about?"

"Sex, lies and videotape."

Her laugh is giddy. "Oh, dear, that boy that works with you has been in my computer. He also rooted around in my underwear drawer. If he's going to be a successful voyeur, he has to learn to put things back in their proper places."

I wait.

"Yes," she says, "let's have a chat. Do you have somewhere in mind?"

"How about Iguana? The tables in the back might offer us some privacy."

She nods agreement and takes my arm. We walk like lovers across the street and into the faux Mexican restaurant. "A hot drink would be nice," she says.

She moves toward a big table in the rear

and takes off her coat. Underneath it, she has on a tight black sweater and a short black skirt. Black stockings descend into black leather boots. Her attire doesn't surprise me. A lot of Helsinki women refuse to succumb to the weather, no matter how severe, at the expense of fashion.

I bring us two Irish coffees and sit across from her. She takes a sip. It leaves an ungodly sexy line of cream along her upper lip. She licks it away, provocative. Linda is drop-dead gorgeous. "Where shall we begin?" she asks.

I decide on the aggressive approach. "The murder of Iisa Filippov has strong fetish overtones, and the fetishes you and Ivan Filippov engage in suggest that I should suspect you of the crime."

She taunts me. "Why, Inspector, what fetishes might you mean? Let me guess, you saw a video in which I perform fellatio on Ivan while I masturbate with a vibrator. He wears a mask and is quite rough with me. I orgasm, then use the vibrator on him, and he comes, too. Did the video you saw go something like that?"

She's embarrassing me, as is her intention. "Yes, very much like that."

She looks at me with impish glee, and although Linda is beautiful, I notice certain flaws. Her right eye is a little slow. Her lips are on the thin side. "It's not as if I'm the only one who enjoys these kinds of sex games," she says. "Your national chief of police does as well. At least, he seemed to."

This comes out of left field, takes me off guard. "You enacted this particular sex game with Jyri?"

"Something like it. On the morning of Iisa's murder. Jyri can serve as my alibi."

"Why do you think both Filippov and Jyri failed to mention this to me?"

She sips Irish coffee and does the cream-lick tongue trick again. "Perhaps because you failed to ask them."

She slides a foot out of a boot, raises it under the table and massages my crotch with her toes. I go stiff, zero to sixty, in about two seconds. She has an amazing knack for turning me on, seems to know what I want even before I do. It's disconcerting in the extreme. My first inclination is to push her foot away, but I'm curious about what I might learn while she plays out her little charade. At least, that's what I tell myself.

She says, "You like it that I look like her, don't you, Inspector?"

"You mean like Bettie Page?"

She keeps massaging. Her toes do amazing things. "Yes," I say, "I like it."

"Me too," she says. "It's nice to be someone else. That's the nature of my fetish, the negation of my personality. That's why Ivan was so rough with me in the video. He treats me not as a person, but as a thing to be used. His fetish, naturally enough, is to be an aggressive but faceless user. Our sexual relationship isn't uncommon. Perhaps you should try it. You're manly. I like that. And I like to be watched. That's why we make the videos. The other detective, Milo, likes to watch. Maybe I could suck your cock while Milo watches and jerks off. You can come in my mouth and Milo can blow on my face. I'll videotape it and watch it with Ivan while we play our sex roles."

My hard-on wilts. I remove her foot from my crotch. "Thanks," I say, "but my wife wouldn't approve."

Her eyes sparkle. "What a stick-in-the-mud she must be. The point I'm trying to get across to you is that I like to be used, not to hurt others. You're barking up the wrong tree."

Maybe I am, or maybe I'm being manipulated. Her skills in that regard are extraordinary.

"Can I ask you about your relationship with Iisa? I gather you two were very close.

And about how you came to have a sexual relationship with her husband. Given your friendship, it seems an unusual state of affairs. No pun intended."

She turns off her overt sexuality, puts her foot back in her boot. Her voice becomes matter-of-fact. "Years ago, I met Iisa at a party. We did a lot of coke — we always did a lot of drugs together — and one night we noticed that we look a great deal alike. We started doing our hair and makeup the same, for fun. We even had sex once, just to see what it would be like to fuck yourself, but we weren't that into it. We were high one night, and Iisa decided we should trick Ivan and get him to fuck me, to see if he would notice the difference. Iisa liked to watch, so she hid and videotaped it. That night, Ivan and I found we have symbiotic fetishes, and history, as they say, was made. Fucking Ivan bored Iisa. She decided to do him a favor, and let me do it for her. Iisa even convinced Ivan to hire me to work at Filippov Construction. I became, in a manner of speaking, part of the family."

"I understand that you worked for Iisa's father as a Bettie Page look-alike escort. Could you tell me about that?"

She stands and dons her coat. "Inspector, I'm tired and have shopping to do. Let's save that story for another day."

Much as in my dealings with Filippov, I have the feeling that Linda is sending me a message, but I still don't know what it is. I decide not to press it and thank her for her time and candor. She thanks me for the drink. We go our separate ways.

## 34

I get home at a few minutes before seven. Jari and company should be here soon. The smell of *karjalanpaisti* drifts through the house. My head hurts. I'd like to lie down in the bedroom and rest for a little while, but the door buzzer rings.

Jari and his family come in, take off their shoes, and I make introductions all around. Jari's wife, Taina, is a pleasant woman in her mid-forties. Their sons, Hannu and Martti, are seven and nine. They take after Taina, have her white-blond hair, look like the products of the *Lebensborn* Nazi eugenics program, like the last bastions of the Aryan race. More confluence. They brought toys and movies with them. They break out Legos and go to work building a pirate ship while they watch *Harry Potter and the Philosopher's Stone*.

We adults go to the dining-room table. I open a bottle of red wine and pour for all of us except Kate and Mary. I get them Jaffa. Mary loves the stuff. Jari and Taina both speak good English. He asks about my migraines.

Despite the pain medication, I feel like my head is in a vise. Even my teeth hurt. "It's okay," I say.

"Have you been using the drugs I prescribed for you?"

I haven't used the tranquilizers yet. "Yeah, they help."

"Your blood tests came back clean, and your MRI is next Monday."

"Good to hear," I say.

"Kate, what about you?" Taina asks. "How is your pregnancy going?"

"There have been some complications. I have preeclampsia, but I've been medicated for it, and the doctors say everything is fine. I'm due in eleven days."

"Mary, do you have children?" Taina asks. She says no.

The conversation bores John. He gets up from the table and goes to the spare bedroom. His suitcase is there. He's taking a couple pops from the *kossu* bottle I gave him.

"How is prenatal care different here from in the U.S.?" Mary asks.

Kate shrugs. "I don't know. I've never

been pregnant in the States, but I feel that I've been well treated. I had my first two exams at seven and twelve weeks. A midwife examined me . . ."

Mary interrupts. "A midwife instead of a doctor?" She sounds disapproving.

"She was quite skilled," Kate says.

"I'm a midwife," Taina adds.

I hope Mary's small gaffe won't grow into something larger. Kate keeps talking to prevent it from happening. "At week nineteen," she says, "they did another ultrasound, and we found out we're expecting a girl. They checked the baby's brain and organs for abnormalities and measured her neck. Somehow, they can diagnose Down syndrome that way. Then a week later, we went to a private clinic and had a 4-D ultrasound made. We have a DVD of it. Watching her move her little arms and legs is so sweet."

John comes back from the bedroom. He took big gulps. His eyes speak of satiety. He browses books and CDs in the living room.

Jari looks troubled. "Why the 4-D ultrasound? It's usually only done if complications are feared. Was it because of the preeclampsia?"

Kate glances at me, looks down at the table. "I had a miscarriage last year. We just

314

wanted to make sure everything was all right this time."

"Why test for birth defects so late in pregnancy?" Mary asks. "Nothing can be done about it."

"In Finland," Jari says, "in case of birth defect, a woman may still abort at week nineteen."

"I see," Mary says, again disapproving.

Taina bristles. "My first pregnancy was terminated under just such circumstances."

Mary sips Jaffa, says nothing.

Kate and I share a fleeting look. This dinner will go wrong.

Taina looks hurt. This is clearly a painful subject for her. "My child, a girl, had a defective heart," Taina says. "Even if I had carried her to term, she would have had a short and painful life."

Mary meets Taina's angry stare with flat eyes, again says nothing. Her silence makes her condemnation more poignant than words.

The room goes quiet. My headache flares. John hee-haws. "What kind of sick joke is this?" He comes to the table brandishing a Christmas card from my parents. "Check it out," he says. "A troll dressed as Santa Claus."

For once, I'm glad for John's drunken

repartee. He bailed us out of a bad moment. "It's our traditional Father Christmas," I say. "His name is Joulupukki, which means Christmas billy goat. It comes from a pagan tradition. Once upon a time, Santa wasn't a benevolent character. He frightened children. He didn't give gifts — he demanded them."

I tell a story in the hope that Mary's implied insult to Taina will be forgotten. I heard it somewhere, and it sounds like complete horseshit to me, but will suffice for this purpose.

"Joulupukki and his flying reindeer originated with the aboriginal people of Lapland. There was a poisonous forest mushroom. Shamans fed the mushroom to reindeer. Their intestinal tracts filtered out the poison, but left hallucinogens. The shamans drank the reindeer urine. They sometimes had out-of-body experiences and flew. They returned to their bodies through the chimney hole of their tent or cottage. And that explains the legend of Santa Claus and his flying reindeer."

John sits down and smiles, pours himself dregs from the wine bottle. "A great story. I apologize for besmirching your *Pyllyjoki*. He's a proud beast."

*Pyllyjoki*. He just called Father Christmas

316

"Ass River." At least he tries to pronounce Finnish.

Kate works with me, trying to guide the conversation in a comfortable direction. "Something smells good," she says.

"Dinner should be ready." I get up and escape to the kitchen.

I set the table, open another bottle of red and bring the *karjalanpaisti*. I ignore what's being said as I come and go, but hear no shouts and see no blood, so a semblance of dinner-table civility is being maintained. Taina calls the children to eat.

I anticipate Mary's wishes. To sweeten her up, I ask her if she'd like to say grace. Everyone understands and bows their heads. She's tactful, keeps it short. We fill our plates.

Jari smiles. "This is Mom's recipe."

"Is there another way to make *karjalan-paisti?*" Kate asks.

"Most people just use pork and beef cubes, potatoes, onions, bay leaves and whole peppercorns," I say. "But Mom adds lamb chunks, and pieces of liver and kidney. It's easy. You just mix it up, cover it with water, throw it in the oven and let it cook."

"She didn't make it this way when we were kids," Jari says. "It was too expensive. When Dad started drinking less and she had more household money, she started making fancier food."

Everyone digs in with relish, except for John and Mary. They pick at it.

I turn to Jari. "Speaking of Mom, I've been thinking a lot about her father lately. Do you remember much about Ukki?"

"Yeah, a lot. Why?"

"I found out that, except for his time at the front during the Winter War, he was a detective in Valpo from 1938 until the end of the Continuation War. I'd like to learn more about what he did in Valpo."

"People used to talk about Ukki being a Winter War hero," Jari says, "but I never heard him say a word about it. Still, it doesn't surprise me. Goddamn, he hated Russians. If he'd gotten to decide whether or not to drop hydrogen bombs on Russia, it would no longer exist."

I think of how much Arvid reminds me of Ukki, except for the bad temper. "I only remember Ukki being calm and kind. Did you ever see him get angry?"

He laughs. "I heard Mummo say one time that she didn't know Ukki had a temper until their wedding day. He couldn't get the wrapping off a present quick enough to suit him. He got frustrated, threw it on the floor and jumped up and down on it."

The image is hard to conjure, makes me laugh, too. "Do you think Mom knows anything about what Ukki did in the war?"

"If Mom knew anything, you would have heard the stories a thousand times by now."

True. I see that Mary and John haven't finished their meals, but have set down their knives and forks on their plates. I should know better, but I have to ask. "You two didn't care for dinner?"

"I'm sorry, Kari," Mary says. "I wanted to be polite and I tried, but I can't make myself eat animal organs. I keep thinking about their functions."

"Me too," John says. "I did okay with the liver the other night, but I have to draw the line at kidneys. Especially after you told the story about drinking reindeer piss."

Fair enough. They're entitled to their likes and dislikes. I clear the table, bring vanilla ice cream with cloudberry jam for dessert. Hannu and Martti are excited. They're good kids, have sat quiet while the grown-ups spoke in a language they don't understand.

Jari says, "Kate, did you get the *äitiyspakkaus . . .*" he looks at me.

I translate. "Maternity package."

He finishes the question. "Did you get the maternity package from the government?" For John's and Mary's benefit, he explains:

319

"Every mother in Finland has the option of either taking the maternity package from the government or four hundred euros to buy things for the baby herself."

Kate beams. "I did and it's wonderful. Such a great tradition. Kari, would you get the box? I want to show it to John and Mary."

I fetch it from the closet, lay it on the table and open it. John, Mary and Kate stand and rifle through the box. Kate shows off a nice selection of pretty much everything you need to embark on parenthood. A snowsuit and sleeping bag. Hats, mittens and socks. Bodysuits and rompers. Leggings and overalls. A mattress and sheets. Bibs and diapers. A picture book and rattle. Nail scissors. Hairbrush. Toothbrush. Bath thermometer. Cream. If we had to buy all this stuff, it would cost a hell of a lot of money.

"Look," Kate says. "There's even condoms and lubricant for Mom and Dad. And the neatest part is that the box itself is designed to be used as a crib."

"You would keep your infant in a cardboard box?" Mary asks.

"Actually," Kate says, "Kari and I thought it would be practical while you and John are here, because it doesn't take up much space. We'll get a proper crib after you leave."

"I see. What are you going to name your baby?"

"We usually don't choose a baby's name until a few weeks after it's born," I say. "There's no need before the christening."

"You don't name your children for weeks?" Mary asks.

"Sometimes."

She rolls her eyes.

John rifles through the box. "This stuff is cool. They must go to a lot of work to choose different clothes for so many newborns."

"No," I say. "Everybody gets the same package. They change the clothing styles every year or three."

"So every kid in Finland wears the same clothes for their first year?" he asks.

"I don't think they much care what they wear."

"That sounds like something Chairman Mao would have thought of," John says.

Mary nods agreement.

"It was only a few decades ago," I say, "that this nation was impoverished. This kind of help saved people a lot of hardship."

Mary sits back down, spoons ice cream, looks thoughtful. "Speaking of poverty and history, do you know that after the war, the United States gave Finland a great deal of aid under the Marshall Plan? I find it odd that Finland accepted U.S. aid but kept such close ties with the Soviet Union, our enemy."

Kate smacks the table with the flat of her hand. "Now, wait just a minute," she says.

I know Kate and her temper. Mary embarrassed her in front of my family. She just reached her limit.

I make a last effort at conciliation. "Mary is right in part. Finland was forced to decline Marshall Plan aid to avoid confrontation with the Soviets. The USSR had its own economic aid plan, called Comecon. However, Finland wasn't included in it. We would have gotten nothing, but the U.S. government sent aid in secret. Clothes. Food. It saved lives. As an example of how desperate we were and how much it helped, after the war, my father and his brother shared a pair of shoes. They had to take turns going to school every day. U.S. aid helped us recover from that kind of poverty."

My attempt at appeasement fails. Kate looks irked because I veered her away from a burst of anger she deserved to vent. Mary looks vindicated. "Thank you, Kari," she says.

Jari looks vexed. Taina stares down into her ice cream bowl. Her face goes red. The boys don't understand but poke each other and giggle. They know something is up. My migraine starts to whisper to me. I can't think straight, want to bang my head off the table.

Taina overreacts, points her spoon at Mary like a weapon. "You come here and pass judgment on us. You live in a country that has never been invaded by a foreign nation, have never had your people's blood spilled on your own soil. You make it clear that you think I'm immoral. I take it you've never been faced with the decision of whether to terminate your child's life or bring it into a world of pain and horror, yet you dare judge me."

Mary remains calm. "The Bible is clear in its message. And if you may recall, our country was subjected to a vicious attack. That day of infamy is called 9/11."

"Nine-eleven was a single goddamned event," Taina says. "How dare you compare an event with the prolonged devastation of a nation by war. Three thousand people died in 9/11, and that's a tragedy, but your country used it as an excuse to colonize Iraq, a sovereign nation, when it was really about oil and money. Your country caused hundreds of thousands of Iraqi deaths out of greed. Your country sent thousands of its own children to their deaths in Iraq for the sake of the almighty dollar."

"My country is the standard-bearer for the world . . ." Mary says and stops, I guess for once uncertain what to say.

Taina cuts her off. "And more is the fucking pity." She switches to Finnish, tells Jari and the boys they're leaving. Now.

Jari pulls me aside, tells me that Taina got so upset because the decision to terminate her pregnancy broke her heart. She never got over it, and Mary hurt her feelings. He tells me he's sorry, that maybe we can get together again after John and Mary are gone. Within five minutes, they're out the door.

Kate, John, Mary and I sit in silence at the kitchen table. I can't read Kate's face. John is amused. His eyes dance. Mary glowers. The migraine booms.

John breaks the ice. "I think this calls for a drink."

I tell him what he already knows. "The *kossu* is in the freezer."

He brings the bottle and two glasses.

"Sure," Mary says. "Start boozing. That's what you two are good at."

I pour us shots. We shoot them down, I pour us another round.

Kate says, "Kari, you don't look well."

Their voices reverberate like my head is in a steel drum. I'm afraid I'll pass out again, as I did at Arvid's. I need to take painkillers, but I don't want to leave Kate alone to deal with this mess, even for a minute. "The headache," I say. "I need to go to bed soon. Kate, will you come with me?"

Kate turns to Mary. "I'm proud of you and John. I wanted to show you off to Kari's family. I had never met them before and wanted to make a good impression. You humiliated me. Why?"

"That wasn't my intention," Mary says. "You know my feelings about abortion, but I said nothing, even though I have a Christian duty to speak out."

Kate glares at Mary and raises her voice. "You insulted nice people. You insinuated that Americans are somehow better than them."

"I pointed out that America's generosity helped make Finland what it is today. I see nothing wrong with that." Mary points at me. "You let your family insult me and my country. That was wrong."

Now it's my fault. Un-fucking-believable. I consider how much shit I should eat to maintain good relations and keep the peace. I think about Kate and the stress this is causing her, and the possibility of losing our child. I would eat all the shit Mary can dish out, but Kate took a stand. I have to back her up.

"I understand that your religious beliefs are important to you," I say, "but Jari and Taina came here in the spirit of family and friendship. You sent a clear message that their culture and beliefs are inferior to your own. And whatever your beliefs, Taina shared an intimate and doubtless painful experience with you. You did it without speaking, but you made your feelings about it clear enough. No matter what you believe, surely you can see that some lines shouldn't be crossed."

She folds her hands, prayer-style, and looks at me. "Kari, I'll be frank. I don't care for your drinking or swearing, and I hate it that my sister lives halfway across the world from her home because of you."

She stupefies me. I can't deal with her, because I don't understand her. "What's the matter with Finland?" I ask.

"You live in a nation where homosexual relationships and abortion are sanctioned by the government. This country lives contrary to God's law."

"But abortions are legal in the States, too.

And some states ratify same-sex relationships."

"Those are missteps on the path to righteousness and soon to be corrected. The Finnish people, however, live in sin."

I shake my head in disbelief. She reminds me of Legion.

John smacks the table with his hand, just like Kate does when she's furious. I picture him learning it from her when they were kids. "Goddamn it, Mary," he says, "leave Kari alone. He's a good guy."

John seems to have depths that belie his outward veneer. He keeps surprising me. "Kari," he says, "I'm sorry, but fuck this. It's time we all start telling the truth around here."

He's going to tell Kate the truth about himself. I'm terrified. "Don't, John," I say.

I watch Kate's face, but can't read it. She presses a thoughtful finger to pursed lips. The migraine screams that stress will make Kate miscarry and it will kill her. All because I couldn't keep her goddamned idiot brother under control. My vision blurs. My ears ring. My heart thumps in my chest so hard it hurts.

Thank God, John takes my meaning and relents. He gets up, puts on his jacket and boots. "I'm leaving now. I've got a date.

Kari, thank you for dinner and all you've done for me. Mary, while we're here, at least try to pretend you're a decent human being."

A date? He takes the spare keys from the nail beside the door and walks out.

Kate, Mary and I look at each other for a few seconds. Without speaking, Mary goes to the spare bedroom and shuts the door.

Kate reaches across the table and takes my hand. "I'm dizzy," I say. "Could you please get the bag with the medicine Jari prescribed for me, and a glass of water?"

She brings them and sits beside me. I drop a painkiller into the water and watch it dissolve, then decide what the hell, I'll try shotgunning dope. I break a tranquilizer and a sleeping pill into chunks and put them in the glass. I have a little *kossu* left and dump it in, too. I drink the cocktail.

"Let me take you to bed," Kate says.

We undress and get under the covers. Kate lays her head on me. I feel silent tears drip onto my shoulder. "I never would have dreamed my brother and sister would become who they are," she says.

The dope kicks in fast. It's hard to keep my eyes open. "I know. I'm sorry."

"I've never doubted how much you love me," she says, "but still, sometimes the lengths you go to prove it surprise me."

I realize she sees through John and knows what he's become and, further, senses that somehow I've been protecting her from it. I wonder what else she knows, if she understands that I've been hiding other things about myself from her, and if so, if she knows what they are. I wrap her in my arms and sleep.

## 35

I wake up at eight thirty a.m. I slept well, feel rested for the first time in I don't know how long. Kate isn't in the bed beside me. I go to the kitchen for coffee. Kate has left a note signed with a lipstick kiss print. She and Mary got up early to do some sightseeing and shopping. I take it they're making an effort at reconciliation. John is nowhere to be seen. His boots aren't in the foyer. I assume his date went well.

I smoke, drink coffee and process my conversation with Bettie Page Linda. This investigation reeks of cover-up, and the national chief of police, if not behind it, is aware of it. I think I know why, and it's time for him to come clean. I call him. He takes the offensive.

"Vaara, your actions go beyond contradicting my instructions. Not only has Rein Saar not been charged with murder, but the press knows that Iisa Filippov and Rein Saar were tased. Why do I think you're the leak?"

I ease in. "I'll get to that, but first, let's talk about Arvid Lahtinen."

"Another case of insubordination on your part. Why hasn't the matter been put to bed yet?"

"Because he's guilty. He and my grandpa and other Valpo detectives committed war crimes. They took part in the Holocaust. Arvid admitted it."

Silence.

"Further, Arvid demands that you make the Germans fuck off. He's blackmailing you. If what he views as harassment continues, he says he'll write a book detailing the government's persecution of Jews. He claims that Marshal Mannerheim was prepared to deliver Finnish Jews to the Germans for extermination. He says Valpo handed over a hundred and thirty suspected Communists to the Gestapo, but that the military turned over three thousand. That we starved prisoners of war and murdered them by exploiting them for slave labor, and that we shared the Nazi ideology and expansionist dreams."

I listen to Jyri breathe for a minute. "Publication of such a book would be unacceptable," he says.

"Arvid says he has more to tell me. I'm going to meet with him again today. I

331

wanted to apprise you of the situation because issuing a simple denial won't make it go away. The truth is going to come out."

"Okay," Jyri says, "I'll bring the interior minister up to speed. We'll make some kind of decision after you meet with Arvid today and we have more information to work with."

Now I lift the ax. "Other truths are going to come out. About the Filippov murder. I think we should discuss it."

Another pause. "What truths?"

I drop the ax on his neck. "Like your rather unusual sexual encounter with Linda Pohjola only hours before the murder."

I hear Jyri gulp.

"I recall that when I investigated the Sufia Elmi murder, your number, as well as the numbers of other politicos, were in her phone. You told me not to release that information."

"So?"

"So you fucked her and used me to cover it up, to save you and others embarrassment."

He recovers his aplomb, tries to regain the offensive. "Everyone — except maybe you, which annoys me — has peccadilloes. I like cooze. That's not a crime. Sufia Elmi was fine quiff. Exceptional. I would have recommended fucking her to anyone, and I don't appreciate your superior tone."

"I don't care if you fucked Sufia Elmi, but the realization that you did and suppressed it told me you have a habit of being disingenuous, and that habit is impeding my investigation. Iisa Filippov had a history of being, shall we say, generous with her favors. I think you fucked her, too, before Linda Pohjola. You fucked both of Ivan Filippov's women, and I doubt he appreciated it. You know something about this murder. It's time to tell me about it."

An angry suck of air. "Fuck you, Kari. I don't know anything about it."

"You're implicated. You're now a suspect."

He swears under his breath, goes silent and waits.

"Where did you and Linda have your encounter?" I ask.

I can almost hear him considering the ramifications of truth versus further duplicity. Seconds tick by. "I had never been there before. Some apartment in Töölö. I was drunk. She took me there and sucked my dick. Then she wanted me to leave. I wandered around, found a taxi stand, went home and passed out."

Jyri is normally so arrogant that I find myself enjoying his humiliation. "Did your sexual encounter include the employment of a green vibrating double-donged dildo?"

I think she stuck it in his ass, and after he knows that I know it, he'll tell me anything I want. He doesn't answer. I picture him on the other end of the phone, wanting to cry.

"I think I know where you were, and I want you to verify it." I give him Rein Saar's address. He gives no indication that he recognizes it. I tell him to meet me there at eleven, and hang up without waiting for him to accept or decline.

# 36

My theratist, Torsten Holmqvist, has on his outdoorsy look this morning, like L.L.Bean laid out his clothes for him. Brown brushed-twill pants, a houndstooth shirt with a lamb's-wool cardigan, moccasins on his feet. The rugged Torsten, a man of contrasts. His various facades still amuse me, but the enmity I felt toward him is gone.

He's in a good humor, and mine is better today. We sit in his big leather chairs. He offers me coffee. His morning tea of choice is chamomile. We smoke, relax. He looks out the window toward the sea. I follow his gaze. Snow is thick on the ground. The ice in the harbor is solid. The sun is rising, the sky is clear. "It's a beautiful day," he says.

I agree.

"I saw you on the news," he says, "stopping a school shooter at Ebeneser School. It's quite a coincidence that you assaulted a man and saved a child at the same location only days apart."

"It was no coincidence. They were the same man."

He raises his eyebrows, sucks his pipe. "Do you think those incidents are related?"

I wish he wouldn't treat me like an idiot. "Of course they're related. My beating him sparked his attack." I haven't said this aloud before, haven't wanted to think about it.

"Do you believe you caused his death?"

"Yes."

He crosses his legs and tugs at the perfect crease in his trousers, strokes his chin — psychiatrist cliché–style — with his fingers. "It's reasonable to think that your bad judgment played a part in his actions, but in my professional opinion, he was a time bomb and would have gone off sooner or later. Don't take too much upon yourself. Could you tell me about the incident?"

I give him a brief account. Tell him I think Legion had no intention of hurting anyone, just went there to die. Describe putting a gun to my own head. Describe Milo's cowboy behavior.

"Your fellow detective seems to admire you," Torsten says, "to the point that he's proud of killing a man so he can be like you."

I hadn't thought of this. "Are you saying I

turned Milo into a killer?"

"Milo probably did the right thing, but his false bravado speaks of an unhealthy relationship between you. But like Vesa Korhonen, he was more than likely a time bomb, and your influence upon him lit his fuse."

I light another cigarette, say nothing.

"Kari," he says, "if you had to choose one word to describe the emotion that has predominantly defined your life thus far, what would it be?"

The use of my name to create false intimacy. I let it go and consider the question. "Remorse."

He jots in his notebook.

"Would you care to explore that?"

"No."

Torsten is smart enough to understand that I need time and distance from the school shooting in order to contextualize it. He changes the subject, asks how my head is, and if I saw Jari.

"Yeah," I say. "He wants me to have tests to rule out tumors, disease and nerve damage in my face. I'm in the unusual position of hoping your theory is correct, and I'm only suffering from sublimated panic attacks."

"How do you feel now?"

"He gave me narcotic painkillers, and I took one before I left the house. They work. I'm pain-free at the moment. I had a bad experience, though. I passed out while conducting an interview."

I tell him about Arvid and the implications about Ukki.

"You seem to want to protect the memory of your grandfather," he says.

I picture Ukki beating the hell out of a starving prisoner, tied to a chair, with a fire hose sap. It splits open and buckshot flies. I shudder. "Wouldn't you?"

He shrugs. "Perhaps not. It would depend on the situation. Tell me about your grandparents on both sides."

"I called Mom's parents Ukki and Mummo. We didn't go there often, but I loved being at their house. They were sweet to me, and my brothers and sister, too. After Suvi died, they doted on me, I guess because I was the youngest after she passed away. I didn't get to know them that well, though, because they died when I was eleven and twelve, respectively. Ukki smoked like a train, and lung cancer killed him. I think Mummo died of loneliness. The only thing I remember odd about them was their intense hatred of Russians. Just the word 'Russia' could send them into tirades."

"Because of the war?"

I nod.

"You told me your father's parents were cruel."

"Mean-spirited in the extreme. Really shitty people."

"So you have no desire to protect their memories in a positive light, as you do your mother's parents."

"They were mean to kids. He was drunk on Midsummer's Eve, stood up in a boat to take a piss, fell into the lake and drowned. Their sauna burned down. She died in the fire. Fitting deaths for both of them."

"That's serious acrimony."

I shrug. "So." I remember something. "They hated Germans like the plague, as much as Ukki and Mummo hated Russians."

"The war affected people in deep ways," he says. "Do you want to talk about the ways in which they were cruel?"

"Not at present."

I light yet another cigarette. Just thinking about them makes me uncomfortable.

He switches gears. "How is the visit from your wife's brother and sister going?"

"Not well. Mary seems to have a good heart, but she's a religious fanatic and a right-wing political nut. Likewise, John seems like a decent sort, but he's a drunk and drug abuser."

I tell Torsten about the fiascos with John.

"This week," he says, "you assaulted a mentally ill person to protect children. You became so intent on protecting your grand-father that you suffered some kind of epi-sode, and you lied to your wife to protect her from her own family. Your desire to protect seems to have no bounds."

"Is that a criticism?" I ask.

"No. An observation." He asks, "Whom have you loved in your life?"

I'm afraid this is going in a silly boo-hoo-hoo direction, but I promised myself I'd try to work with Torsten. I think about it. "My parents, Ukki and Mummo, my brothers and sister, my ex-wife, when we were young, and Kate."

"No one else?"

"No people, but I loved a cat, named Katt." I laugh aloud at the maudlin idea of it. "The dumb bastard choked to death on a rubber band."

He appears thoughtful, fills his pipe again and lights it. "May I offer a conjecture?" he asks.

"Be my guest."

"Your father beat you when you were a child, but you say you bear him no ill will.

Yet you have little contact with your immediate family. Is it possible that you don't see them now, because you were the youngest, and none of them did anything to protect you from your father?"

"They were afraid of him, too."

"Failure to protect is a form of betrayal. Your sister died. She left you. Another form of betrayal. Your ex-wife betrayed you in the literal sense and abandoned you. Even Katt died and left you. Your Ukki has turned out to have been a war criminal and this tarnishes your image of him. A betrayal. Is it possible that you're overprotective of Kate because she's the only person in your life who has loved you without betrayal, and that, deep down, you fear that if you lose her, you'll never know love again?"

"I have to think about it," I say.

"You told me that during the Sufia Elmi investigation you felt that a suspect threatened Kate. You developed symptoms similar to a heart attack, pulled your car to the side of the road, put a gun to his head and threatened to kill him."

"I'm not proud of it."

"That's immaterial. The point is that your symptoms and responses are consistent with those of severe panic attacks. This lends credence to my suggestion."

He's right.

He leans forward. "Has it occurred to you that Katt and Kate are almost the same name? A curious coincidence."

I've had enough, can't take such ridiculous Freudian bullshit, and resist the urge to mock him. "Let's call it a day," I say.

Torsten is professional and means well, but I doubt I'll see him again. I realize that if I'm ever really going to open up to anyone, it can only be Kate.

## 37

The snow, already almost waist-high, pours down in a torrent. Lucifer doesn't relent. Dante states that the devil resides in the ninth circle of hell, trapped in the ice like the rest of us, and I feel that he's here, watching over us with approval. Except for the fact that the extreme cold makes my bad knee useless, I couldn't care less. Let the snow fly.

I find Jyri Ivalo shivering on the stoop of Rein Saar's apartment building. We nod greeting but don't speak. We take the lift to the fourth floor. I break the crime-scene tape and unlock the door. We step inside.

"Look familiar?" I ask.

Jyri's face sags. He fumbles with the buttons on his overcoat, but trembles so hard that he can't open them. He's experiencing déjà vu and horror. I wait and let the truth sink in. The meanings of the veiled cryptic messages in my conversations with Filippov and Bettie Page Linda are now clear to me. They have no fear of conviction because they've framed Jyri for Iisa's murder. If Rein Saar doesn't go to prison, Jyri will take his place. He'll never let the investigation look in their direction. Who better to protect them than the national chief of police?

Jyri wanders into the bedroom, looks around in disbelief, sits on the bloodstained bed. "Why is this happening to me?" he asks.

"Describe — exactly — what happened when you came here with Linda," I say.

He pulls it together enough to answer. "I told you I was drunk, it's all a bit blurry. But it happened here, in this room."

I stand over him. "I said exactly."

"We came into this bedroom and she wasted no time. She stripped her clothes off except for black stockings, and told me to take my clothes off. She had a dildo, as you thought, and took it out of the closet. She sucked me off and used it to masturbate." He averts his eyes. "Then she used it on me."

"Show me where you were and the position she was in when she blew you," I say.

He gets up and moves to a spot beside the bed, across from the closet. "I stood here." He moves his hands to where her head had been. "And she knelt here. The whole thing lasted for maybe ten minutes."

"And then what?"

"Then she went to the bathroom, I guess to wash her mouth out."

I shake my head at his stupidity and point at the hole in the closet door. "She positioned you so that she could make a video through there." I open the door and show him the stool. "That's where the camera was."

He sits on the bed again and buries his face in his hands.

"You're known to have had sex with Iisa Filippov. Linda and Iisa look alike. She placed herself so that, with her back to the camera, no one could tell the difference between them. She went to the bathroom to spit out your come and save it, to have a sample of your semen and DNA, damning proof of your affair with Iisa, should it be required."

He looks up at me, haggard. His mouth spasms. "How do we fix this?"

I kneel down and stare into his face. I've seldom seen a man look so broken. "When you tell me why they framed you, maybe I can answer that question."

He forces himself to focus. "As you said, I had sex with Iisa and Linda. Cuckolding

Filippov twice must have driven him to murder and revenge."

Jyri needs a moment to come to grips with a situation that could destroy him. "Let's go to the kitchen," I say.

He follows me. I find an ashtray and we sit at the table. I shake Marlboros out of my pack for both of us. We smoke and let a few moments pass in silence.

"You're being evasive," I say. "Stop hedging and tell me the truth. All of it. Otherwise, I can't help you."

He nods, steels himself. Coming in here and realizing what has been done to him was a hard jolt, but he's a tough bastard. I watch him recover by degrees. It doesn't take long.

"I don't know the particulars about Filippov's relationships with his wife and Linda," he says, "but I can tell you about his business affairs . . . and a few other things."

"Tell."

"Filippov wanted to expand his construction business. He wanted government contracts for big projects. He spread a lot of money around in order to get them."

"You're saying he bribed government officials."

"Correct."

"Which ones?"

"At this point, their names are inconsequential. I'll tell you later if the need arises. He spent a lot of money on bribes and was dissatisfied with the results. The reason he came to the party on the night his wife was murdered was to express that dissatisfaction in strong terms."

"And the result was?"

"None. He was told that he'll get what he gets, when he gets it."

"And the 'few other things' you mentioned?"

"I wasn't the only one to have sex with both Iisa and Linda. There are four of us — officeholders — that I know of. There could be more."

"So, in addition to bribing you with money, he was pimping out his wife and mistress to get these contracts."

"In retrospect, it appears so."

I sit back and take a second to put the pieces together. "My guess is that Filippov and Linda set up the others the same way they did you. Filippov more than likely acquired sex videos and DNA samples from all the corrupt politicians who took his money and fucked his wife. You fucked *him* as well, pushed him too far."

"But why kill his wife?" Jyri asks.

To give him the whole picture, I tell Jyri

about Milo black-bagging Linda's apartment, about the audio track of the murder and about the video he turned up. Jyri takes it all in.

"Aside from some bizarre sexual-fetish issues," I say, "Filippov is a straitlaced guy. His wife was a whore and a constant embarrassment. She refused to have sex with him. She fucked everybody under the sun except him. He had what was apparently a gratifying affair with Linda and got what he needed from her. Iisa became an irrelevant millstone around his neck. Murdering her was both revenge on her and a way of getting what he wanted from the establishment. And also, because of the nature of his and Linda's fetishes, it got them off."

I'm confident that when Iisa was murdered, although he didn't understand the particulars, Jyri knew that he and other politicians were being set up. He planned to frame Rein Saar to save himself. I'm sure he eased his conscience as Arvid claims Marshal Mannerheim did in regard to Jews. Like Mannerheim, the chief is prepared to throw innocents to the dogs for what he conveniently perceives as the good of the nation. Rein Saar is intended to be a sacrificial lamb.

We both chain cigarettes off the last ones.

"Tell me how you're going to get me and the others out of this," Jyri says.

"The murder was videotaped. More than likely, all of you were also videotaped. And there are your DNA samples. Plus, Iisa Filippov kept a diary. It may contain information damning her husband. If all those things are recovered, it might be possible to cover this up."

"Do it," Jyri says. "I'll make sure you get all the resources you need. Just do it."

I shake my head. "The thing is, I'm not sure I want to. I won't let Rein Saar get sent down for a murder he didn't commit. Filippov has to be convicted of the crime. When he gets his day in court, no matter how much evidence gets buried, all of this is going to come out, and all your careers will be ruined. And, I have to say, you all deserve it."

Jyri drums his fingers on the table, thoughtful. "Filippov killed his wife at least partly out of embarrassment. If you recover the fetish videos of him and Linda, I can threaten to release them. I'll offer to let him commit suicide and leave a confession letter to save himself the humiliation. Given his mind-set, he might take the deal."

At first, I have trouble believing he said it. I didn't realize I was sitting across the table from Machiavelli. If he'll go that far, I wonder if he would go one step further, fake Filippov's suicide and have him murdered.

"I'll give you anything you want," he says, "just make this go away."

"That's another problem for you," I say. "I don't want anything."

He leans toward me. "I've been thinking of putting together a black-ops unit. Anti-organized crime. The mandate is to go after criminals by whatever means necessary, to use their own methods against them. No holds barred."

"We already have such a group. It's called SUPO."

"There's a problem with SUPO," he says. "They don't work for me."

I shake my head again, this time in amusement. "So you want to be some kind of Finnish J. Edgar Hoover."

"Yes."

This makes me laugh in his face. "No," I say.

His face twists so much that he reminds me of a gargoyle. "You think I don't know you, but I do," he says. "You suffer from a pathetic need to protect the innocent. You think you're some kind of a Good Samaritan in a white hat, but you're not. You're a rubber-hose cop, a thug and a killer, as you've demonstrated. You'll do anything to get what you view as justice. Let me give you an example of how badly we need this kind of unit. Only about a half dozen cops in Helsinki investigate human trafficking. In Finland and the surrounding countries, thousands of gangsters orchestrate the buying and selling of young girls, and hundreds or thousands of those girls pass through this country every year. With our limited legal resources, we can't possibly make even a dent in the human-slavery industry. Picture all those victims and how many of their bright shiny faces you could save from abject misery, abuse and terror, from being raped time and time again."

He's got something there.

Jyri senses I'm beginning to be intrigued. "Milo knows black-bag work," he says. "He's a genius with great computer skills, and he's also a killer. He could be your first team-member acquisition. Then you can staff it with whoever you want."

"I'm not killing anybody," I say.

"I'll leave that to your discretion."

"Milo is a loose cannon and a liability."

"Milo is a nervous puppy. He needs a firm hand to guide him. Yours."

"It would take a hell of a lot of money," I

say. "Computers. Vehicles. Surveillance gear."

"In two weeks, Swedish and Finnish gypsies are going to make a big drug deal for Ecstasy. A hundred and sixty thousand euros will trade hands. You can intercept it and use the money for the beginning of a slush fund."

I'm tempted, but not that tempted. "No."

Frustration wells up in his face. For a second, I think he's going to punch me. "I told you I know you, and I do. I can see into your soul. You hate your job. You're frustrated because you can't make a difference. You're a failure. To your dead sister. To Sufia Elmi and her family. To your sergeant Valtteri and his family. To your dead ex-wife. To your dead miscarried twins and, as such, to your wife. To that pathetic school shooter Milo capped. You're a failure to yourself. You failed everyone you've touched, and you're going to have to save a hell of a lot of people before you can make it up. You'll take this job to save yourself. I'm offering you everything you ever wanted."

He's worked hard at building a dossier on me to have all this information at his fingertips. He's been considering me for this position for a long time. "Why me?" I ask.

"Because of your aforementioned annoying incorruptibility. You don't want anything. You're a maniac, but you're a rock. I can trust you to run this unit without going rogue on me."

I'd like to dismiss the idea, but I can't. "I'll think about it."

He reaches across the table and takes my hand. It shocks me. "No one ever finds out about any of this," he says. "I'll organize everything, get you the manpower. This evening, you and Milo oversee while they tear apart Filippov's and Linda's apartments and his business. Rip the walls down to the studs with crowbars if you have to, but you find that evidence, show it to me, then burn it."

I don't trust Jyri. I'll find the evidence and keep it, in case of a contingency, such as betrayal. "Okay," I say.

He shakes my hand with both of his. "Fix this for me," he says, "and run my black-ops unit."

I'm not ready to agree yet — I don't want to give him the satisfaction — but I know that I will.

# 38

On the way to Porvoo, snow and fierce winds batter my Saab, make it hard to keep it on the road. My phone rings. It's Milo. I don't answer. It rings again. I don't recognize the number but answer anyway. "Vaara."

"This is the interior minister."

I'm feeling a bit flip. "How ya doin'?"

"I'm fucking pissed off is how I'm doing. You were supposed to bury the Arvid Lahtinen matter. I'm told you now claim he's a war criminal. That wasn't what you were instructed to do."

What a fucking asshole. "I only repeated what Arvid told me."

He screams in my ear. "I don't give a rat's ass what that old man says! There are no fucking Finnish war criminals!"

"In fact," I say, "that's not true. Several thousand Finns were accused of war crimes — usually killings of or violence toward

POWs, according to the standards of the Nuremberg principles — and hundreds were eventually convicted."

He keeps yelling. Louder now. "Listen, fuckwit, I repeat, there are no Finnish war criminals! Get that through your thick head!" He calms down, lowers his voice. "Write the report the way you were told, or I'll have you fired. You'll never work as a cop again. We clear?" He rings off.

I'm not concerned. If he hadn't hung up on me, I would have told him to fuck himself. His ire doesn't surprise me. One of the anomalies of Finnish self-understanding, regarding the war, is that these trials have failed to make any impact on the national consciousness whatsoever, and most people would say there are no Finnish war criminals. I suspect most Finns of our generation would be shocked to learn otherwise.

I'm looking forward to lunch with Arvid and Ritva. I haven't enjoyed the company of others besides Kate so much in a long time. Arvid opens the door before I knock. He's been waiting for me.

"You're late," he says.

Arvid looks tired, seems nervous. Maybe the war-crimes accusations have gotten to him. For the first time since we met, he seems old to me. "I got hung up with a case. Is it a bad time?"

He points at a snow shovel in the corner of the porch. "Ritva isn't feeling well. I have to tend to her for a little bit. The boy that shovels snow for us didn't come today. Could you do it for me?"

I suppress a smile. He's treating me like I'm twelve years old. "Sure, I can do it."

"Come in and make yourself at home when you're done."

He closes the door.

It's minus eighteen, but shoveling his porch and walk only takes about twenty minutes, and I don't mind doing it for him.

Afterward, I go inside and take off my boots and coat. He's got a good blaze going, and I warm up in front of the fireplace. He comes downstairs and sits at the table, tells me to join him. I sit across from him.

"Got any cigarettes?" he asks.

I lay a pack and a lighter on the table in between us. "I didn't know you smoke."

"I don't much, but once in a while, I get the yen."

He goes to the kitchen, comes back with two cups of coffee and an ashtray. "Son," he says, "I'm not up to making lunch today. If you're hungry, I'll make sandwiches for you."

"That's okay, I don't much feel like eating."

He gives me his appraising look. "How's your head?"

"Hurts."

"They know what's causing it yet?"

"No. I'll have some tests run soon. What's wrong with Ritva?" I ask.

"We suffer from old people's maladies. She'll get past it."

We share an uncomfortable silence for a few minutes. I get the idea he has a lot on his mind and would rather be alone to sort it out. We smoke and drink coffee in silence for a while.

"Got any interesting cases?" he asks. "I mean, besides mine."

I nod. "Some real interesting stuff. I shouldn't talk about them, though."

He forces a smile. "You want to hear all my secrets. You're going to have to tell me yours if you want to get them. Let an old man vicariously relive his detective years through you."

Much like when Arvid told me to call him Ukki, this raises my suspicions about his motivations, and I wonder if he's looking for information to augment his blackmail strategy. Then I decide, if he is, why not let him? Let the truth prevail. Besides, I can use him for a sounding board. Sometimes articulating problems helps me solve them. I tell him about the Filippov murder, about its bizarre and aberrant circumstances, how in the end it's come down to a blackmail scam, and that if I can make it go away, I'll be put in charge of a special black-ops unit.

He nods approval. "A good story," he says. "But what happens if you don't recover and bury the evidence? You'll have a lot of dirt on important people and have done nothing for them. They won't like it. They'll try to burn you somehow."

I shrug. "What can they do?"

"It depends. What have you fucked up? You were involved in that school shooting and somebody died. Any way they could turn that around on you?"

In fact, they could. The realization startles me. "I beat the shit out of the school shooter just days before the attack. They could say I caused the incident, and they'd probably be right."

"That's how they'll come at you then," he says. "They'll call you an abusive rogue cop, discredit you and kick you off the force."

We light more cigarettes. "Any idea how I can get out of it?" I ask.

358

"I'll put my detective cap on and think about it. I have to say, though, boy, that you're fucking naïve. It's going to cost you one day."

He's not the first one to say it. "Your turn," I say. "Tell me some good stories."

His grin turns sly. "All right, boy, I'll tell you how your great-grandpa, my dad and the former president of Finland became executioners and mass murderers together."

Like Milo, he enjoys astonishing me, and he's succeeded. He beams pleasure. "And under the auspices of Lord and Savior Marshal Mannerheim."

He got me again. I'm riveted. "History records Kekkonen only executing one Red," I say, "and if I remember correctly, he expressed remorse about it."

"You ever been to the Mannerheim Museum?" he asks.

I'm itching for the story of our families, but he's going to make me wait. "No."

"When Mannerheim died, they turned his home into a memorial for the great man. I went there once. They have tiger-skin rugs on the floor, knickknacks and keepsakes he slogged home from all over the world. Like me, Mannerheim loved fine wine and spirits. I told the tour guide I wanted to see the wine cellar. This pretty little girl with big tits and a skinny waist told me it's off-limits. I decided to fuck with her a little bit. I said, 'I served under Mannerheim, and I'm a goddamn war hero, and I will look at the marshal's booze and if I fucking feel like it, I'll open a bottle and drink to the marshal's goddamned health.' "

It's easy to picture Ukki doing it, makes me laugh.

"She got nervous and admitted to me in confidence that a few years ago, some workers were instructed to clean out the cellar. Like good Finns, they did what they were told. They pulled up a dumpster and smashed all those fine bottles of wine and cognac in it. Destroyed it all. It would be worth hundreds of thousands or millions today. Mannerheim would come out of his grave in a screaming rage if he knew."

He's digressing to increase my anticipation. Like Milo. I wait. He sees I'm only indulging him.

"Okay," he says, "it went like this. I'll just tell the story to you as Dad told it to me. President-to-be Urho Kaleva Kekkonen was seventeen when the Civil War broke out in 1918. At the time, he was a schoolboy in the northeast, in Kajaani. He had war in his blood. In the summer and autumn of 1917, he served in the local civil guard. At the end

360

of 1917, he decided to go to Germany to get a military education. His plan was ruined by the German announcement that there would be no more recruiting from Finland. Kekkonen was disappointed, but then the Civil War enabled him to join the military on the side of the Whites. The civil guard in Kajaani was organized into what was known as a flying cavalry unit called the Kajaani Guerrilla Regiment."

Arvid is telling me what I already know. Information readily available in history books. It takes me back to that gray area: can I trust him, or is he manipulating me with half-truths and lies.

"Kekkonen was an ordinary soldier, and his comrades were boys from the same school. These included my dad and your great-grandfather. First, they went to Kuopio, where the situation was already under White control. From there they went to Iisalmi where they imprisoned local Reds. Dad said they executed a Red there. Their first one. The next stop was Varkaus, a Red stronghold deep in White Finland. White troops were concentrated around Varkaus, among them the Kajaani Guerrilla Regiment. Near the end of the fighting, the Reds withdrew to a factory and finally surrendered when it caught fire. The prisoners were taken out on the ice of a nearby lake. Locals identified the worst of the Reds, and they were taken out of the line and shot. The Whites executed over a hundred people. They also picked every tenth man from the line and executed them, too."

I've read, in Kekkonen's memoirs, that he saw the bodies on the ice after the event, but he didn't admit to taking part in the killings. "There's no proof that Kekkonen executed anyone at Varkaus," I say.

Arvid shrugs. "I'm just telling you what Dad told me. You want to hear it or not?"

"Yeah. Sorry."

"After Varkaus, the regiment fought on the front in Savo. At the end of April, they were sent to Viipuri. The Battle of Viipuri was the last major fight of the war, and several hundred were killed in action. Some two hundred Russian inhabitants were rounded up, taken to the old city walls and executed. Machine-gunned to death. The shooting went on for almost twenty minutes, and the shooters were none other than the Kajaani Guerrilla Regiment."

Rumors and speculations given the stamp of truth — secondhand — by a Winter War hero. I have no idea if he's making all this up as he goes along, but he would sure as hell upset a lot of people if he said it publicly. The Civil War remains the most emotionally charged event in the history of this country. After almost a hundred years, we haven't even agreed on a name for the conflict: the Civil War, the Red Rebellion, the Freedom War, the Class War. The list goes on.

"The war was essentially over," he says, "but by then Dad and the others had a taste for Red blood. In Hamina, during the second week of May, they executed over sixty prisoners. In the last week of May, they shot another thirty-something prisoners. Kekkonen made the leap from shooter to leader and ordered the execution of another nine Reds in Hamina. In June, Kekkonen, Dad and your great-grandpa were sent to Suomenlinna as prison camp guards. It was essentially a death camp. And the result of all this was that Kekkonen became a celebrated war hero. After the war, Kekkonen spent seven years as an investigator for the state police, during which time he was a Communist hunter. Like me. Like your grandpa."

Kekkonen was a hero — even a God-like character — to me as a child. I guess to most of us. He was a gifted athlete, a war hero, he protected us from the Soviets. Except for a brief period, he served as prime minister from 1950 to 1956, and as president from 1956 until 1982. He was essentially an absolute ruler. At a certain point, he humiliated his opponents in presidential elections by neglecting to show up for televised debates. He knew he was unbeatable. As a child, I thought "Kekkonen" meant "president." I remember asking Mom who she thought would be the next Kekkonen.

"During the Civil War and its aftermath," Arvid says, "the Reds executed about fifteen hundred White prisoners, and the Whites executed upwards of ten thousand Reds. Do you know who ordered the execution of those almost ten thousand people?"

I shake my head, weary from his terrible tales. "Who?"

"Lord and Savior Marshal Mannerheim. That's who. The great men of our nation saw to the extermination of Communists. I shot a few commissars in a POW camp, less than nothing in comparison. Why bother me about it? It just doesn't make any sense."

Under the influence of his revisionist version of history, it doesn't make any sense to me, either.

"The great man, Kekkonen," Arvid says. "Don't make me laugh. He was a drunken whoremonger. He got more pussy than JFfucking-K, and his wife, Sylvi, put up with it. And those fucking propaganda films about him they show every year around Independence Day. More Leni Riefenstahl–type stuff that would have done the Third Reich proud. See the great athlete Kekkonen. See Kekkonen go to sauna. See Kekkonen swim in the lake. See Kekkonen chop wood. See Kekkonen, contemplative man of the people, sit on the edge of a dock and fish."

"Why such acrimony?" I ask. "Kekkonen did a hell of a lot for this country. He kept good relations with the Soviet Union and maintained our sovereignty through Finlandization."

"Because I detest hypocrisy, and I'm its victim. I'm just pissed off at the moment. Kekkonen paid a price for his success. He was a Communist-killer, just like I was raised to be. How do you think that must have made him feel, sucking Russian ass to save this nation. Taking orders from people he wanted dead. It must have been a living hell sometimes."

I get his point. "And so, because of their connections from the Civil War, your dad and my great-grandpa were able to secure positions for you and grandpa in Valpo."

He nods. "That's right. Killing Communists. The family business. Mine, and yours, too, by way of inheritance."

And now Jyri wants me to run a black-ops unit, mandated to fight crime organizations that rose from the ashes of the Soviet Union. Confluence.

Arvid looks across the table at me with sad eyes. We share a quiet moment, but the silence is comfortable this time. Finnish silence. After a while, he says, "Son, you better go soon. I'm tired. All this talk has worn me out, and I have to look after Ritva."

"Yeah," I say, "I better get back to work."

I'm tired, too, and melancholic, worn down by so much ugliness. Compared to relearning the history of my country in this new light, even the Filippov murder seems cheerful.

## 39

I start back to Helsinki and turn on the radio. The weather forecast announces that the worst snowstorm of the season is on the way. Given the severity of what we've already experienced, this seems near impossible, but within minutes, thick sheets of snow start to pound the landscape. Road visibility sinks to almost nothing. I drive slow.

Jyri calls. He says, "Ivan Filippov and Linda Pohjola are at Filippov Construction, and their vehicles are there, too. I got you sixteen detectives. Twelve are on-site, waiting for you to orchestrate the raid. Two detectives each have sealed off Linda's and Filippov's homes. They'll wait for you and the other detectives before beginning the searches. Is that everything you need?"

"For the time being."

He rings off, and I change direction toward Vantaa. I call Milo and tell him to meet me at Filippov Construction.

I get there before Milo. The other cops are hidden in their vehicles around the area. I park. They spot me and follow to the front door. I explain to them that we're looking for video disks, which they're not to watch but to hand over to me for inspection, for camcorders and cell phones, for any device capable of shooting video, for bloodied protective gear and a taser.

I assign three detectives each the task of searching Linda's Mustang and Filippov's Dodge Journey. Filippov must have been watching us on a security camera and sprints out of the building in a rage. He's not even wearing a coat. "Inspector, who the fuck do you think you are, and what the fuck do you think you're doing?"

"What does it look like? Search and seizure of your property."

He screams. "This will not stand! Show me your search warrants!"

"In urgent cases," I say, "any police officer can conduct a search without a search warrant. Additionally, I have verbal authorization from the national chief of police. Give me your car keys."

He folds his arms, adamant. "Not a chance in hell."

Jyri wasn't joking, the detectives have

brought crowbars with them. I borrow one and use it to snap open the Dodge's passenger's-side door, then take out my pocket knife and slash a seat open. The cushioning comes spilling out. "I can search your houses and vehicles like this if you want, or I can be a little more gentle. You pick."

He's near to foaming at the mouth from fury, calls me a fucking cocksucker. I hold out my hand. He slams a key ring into my palm.

"Do these open all the locks to your vehicle, home and business?"

"Yes, you motherfucker, they do. I'll get you for this."

"Maybe," I say.

"Where do you expect Linda and me to go while you violate our property and privacy?"

I stamp my feet and rub my gloved hands together against the cold. "I couldn't care less. Take a taxi somewhere. Have a couple drinks and something to eat. Enjoy yourselves."

He's already fringed white with snow, calms down, sees the wisdom of this. "When can we have our property returned to us?"

I shrug. "It depends. I've got a lot of manpower. Probably just a few hours."

"And when will you release my wife's body to me for burial?"

"When I'm done with it."

He goes back into the building in a huff. I follow, repeat the routine with Linda, take her keys and both their cell phones.

The detectives begin to search in earnest, rip construction equipment from shelves, go through it, dump it on the floor.

Milo arrives. I usher him into Filippov's office so we can speak in private, and we sit at his worktable.

Milo looks pissed off. "You've been hard to reach," he says.

"I've been busy."

"You've been cutting me out of this investigation."

"Now you're back in."

I fill Milo in on the deal Jyri offered me. I ask him formally, but, of course, I already know the answer. "Do you want to be part of a black-ops unit? Are you in?"

His smile is broad. The circles around his eyes gleam. He's in heaven. "I want certain things," he says.

"What?"

"An H&K machine gun. A .50-caliber Barrett sniper rifle. Flash-bang stun grenades."

Milo, the boy and his toys. "We can arrange that. Maybe even get somebody to teach you how to use them."

He ignores the slight. "Then I'm in."

"First, we need to recover the evidence against Jyri." I point at Filippov's computer. "You can start there."

"I've already been through the computers here. There's no evidence in them."

"How did you do that?"

"With intrusion software. I uploaded the hard drives to a server in Amsterdam and created mirrors of them. I found nothing related directly to Iisa Filippov's murder, but turned up some financial discrepancies of some hundreds of thousands of euros. The money was deposited in numbered offshore accounts."

I'm impressed. He's the right guy for black-bag work. "Did you go through their home computers, too?"

"No, they weren't booted up, and I couldn't get it in. However, I got in touch with a staff member at Oulun Palvelukoti, where Linda's mother, Marjut, died. He's worked there for twenty years and knew Marjut well. He checked the guest logs for me. Linda had visited semiregularly and saw her mother on September 9, 1998. Linda's eighteenth birthday. After that, she never saw her mother again. Marjut had been in good spirits, but after Linda's visit, went into a funk that lasted until she died. Marjut entered care in 1990, when Linda was ten. Linda was in foster care until she was sixteen, then disappeared and went off the radar until she came of age. Around the time that Marjut conceived Linda, she lived in Helsinki and worked as an escort or prostitute."

"For Jonne Kultti?"

"Bingo. And Kultti offed himself seven days after Linda visited Marjut, after which the mother and daughter were estranged. I think Marjut wrote to Kultti."

"And the contents of the letter drove him to suicide. A viable theory."

Milo lights one of his tough-guy cigarettes. "I also took your advice and Web-searched Bettie Page. A good call. It turned up some interesting stuff."

He pauses. I'm afraid he's going to sidetrack again. *And a child was born in Bethlehem.* But he doesn't.

Milo says, "Bettie Page was placed in an orphanage at age ten, much as Linda was placed in foster care at the same age. Bettie Page's father sexually abused her after she left the orphanage. I think it's possible that Marjut bore Kultti's child. She never told him, but she told Linda, and Linda went to look for him. Maybe Linda was afraid of rejection and never told Kultti he was her father. Maybe she thought the only way of having a relationship with Kultti was to work for him, and she re-created herself as Bettie Page to the extent that she had sex with her own father. She told her mother, who, consumed by grief, wrote to Kultti and let him know his own daughter was sucking his cock. Then he went to pieces and shot himself."

"That would make Iisa and Linda half sisters and explain their close resemblance," I say.

"We would need to run a DNA test to find out."

I stretch out in Filippov's chair. This line of inquiry feels right to me. If Linda and Iisa were half sisters, it might explain motivations for the murder that we're as yet unaware of. "That's a tough one. With half siblings, it's hard to determine parentage without the cooperation of the potential parents, and in this case, they're all dead. It could be done, but might take weeks."

"I wonder if Iisa knew Linda was her sister?" Milo asks.

Then the lightning bolt hits me and I sit up straight. "I wonder if the dead woman in Rein Saar's bed was really Iisa, or if it was

Linda?"

The idea jars us both, and we ponder it in silence for a while. "Let's split this team up," I say, "and search all three places at once. We leave some guys here, you take some to Filippov's house, and I take some to Linda's, since I haven't been there before. Maybe we can find some documentation to substantiate all this."

Milo and I finish up at Filippov Construction, go through their phones and all the video disks we run across. We find nothing and leave to search Linda's and Filippov's homes.

# 40

I take my Saab, four detectives ride in a separate vehicle, and we drive through blizzard conditions back to Helsinki and Linda's apartment. It's a dumpy little one-bedroom, but neat and clean. Vintage Bettie Page posters line the walls.

The other detectives know their business. They run long needles through sofas and mattresses, looking for obstructions sewn into them. They tap the walls, looking for plastered-over safes or hidey-holes. They turn appliances over and look inside.

In her bedroom, I go through Linda's things. I find a small trunk brimming with Bettie Page memorabilia, magazines and movies. I open another box and the rich smell of oiled leather hits me. It's filled with fetish accoutrements: high-heeled shoes and boots, whips, leather costumes and restraints, ropes and gags.

I boot up her computer. It has a Bettie

Page screensaver. It's chock-full of videos, including what I take to be a complete collection of Bettie Page footage. I take a quick look and find scenarios of abduction, spanking, domination, restraints, slave training with bondage. Page sometimes played a stern dominatrix and sometimes a helpless victim, bound hand and foot.

Then I find Linda's personal files. Videos she made of herself, reenactments of the Bettie Page movies. Videos of her and Filippov and their sexual role-playing. They have only a few variations on the themes I saw in the video Milo took from here. I see nothing from Rein Saar's apartment, no images of Jyri or his political cronies, nothing to connect them to the murder. Just personal stuff. I'll take the computer into evidence, but I'm sure they've covered their digital tracks.

I go through Linda's clothes. She dresses well. I open her underwear drawer. She likes expensive, fetish-variety lingerie. Underneath it, I find her famous big, soft, green double-donged vibrating dildo. I picture her sticking it up Jyri's ass and laugh, then bag it for DNA testing.

By Linda's bed, in a desk drawer, I find a family album. It contains pictures of Linda and her mother from Linda's infancy through the time of her mother's death. Their correspondence, beginning at the time Marjut entered the mental rest home, is also here, all in original envelopes. The letters from her mother are touching, always assuring Linda that she's getting better and will be out before long. Then she and Linda will build a new and better life. The final two letters are dated September 9, 1998, Linda's eighteenth birthday and the last time she saw her mother alive. Both letters are short.

The one to Linda reads: "I love you dear, but what you've done is more than I can stand. Please stop. Love, Mom."

The one to Kultti reads: "You may not remember me, but you told me you loved me once, when I was young. I bore you a daughter named Linda. You're raping her, your own child. Please stop. Love, Marjut."

I wonder if Linda saw this letter before her father blew his brains out, or after.

My phone rings. "Vaara."

"This is Stefan Larsson, the owner of the Silver Dollar."

"How did you get my number?"

His tone says I'm a moron. "I called information."

Stupid of me to have it listed. I make a mental note to have it removed from the phone company's public registry. "What do you want?"

"You're investigating the death of a patron on my premises. Now you have something else to investigate."

"What might that be?"

"After two days in jail cells, punishments they didn't deserve, my bouncers were cleared of responsibility and released. They came back to work. A man wearing a hood attacked them this evening. In one hand, he had a set of keys, a couple sticking out between each of his fingers, and used it to punch them in the face. The beating left terrible puncture wounds. In his other hand he held a box cutter, which he used to stab them repeatedly. It was attempted murder. My bouncers are hospitalized."

"So what are you calling me for?"

"The attacker was a giant in a hooded sweatshirt. I know goddamned good and well it was Sulo Polvinen, but when the investigating officers went to his house, his parents provided him with an alibi and said he was home all evening watching TV with them. I demand that you do something about this."

"One," I say, "I'm on the homicide squad, and the bouncers aren't dead, so it's not my concern." Actually, it falls within my pur-

378

view, but I doubt he knows that. "Two, I think the bouncers got what they deserved. Three, you can go fuck yourself."

I hang up on him.

The bedroom is clean. I walk out to check with the other detectives. The apartment is a shambles — they've turned it inside out. They've found nothing.

I call Milo. "I'm disgusted to say," he says, "that I'm holding in my hand four freezer bags, all of which appear to contain sperm. I assume one sample came from Jyri and the three other come-wads are from his buddies. They were in Filippov's freezer, numbered one to four instead of labeled by name."

It's something, anyway. Beyond that, his report is also negative, and their search is near conclusion. Filippov sticks his head in the front door. I hang up on Milo.

"Hi, Ivan," I say. "What can I do for you?"

He strides in, has recovered his self-possession and intimidating manner. "I trust you haven't found what you had hoped for," he says.

"No, I haven't, but I remain confident that I will."

He leans against the wall with his arms folded, cocky. "I came here to let you know that I intend to ensure that the investigation of my wife's murder is speedily concluded, and that Rein Saar is prosecuted. And I intend to file a complaint against you for harassment. You've searched my home and business without cause. A grieving widower should be left in peace to mourn, not treated in such a fashion."

"Your wife was a slut," I say, "and so is your mistress. We turned up four semen samples in your freezer. I'm pretty sure I know where they came from."

His voice takes on a sadness both out of context and character. "Poor Iisa was given toward promiscuity, but Linda has always been faithful. If she was unfaithful, it was for me, for our common good."

I pretend confidence I don't feel. I may well be unable to convict Filippov. The murder was well planned and executed, all the way down to the blackmail scam. I come on conciliatory and bluff, as if I'm prepared to negotiate on Jyri's behalf, just to see what comes of it. "Listen," I say, "it's possible that we could set aside our differences. You want things, Jyri and I and others want things. Let's get together and discuss it."

Now he realizes Jyri put me in the loop and I know the truth, but he hedges to buy time and process what it might mean. "I have no idea what those things might be," he says.

"Maybe we could both think about it overnight. What those things are — and how to get what we want — might come to us."

He studies me, skeptical. "All right, Inspector. Let's meet at Kämp tomorrow at five p.m. You can buy our dinner."

"Deal," I say. We don't shake hands. He walks out.

I have no idea what I'm going to say to him tomorrow, but for his vengeance to be complete, Rein Saar has to go to prison. If I can't come up with something, it might happen. That's unacceptable to me. Unfortunately, Jyri won't share my concerns. I have to figure this out by myself.

My phone rings again. It's Kate, and she's crying. "Kari, where are you, it's one thirty in the morning."

"I'm sorry, it's this murder investigation."

She sobs. "Can you please come home now? I need you."

"I'll leave this minute," I say, put on my coat and head out the door.

## 41

I find Kate lying on the couch in the dark, in a bathrobe, her hands folded atop her big pregnant belly. I pick her legs up, slide under them, rest them in my lap and sit next to her. The dull glow of a streetlight shows me tears glistening in the corners of her eyes. She's sniffling.

"What happened?" I ask.

She whispers. "It's true, what I said before. I failed my brother and sister."

"Tell me."

"Mary might hear. Help me up and let's go to the bedroom."

I stand and hoist her onto her feet. As she comes close to term, she's having a harder and harder time getting around.

We go to our room and lie on top of the covers. Kate takes her usual position, her head in the crook of my shoulder, her face nuzzled into my neck. "Mary is only twenty-five," she says, "but she acts like an old woman."

"I noticed."

"I wanted to find out what's wrong with her. Why she's so stern. Why she's so obsessed with fundamentalist religion. I talked to her for a long time today, and asked without asking what happened to her after I left for college when she was eighteen."

Kate chokes back a sob, takes a second and composes herself. "Mary told me that after I left for college, Dad started bringing his friends home to drink with him. I pushed her to tell me about it, because I could tell Mary was hiding something. I kept pressing her about what happened and asked her point-blank if she was raped. She denied being raped, but said one of Dad's friends used to make her drink hard liquor and then do something to her that 'tasted bad.' "

Kate's composure dissolves. She grabs my head in her hands and pushes her face against mine to stifle the sound of her sobs. She spits out broken words. "Mary was abused and forced to do awful, disgusting things. I don't think she even remembers what happened."

I pull her closer. "If she doesn't remember, maybe it's for the best."

She wipes snot and tears off my neck and

onto her bathrobe. "Do you believe that?"

"I don't know. Maybe."

"And I thought she's happily married, and maybe she is, but I got the impression that her husband isn't good to her, that they live some sort of severe religious lifestyle, and when she doesn't conform to it, he beats her. I think that's why she acts so old."

I wish I had some comforting words, but Kate's explanation of Mary's personality makes sense to me. "I'm sorry," I say.

"All I wanted was for all three of us to be happy," she says.

"I know."

"How is your head?" she asks.

"Fine."

With difficulty, Kate rolls over and flips on the bedside lamp. She rolls back to me. "Look in my eyes," she says.

I do.

"When your headaches are bad," she says, "your pupils get so small that I can hardly see them. When your migraines are very very bad, I can't see much more than the whites of your eyes. Right now, your pupils are almost invisible. Your head is killing you, isn't it?"

She's got me. "Yes."

Anger and frustration creep into her voice. "You lie to me. Why?"

I take a second before answering. "Because I'm afraid for you and our baby. Because I don't want to cause you needless stress and worry."

"When you lie to protect me, you treat me like a child. It's not fair and it's not right. I also had a talk with John today."

I suppress a sigh. I guess she's got all the goods on me. "And?"

"And I knew there was something going on between you two, and I made him tell me what it was."

She put John on the spot, but I told him to keep things between us between us. It pisses me off. "He wasn't supposed to do that."

"He said that, too, but he said you told him to be my friend, and he thought the best way to do that was by telling me what a good husband I have. He told me the truth about himself, about getting fired from New York University and why. Then he told me about his screwups since he arrived in Finland and how you fixed them all. About how you got his boots back."

I say nothing, prepare for her well-deserved anger.

Kate wraps her arms around my neck and hugs me tight. "Thank you so much," she says. "John is right, you're a wonderful husband."

I think I know Kate so well, but she continues to amaze me.

"But still," she says, "you should have told me the truth."

"I was afraid to. John's life is his own, and I didn't see how upsetting you with his problems could help."

"He's my brother, and you don't have the right to make those decisions for me. And this discussion goes deeper than that."

I was afraid of that. "How?"

"You keep all sorts of things from me. We've been together for almost two and a half years, been through a lot together, but still you hold things back. I know things hurt you. I want you to tell me about them."

"I don't see how it would help."

"Maybe you should try and find out."

Back against the wall. I let out a sigh. "Tell me what you want to know."

"Everything. But this thing with Mary has taught me that I need to know about your childhood."

"Like what?"

"People were mean to you, especially your father. I want to know about it."

I try to make myself tell her, but I can't. I don't want her to know. "Maybe one day," I say, "but I'm not ready for that."

"Don't you trust me?" she asks.

"Yes, but it's not about you. I'm just not ready."

We hold each other in silence for a while. "I shouldn't have pressed so hard," she says, "but please don't lie to me anymore."

I consider if this is possible for me. It is. "I won't," I say, "but sometimes I need time to work up to telling you things. You have to let me do it in my own time and in my own way."

"Okay," she says.

Kate falls asleep. I lie awake thinking. We hold each other tight, in a state of détente.

## 42

I get up early Saturday morning, thinking about Sulo Polvinen. He seems like a good kid who took a hard knock. No doubt he assaulted the bouncers at the Silver Dollar, and alibis from his parents or no, he's going to get caught. If he turns himself in, he'll get a reduced sentence. I decide to have a friendly talk with him. I check my case notes and find his address.

He lives in East Pasila, not far from the police station. It's a crappy neighborhood, built in the 1970s. It's frequently called the DDR, because its concrete and bunkerlike buildings call to mind the architecture of East Germany during the Soviet era. I drive over without calling first, because I think if I asked, he would refuse to see me.

The temperature remains around minus twenty, the snow still flies. Driving is difficult.

Mama Polvinen opens the door of their

dreary apartment. I introduce myself. With a look of distaste, she lets me in. The furnishings are all old and worn. Papa Polvinen sits on a dilapidated couch, reading a newspaper, sipping his morning hangover beer. Sulo sits cross-legged on the floor in front of the TV, playing video games. They should be called the Family Big. Mama Polvinen is two ax handles broad. Papa Polvinen is even bigger, his body built out of thousands of gallons of beer. Monster-sized Sulo takes after them.

"Sulo," I ask, "is there somewhere we could talk in private?"

Papa doesn't approve. "Anything you got to say to him, you say in front of me."

Sulo shrugs, that's the way it has to be.

No one invites me to sit down, so I stand in the doorway and keep my boots on. "I just came to offer some friendly advice," I say. "You stabbed those bouncers yesterday evening. They probably got what they deserved, but you're going to get nailed for it. It'll cost you years of your life. I'd like you to consider turning yourself in. You'll still have to sit for the crime, but maybe for three years instead of five."

Sulo starts to speak, but Papa speaks for him. "Sulo was here with us, as I told you bastards yesterday. Fuck off and leave him alone. He lost his brother. This family has gone through enough."

"You've gone through a lot," I say, "but losing Sulo to a long stretch in prison won't make it better."

Papa chugs his beer dry and throws the can down beside the couch. "If Sulo had stabbed those cocksuckers, which he didn't," he shoots Sulo a dirty look, "he did a shit job of it. They're alive, and our Taisto is dead."

So, Papa put Sulo up to the attack.

Sulo finally speaks for himself. "Inspector, it's nice of you to come here. I know you did it out of concern, but I didn't do anything wrong. And besides, I'm thinking about leaving the country soon. I don't have a job. I may go to Sweden and look for work."

As if we can't extradite him from Sweden. That doesn't leave much to be said. At least I tried. "Okay, Sulo, I wish you luck." I take a business card out of my wallet and flip it over to him. "Call me if you need anything," I say, and leave for work.

I drive the few minutes to the Pasila police station and sneak to my office, bypass the common room. I sit for a while and contemplate *December Day,* my print of the Albert

Edelfelt painting. It portrays houses near the frozen sea in sepia and monochromatic colors. I hung it here because it soothes me.

I think about my meeting with Filippov later and what I could possibly say to him. I come up with nothing. I call Jyri and fill him in. I don't want to, because his input will be Machiavellian, but I have little choice. He takes a while, turns it over in his mind. I turn on the recorder in my cell phone and document the conversation, to protect myself in case all this goes wrong.

"Why do you think he left the semen in his freezer, in clear view?" Jyri asks.

"Arrogance. He didn't think we'd figure out that DNA samples were part of his blackmail scheme."

"Then he's made other mistakes, too. We just need to buy some time to find out what they are."

"I'm not sure we have much time. Filippov might get pissed off or feel cornered and pull the trigger on you and the others. Release the videos to draw attention away from himself."

"Maybe." Jyri pauses. "Tell him we'll give him the business contracts he paid us for."

I note the use of pronoun, *us.* Jyri also takes bribes.

"And tell him if he returns the videos,

we'll guarantee that he never becomes a suspect in his wife's murder investigation."

This was my fear. Jyri will go the obvious route and hang Rein Saar out to dry. "You'd let an innocent man sit for murder?"

"Do you have a better plan?"

I think yes, let the truth come out and justice be done. "Not at the moment."

"The only other option," Jyri says, "is to let the case go unsolved. Release Rein Saar on the grounds that he couldn't have been tased and then murdered Iisa Filippov."

This is the lesser of two evils, but unsatisfactory. Ivan Filippov deserves punishment. "What about your precious *murharyhmä* track record?"

"An unfortunate necessity."

"Because I ruined it, I'll look like an asshole, like a shitty detective. And it's not a great start for Milo's career, either."

"True, but on the other hand, you two are both famous hero cops at the moment. Discrediting you and making you disappear would be a way of keeping the black-ops unit secret. I believe the term is sheep-dipping. You go away, then quietly reappear, out of the public eye."

And I'm supposed to trust him with this. Not a fucking chance. I make up my mind. One way or another, the murder of Iisa Filippov — whether it's Iisa, and not Linda, in a cold drawer in the morgue — will be punished. I just still don't know how to accomplish it. I lie. "Okay, Jyri, we'll do it your way. I'll call you later and let you know what Filippov and I work out."

"Just buy us some time to find his other mistakes. Make some cockamamie deal, then later, no matter what you agree to, we'll put the fucks to him."

As is Jyri's habit, he hangs up without saying thank you, fuck you or good-bye.

I turn back to *December Day,* think about calling Milo to get his opinion, but decide I don't want it. I turn my latest conversations with Filippov and Jyri over in my mind, try to find chinks in their armor I can chisel open, but I can't. My cell phone rings. It's Arvid.

"How are you doing?" I ask.

He doesn't answer straight away, and when he does, his voice cracks. "Son, I've been better."

Arvid keeps his emotions, except anger, tight. I'm worried. "What's the matter?"

"Can you come here? Right away?"

I look out the window at a blizzard. Snow comes down in a deluge. "I don't know if I can. The roads might not be passable."

"I'm asking you, please."

"What's the matter?"

Long pause. "It's Ritva. She's passed away."

It almost brings tears to my eyes. "Jesus, I'm so sorry."

"I need you to do her death investigation."

"Even if I wanted to, it's not my jurisdiction."

His sigh is long and full of sorrow. "It has to be your jurisdiction. Ritva had bone cancer. I helped her to die. I need you to cover it up."

I don't know what to say, and say nothing.

"It was her wish," he says. "I know you can't just take my word for it. We've known this day would come for a long time and planned for it. Ritva wrote you a letter to explain."

I still don't know what to say.

"Please help me," Arvid says.

"Hang tight," I say. "I'll be there as soon as I can."

# 43

The drive to Porvoo is treacherous. My Saab slips and slides all over the road, and visibility is nothing. The trip, usually little over half an hour, takes me two hours.

Arvid ushers me in. He's wearing his usual starched and pressed pants and his hair is perfectly combed. I get the idea that he made himself as presentable as possible before seeing his wife off to the next world, made their last moments together as special as he could.

We take our now customary places at his kitchen table. He brings us coffee and cognac. "Let's drink to her," he says, and raises his glass.

I raise mine, too.

"To Ritva, may she rest in peace," he says.

I repeat it after him, and we drink.

"Do you want to tell me about it?" I ask. "You don't have to if you don't want to."

"Boy, are you going to do me this favor

and sign off on her death? I'll get Ritva's letter for you."

The pain in his voice makes further proofs unnecessary. "I don't need to see the letter, unless you want me to read it. And of course I'll help you."

"Ritva was eaten up with bone cancer. Her pain got worse and worse, and the days she could even get out of bed were fewer and farther between. In the end, she was in near-constant agony."

"Like I said, you don't have to tell me this if you don't want to."

"I want to. She was only seventy-six, but I'm ninety. I do my best, but I'm not strong enough anymore to take care of an invalid. The time came where she had to go to a hospital to die, and she didn't want to do that. She wanted to die here with me. In our home, and in my arms. So today, we renewed our wedding vows, and I overdosed her with morphine. She fell asleep and passed without feeling any pain."

He starts to cry a little. He needs privacy. "Let me go have a look at her," I say, "just to make sure you didn't leave any clues somebody might pick up on."

He nods.

I go upstairs and find their bedroom. She's covered with a sheet. Ritva's eyes are closed and her arms are folded across her chest. Her hair is done up in a neat bun. I pull back the sheet. She's wearing a long silk nightgown. I don't see anything that might cause suspicion of anything but death due to cancer, no reason for an autopsy.

I go back downstairs. "Everything is fine," I say. "You did everything just right. Do you want me to call the mortuary now?"

"Give me a few minutes with her first," he says.

I sit by myself for a while. When he comes back, he tells me to make the call. I do, and sit with him while we wait.

"Tell me about your goings-on with the Filippov case," Arvid says.

At this moment, he looks every day of his ninety years. He just lost his life partner of more than fifty years. His face is all grief and pain. I guess he wants to think about something else for a little while.

I bring him up to speed, tell him that it looks to me like Filippov — protected by the powers that be — will walk away from murdering his wife. If it is his wife and not her half sister. An innocent man may be made a scapegoat and have his life ruined. And I have a feeling I'm going to be hung out to dry and have my career destroyed. I say I have no idea what to say or do when I meet Filippov at Kämp at five, but come hell or high water, I'm determined to convict him.

"Kämp," he says. "I used to love that place back in the war years. Great food. I miss that food."

"My wife is the general manager of the hotel," I say. "Come there sometime, I'll ask her to comp us and we'll have a nice meal together."

"Sounds good," he says. "But this Filippov case. It's going south on you. One way or another, you're going to be the one hurt by it, and the bad guys are all going to walk away like it never happened."

I light a cigarette. He takes one, too. "I smoked like a train when I was young," he says. "Always loved smoking. I'm going to take up the habit again."

"Sometimes, Arvid," I say, "I think these cigarettes are the only things keeping me alive."

He stubs out a cigarette, lights another, finishes off his cognac. "You're a good boy. This situation of yours. We're going to have to do something about it."

I have no idea what he means by "we." Sometimes I wonder if he's still whip-smart or mentally feeling the effect of his years.

"You have your own problems at the moment."

His smile is knowing. The old man has depths I don't fathom. "Well," he says, "I guess we better do something about them, too."

He switches gears. "You know anything about the *Arctic Sea* case?" he asks.

"A little. Why?"

"The ship the *Arctic Sea* left Kaliningrad, in Russia, in July of last year and picked up a little less than two million euros' worth of wood in Finland. Depending on who you listen to, the ship either was or wasn't tested for radiation. If it was, the paperwork has disappeared. Shortly after departing Finland, it was hijacked by eight men, supposedly of various nationalities from former Eastern Bloc countries. But the hijackers spoke English to the Russian crew. In this day and age, despite current technology, the ship disappeared. When finally located, the *Arctic Sea* was three hundred miles off Cape Verde, thousands of miles from its original destination. Who the fuck commits piracy for timber?"

He seems fascinated by the event. "What's your interest?" I ask.

"It's clear that the ship was loaded with secretly sold nukes, their destination unknown. High-level cover-ups always interest me."

The hearse arrives and stops our conversation. I stay with Arvid while he sees Ritva out of the house.

"You better go," he says. "With this weather, you won't make your appointment with that murderous Russian bastard if you don't."

Right now, the Filippov case doesn't seem so important to me. "Fuck that Russian bastard. I can stay here with you for a while. Or if you want, come and spend the night with me and Kate. The house is a little full at the moment, but we'll make room."

He pats my back. "Thank you, son, but no. This old man needs to be alone for a while."

I would, too. I leave him to his memories and his grief.

# 44

I drive back to Helsinki at a crawl. The migraine snaps on sudden and bad. The white of the snow hurts my eyes. It's hard to see. I think about poor Arvid, alone after all those years with Ritva. I picture her pretty, dead face. Then a procession of dead faces from childhood forward.

My sister, Suvi, her panicked dying eyes looking up at me through a sheet of ice on a frozen lake. A slew of murder victims from over the course of my career as a policeman stare at me, judging. Then Sufia Elmi, but she can't look at me because her eyes are gouged out. My ex-wife, Heli, who can't look at me because her eyes are burned out. My ex-sergeant, Valtteri, his eyes fish-dead, his brains blown out. His son, Heikki, hanging from a basement rafter, his eyes bugged out. Sufia's father in flames, eyes open wide and angry. Iisa Filippov, if it is Iisa, her face destroyed by cigarette burns and lashings, glares at me with her one remaining eye and demands justice. Legion, his eyes at peace. I see starving and helpless prisoners of war looking up from inside a bomb crater, their eyes imploring. Arvid and my grandpa machine-gun them to death, and a tractor covers the pit with dirt.

My cell phone rings and breaks my unholy reverie. It's Milo. I don't want to answer but do it anyway. "Guess where I am," he says.

"No guessing games today. Where are you?"

"I'm at Meilahti hospital. Guess why."

My mood is foul. "What the fuck did I just say?"

"Jesus, don't have a cow. Sulo Polvinen's father took matters into his own hands. He came here and stabbed the bouncers to death in their hospital beds."

I can hear the glee in Milo's voice.

"He plugged them in their chests with a hunting knife and didn't even try to escape, just sat down in a chair after he killed the second one and waited to be arrested. He confessed to the attack at the Silver Dollar, too."

"He didn't attack them at the club. Sulo did. I'm sure of it. He confessed to keep Sulo out of prison so he wouldn't lose a second son."

"So? Taisto Polvinen got some justice, after all."

I resist the urge to scream at Milo. "Has it occurred to you that Sulo has now lost his brother and his father? His mother lost a son and a husband. He's going to rot in a cell for ten years for avenging his child."

Remorse isn't Milo's strong suit. "Well, no, I hadn't really thought about it, but still. . . ."

I hang up on him, can't stand to listen to unadulterated stupidity at the moment. I'm ten minutes away from downtown Helsinki and Hotel Kämp, and I still don't have a fucking clue how I'm going to deal with Ivan Filippov.

# 45

Despite the cold and snow, Kämp's restaurant is bustling. The hotel's guests, mostly foreign businesspeople, need a place to eat and drink, and it's easier to do it here than to go out in the cold and snow. Filippov and Linda sit side by side at a window table, he on the inside, she next to the glass. The table next to them is reserved and so unoccupied for the moment. I take a seat across from Filippov. They're noshing on caviar and drinking Dom Pérignon.

"It's a pleasure to see you again," Linda says. "Ivan, did I tell you how charming the inspector is?"

"You mentioned it." Filippov gestures toward the champagne. "Inspector, would you care for a glass? Since dinner is on you, we thought it best to show no restraint."

"No, thank you," I say.

A waiter takes my drink order. I take *kossu* and beer.

"So," Filippov says, "you have a proposition for me. What is it?"

I aim for middle ground, just to see if it will work. Jyri was right, I should promise him anything he wants to buy time, but if I seem soft, he'll smell the lie.

"The murder goes unsolved," I say. "You and Linda walk. You get the contracts you felt you were promised. We get the videos."

The waiter brings my drinks, and a dozen raw oysters for Filippov and Linda. He takes a break from speaking to chow down, slurps an oyster, dabs his mouth with a linen napkin. "Unacceptable. My wife was brutally murdered. The culprit is Rein Saar. He has to serve a lengthy prison sentence."

Strike one. Filippov is negotiating from a position of strength. He won't compromise.

"Be reasonable," I say. "You and Linda murdered your wife, but you'll go unpunished, and the matter will be forgotten. Saar is innocent. Leave him be."

He sticks a finger in my face. "You're wrong. Saar is guilty. He fucked my wife for two years." He raises his voice. "My wife! Mine! He deserves prison. He deserves worse. He's getting off easy."

Filippov pauses, slides another oyster down his throat. "As you pointed out last night," he says, "my wife was a miserable

405

slut. I can't punish everyone who fucked my wife, but I can punish him. If he and others like him had respected my marriage and kept their hands off my wife, Iisa would still be alive, and we wouldn't be having this conversation. The value of punishing Saar is symbolic to me. His incarceration is non-negotiable."

I have to admit, he makes an extreme but compelling argument. I look at Linda, hoping for help, but she only winks at me and chases an oyster with champagne.

The waiter brings their main courses. We halt our conversation while he sets their plates in front of them. Arvid walks in. My bewilderment mounts. The waiter leaves.

Arvid walks over to the table and stands beside Filippov.

"How did you get here?" I ask Arvid.

"By taxi. Cost me two hundred euros. Is this that Russian bastard?" he asks.

"That's him. What are you doing here?"

He pulls a chair over from the next table and sits next to Filippov. Arvid has on a long overcoat. He shoots the sleeves and shows us the little Sauer suicide pistol that sat on the mantel over his fireplace, only now it has a silencer attached to it. He pulls his sleeve down again to hide it, and jams it against Filippov's ribs. "As I said earlier,"

Arvid says, "fixing our problems."

Filippov blinks and licks his lips, confused. He knows something has gone wrong. I do, too, but haven't the vaguest idea what it is.

"Old man," Filippov says, "who the hell are you and what do you want?"

"Admit that you killed your wife," Arvid says.

Filippov shrugs his shoulders. "Okay, I admit it."

"Don't move a goddamned muscle," Arvid says.

Filippov senses that Arvid isn't fucking around. He sits stock-upright in his chair and stares straight ahead.

Arvid takes a wineglass from the table with his left hand, stands up, and with his right hand presses the pistol against the back of Filippov's head. Low, where it meets his neck. Arvid smashes the wineglass on the floor and pulls the trigger, simultaneous. He shoots Filippov at the junction of his brain and brain stem, in the same way that Milo shot Legion. It's obvious that Arvid has done this many times before. Arvid pockets his gun and holds Filippov up so he doesn't pitch forward onto the table.

The silencer muffled the sound of the shot and changed its pitch. Diners look around, curious. Arvid goes sheepish and shrugs.

His look says, *Sorry, folks, I'm just a clumsy and silly old man.* They think the sound was only from the breaking wineglass and go back to their conversations. Arvid balances Filippov so he stays upright, and sits down beside him again. Filippov doesn't look dead, just bored. Arvid's peashooter didn't pack enough punch to make a mess. A busboy scurries over, sweeps up the broken glass in ten seconds flat and departs.

I'm so shocked that I start to giggle. Linda gets up, goes over to Arvid and kisses him on the cheek. "You've rather changed my plans," she says, "but thank you. That was the nicest thing anyone ever did for me. Who are you?"

He shakes his head. "I don't know anymore."

She sits down again. "Would someone please explain to me what just happened?"

"Yeah," I say, "as soon as I understand it myself."

Arvid slides Filippov's plate over and eyes his dinner. "What was he having?"

I've eaten here a lot and know the menu. "It's a grilled fillet of beef with haricots verts, mushrooms, caramelized onions and potatoes au gratin. Can you please tell me why you just killed a man?"

He takes a place setting, cuts a slice of

beef and digs in. "You were going to get fucked by this murder investigation. Now, your killer is apprehended, but unfortunately unable to stand trial. You solved the crime and closed the case."

Arvid helps himself to Dom Pérignon. I knock back my *kossu*. I need it. Filippov remains upright. His eyes are open, staring at me like the dead I imagined earlier on my drive here. Sooner or later, he'll pitch forward. We don't have much time. I turn to Linda. "Who are you?" I ask.

She sips champagne. "Iisa."

"Why did you kill Linda?"

Her Bettie Page facade has disappeared. She's all business now. "First things first." She points at Filippov. "Like the old man said, you've got your killer. After this brief discussion, I'm going to get up, walk out of this hotel, embezzle the assets from Filippov Construction — which rightfully belong to me anyway — and never be heard from again. If not, I'll expose everyone involved."

It may be the most reasonable way out of this mess for all of us. "If your story satisfies me, it's a deal. Tell it fast."

She kills half a glass of champagne to steady herself. Her voice changes, I presume from a facsimile of Linda's to her own. "I had agreed to meet Rein at his apartment on Sunday morning. I decided the easiest thing would be to just sleep in Rein's bed and wait for him."

"You were going to watch him fuck another girl?" I ask.

She nods. "About five a.m., I hear the door unlock. I think they've arrived early and hide in the bathroom. I hear two voices, Linda's and a man's. I'm wondering what the hell Linda is doing in my lover's apartment with some guy, so I wait and listen. She sucks his cock and shoves him out the door."

"No one saw you?"

"No, I'm good at this game. After the guy left, Linda called Ivan so she could gloat about their plan to murder me. She got off the phone and started getting ready, laid out her toys. I came out of the bathroom, took the taser, snuck up behind her and zapped her with it."

It's all clear to me now. "You decided to punish them both. You tortured Linda with cigarettes to disfigure her beyond easy recognition, tasing her occasionally to keep her under control, and made her tell you their plan in detail."

"And after she did, I put on the protective clothing, so Ivan couldn't tell the difference between us, and waited on him."

"Torturing with cigarettes wasn't part of the plan. Didn't it piss him off?"

"I told him I got excited and overzealous. He accepted it."

"And your lover, Rein Saar. You were willing to let him be framed and go to prison?"

She shrugs. "I was in a bit of a predicament. At the time, it seemed like it was him or me."

"So you just acted out the murder, as explained by Linda."

"And afterward, I put on Linda's clothes, did my look-alike thing with makeup and hair, mimicked her voice and pretended to be her until we got to Filippov Construction. Then I switched from Linda's voice to my own and said, 'Surprise.' "

I can picture it clearly enough. She only had to fool him long enough for them to drive to work. He was in such a heightened state of excitement after the murder and completion of a dream-like sex act, it wouldn't have been hard to deceive him. How could he suspect he killed Linda, not Iisa, after just sharing such an act of demented intimacy?

"I'm surprised he didn't murder you on the spot," I say.

"He knew he wouldn't be able to cover up a second murder. We struck a bargain to

411

sell Filippov Construction, take my life insurance payment, split it all and never see each other again."

"And pretending to be lovers when I saw you and Ivan here at Kämp on the evening of the murder?"

"As when we spent the night together in Linda's apartment, we were maintaining a facade."

"Didn't you want him punished for planning your torture and murder?"

"I tricked him into torturing and murdering the woman he loved. I felt he was sufficiently punished."

"And recording the murder, even setting it to music?"

"Part of Ivan's aforementioned punishment. They had intended to do so when they murdered me, for their further listening enjoyment while they fucked. I simply completed the plan, so that Ivan could listen to the sounds of his lover dying again and again, guilt-ridden, as he mourns her."

Even after all my years as a cop, the darkness inherent in human nature still shocks me. Sometimes I feel I'd like to take Kate and our child to live deep in the forest, away from the beasts we call humans. Somewhere peaceful and safe.

"Did you know Linda was your half sister?" I ask.

She cocks her head, uncomprehending. "Half sister? Impossible. She used to have sex with my father."

"I think that's why she wanted to murder you. During our last chat, you told me that her fetish was self-negation, that she wanted to be other people. I'm guessing that was because of the self-loathing incest caused her. Your father had an affair with her mother, but didn't know it resulted in a child. Linda's mother wrote to him and told him, and he committed suicide out of grief."

Her breath catches, but she doesn't interrupt and so must want all of this bitter truth. I also want her to have it, and I give it to her. "You received unconditional love from your father. Linda had to suck her daddy's dick to get it. She must have hated you for it. You were cruel to your husband, but she loved him. You had everything she wanted. With you dead, she could become you, a new and improved version, and Linda, the unwanted and abused child, could cease to exist, once and for all."

She stands, expressionless. I have no inkling of how she feels. "I believe our business is concluded," she says.

"Not quite. I need the videos."

"I'm keeping them."

"Nope. That's the deal-breaker. I'll let you embezzle the money and disappear, but if you don't give me the videos, or if I find out you made copies of them, I'll find you and prosecute you for your sister's murder."

She eyes the door, anxious to leave, considers the ramifications. "They're buried in snow, triple-wrapped in freezer bags. Walk four paces off my back porch, turn left and take four more paces, and dig. Are we done now?"

"Disappearing isn't as easy as you might think. If you're lying to me, I'll track you down and see you punished. I doubt it would take me more than a couple days."

"I'm not lying."

"Then yes, we're done."

I watch her walk away and wonder how she can live with herself. I suspect she won't be able to, and I may find myself investigating her suicide. She may not pay for murder, but she stands punished.

Arvid is busy scarfing Filippov's meal. I say to him, "The crime is solved and the case closed, but you're going up for murder."

He washes down steak with champagne. "*Au contraire,* quite the opposite. I faced extradition to Germany and a lengthy trial for accessory to murder. Now that I've committed murder in Finland, I'm not liable for extradition until my trial here is concluded. While I await trial in this country, as an old and frail man, and a war hero to boot, I'll be released on my own recognizance until I'm convicted and sentenced. You'll be the investigating officer in this case, a number of important officials want the truth buried, and I'm sure that between us all, we can delay my trial for some years. Years I don't have. I'll be in a grave before it goes to court."

This smacks of pure and crystalline genius. I can only shake my head in wonder and amazement.

"Besides," Arvid says, "with Ritva gone, I don't have anything left to live for, and I wanted to kill one more goddamned Russian before I die."

He pulls Linda's plate over. I don't wait for him to ask. "Sautéed hare, globe artichoke, fava beans and roasted pine nuts over pasta. How are you going to explain why you shot a suspect in my case?"

"Over the past couple days, I've been busy making phone calls. To the president and various ministers and generals. Out of respect for my service to my country, they're willing to take my calls and listen to an old man ramble for a few minutes. I intend to claim that Filippov was a Russian spy and saboteur involved in the *Arctic Sea* affair, and I killed him because it was my patriotic duty. As phone records will show, I learned of his involvement through chats with highly placed government officials, who regularly take me into their confidence in the hopes of gaining insight into weighty matters through the sage wisdom of a revered elder. Because the killing of Filippov involves issues of national security, my trial must be conducted in a closed courtroom, the details never released to the public. In addition to my achievements as a war veteran, I'll pass into the annals of Finnish history as one of its greatest heroes."

"You seem to have thought of everything," I say.

He wolfs pasta. "Yes, I have."

"Fancy silencer on that pistol," I say. "Where did you get it?"

"I bought it yesterday. No law against it. Should we order dessert?"

I smile and shake my head. "Sorry, there's no time. You have to go to jail soon."

He nods agreement.

"All this 'boy' and 'son' and 'call me Ukki' stuff. You've been playing me all along, haven't you, preparing for this moment?"

He leans forward and folds his hands on

the table in front of him. "Boy, I said you were naïve beyond words. Not this *specific* moment — I didn't know for certain that I would kill this Russian bastard beside me until yesterday — but yes, I planned all along to use you to keep me from being extradited to Germany after Ritva was gone. But it wasn't all a lie. You really are a good boy, and in truth, I've come to feel affection for you. And I did save your ass, didn't I? It's not as if I'm not grateful for all you've done for me."

"And everything you told me about the Civil War and the Second World War and about my grandpa. Was it all one big lie?"

"No, I told you the truth about Toivo and myself at Stalag 309. About the rest of it? Well, let's say the *exact* truth about this country's history is going to die with me. I believe it's for the good of the nation."

Maybe he's right about that. My cell phone rings. It's Kate. "Kari," she says, "I'm in labor. Could you come home and take me to the hospital?"

My heart thumps in my chest from both fear and joy. "Are you sure? You're not due for nine days."

She laughs, lighthearted. "The baby disagrees. My water broke."

"I can be there in half an hour. Is that too long?"

The panic in my voice makes her chuckle. "It's fine, dear. I'll see you soon." She hangs up.

"I'm sorry, I've got a baby on the way, and I have to take my wife to the hospital. That means you have to go to jail now."

He reaches over and pats my arm. "Congratulations, son. And please do call me Ukki. I like it. If you were really my grandson, I would be proud." He takes his pistol out of his coat pocket and lays it on the table between us. "You better take that."

I put it in my own pocket and call for a cruiser.

## 46

I drive home as fast as road conditions will allow, pull up in front of our door, call Kate and tell her I'm here. She says I don't need to come upstairs and get her. John and Mary will bring her down. For once, I'm glad for their presence. Kate didn't have to be alone while she waited for me.

They pile into the Saab, and we set out for the hospital together. Kate is calm and smiling. I'm a nervous wreck. The car skitters and shimmies. I picture having an accident, and Kate giving birth in a freezing car by the side of the road.

But we arrive at Kätilöopisto hospital without incident. I help Kate inside. We get her checked in. John carries Kate's hospital travel bag. Kate packed it weeks ago, just in case. It has everything she thought she might possibly need to make herself comfortable. Massage aids: tennis balls, a rolling pin, frozen juice cans. Comfort aids: a heat pillow, aromatherapy, socks for cold feet. Clothes and toiletries for after the baby is born. She brought extra, in case there are complications because of her preeclampsia and her stay is longer than the normal two days.

We opted to not bring a camera. Kate said our memories would suffice. She would prefer to maintain a bit of decorum and not have her sweating and grunting recorded for all time to come. I offered to attend childbirth classes with her and be her coach, but she declined. She said she couldn't picture me huffing and puffing along with her, and holding her hand would be enough.

An orderly and I situate her in a bed in a private room in the maternity ward. John and Mary don't try to intrude, and they go to the waiting room, for which I'm grateful. I sit in a chair beside Kate's bed and try to maintain an air of composure I don't feel. Over the next few hours, Kate's contractions come harder and faster. At first, they had come about once every fifteen or twenty minutes and lasted for about thirty seconds, and they've gradually accelerated to every three or four minutes and last sixty seconds. Kate doesn't complain, seems to take it in stride, says she doesn't even need the comfort aids she brought with her. I ask her occasionally if the pain is bearable, and she answers that it isn't that bad at all.

To take her mind off her contractions, I do something uncharacteristic and tell her stories. I begin with the cases I've been working and tell her in exquisite detail about the Filippov affair and how it ended with Arvid shooting Filippov to death in a restaurant she manages. I pause the tale when the midwife comes in to check on her, then tell Kate about how Arvid helped Ritva die, and then he managed to save me and himself, and punish the guilty. Strange childbirth talk, but the tale is so morbid and bizarre that it holds her rapt attention. I leave out the possibility of heading up a black-ops unit for the moment.

A day ago, Kate wanted to hear stories about my childhood, so I tell her some, but pleasant ones. About how, when I was a kid, Dad and his friends would get together, drink and sing waltz and tango songs accompanied by an accordion. I tell her about how we went to a dog show once. My brother Timo looked around and said, "It's been raining cats and dogs," even though the ground was bone-dry. "Look," Timo said, "there are poodles everywhere." Kate hee-haws despite a tough contraction.

The doctor comes in to check on Kate

occasionally, and finally says it's time to get down to business. The baby's head is crowning. He tells Kate to start pushing. She says she wants this over soon and pushes like hell. It works. After only about an hour, our child, a girl, is out and into this world. The doctor gives her a slap. She sucks air and squeals, and he cuts the umbilical cord. Kate flops back against her pillows, exhausted. From her first contraction at home until now, her labor lasted sixteen hours.

A nurse takes our baby, who resembles a bullet-headed frog covered in blood and viscous ooze, wipes some of the mess away, wraps her in a blanket and hands her to me. I'm nervous at first, afraid I'll make a mistake, hold her too tight, drop her. Irrational fears. But they fade within seconds, and I realize that I love this little bullet-headed frog as much as anything in the world.

The doctor tells me that Kate's delivery was one of the easiest he's ever seen. No complications, no vaginal tearing, no nothing. Kate didn't even require an episiotomy. Kate begins contractions again, and within a few minutes expels the placenta and the umbilical cord. And it's over. All my fears came to nothing.

I hand the baby to Kate, and she asks me

to get John and Mary. I bring them into the room. We exchange hugs and share joy. For the first time since they arrived, I feel that they truly are part of my family, and it gratifies me.

John and Mary go back to the waiting room to give Kate, me and our bullet-headed-frog privacy. Kate and I sit in the silence for a while, bask in our moment. After about half an hour, Kate tells me she's tired and wants to sleep. She wants me to sleep, too. I don't want to leave, but know it's for the best.

I talk to John and Mary. John wants to come home with me. Mary says she's slept while waiting, and she'll stay in case Kate needs something. Mary tells me not to worry, if anything happens, she'll call me straightaway. For a woman who doesn't like me, she's working hard to be my friend.

## 47

We get back to my place. John crashes on the couch. I go to bed, and for the first time in I don't remember how long, I have no headache and feel no anxiety, and sleep the sleep of the dead.

I wake up in the middle of the afternoon and check my cell phone. I kept it on silent while I slept. I have seventy-two missed calls. Press, police and God knows who else are trying to contact me to find out how it came about that in my presence, in the restaurant of the city's finest hotel, a ninety-year-old Winter War hero put a bullet in the brain of a Russian businessman whose wife had recently been murdered.

I go back to the hospital to be with Kate, but she's sound asleep. I hold our baby, enjoy the quiet and sit next to her. Finally, I decide Kate may not wake for hours, and go back home to get something to eat. Mary continues to wait, in case Kate wakes and needs something.

I find John in the kitchen, a bottle of *kossu* in front of him. He's not tanked, just drinking. "I guess you know I told Kate about myself and everything you did for me," he says.

"Yeah, I know."

"Are you pissed off at me?"

"No."

"Can I give you a brotherly hug to congratulate you on the birth of your child?"

It makes me laugh. "If you have to."

He stands and gives me a hard squeeze. "Want to have a drink with me?" he asks.

I sit down with him. "Sure."

He fetches me a glass and pours me a drink. We nurse our vodkas and share a comfortable silence, something I wouldn't have thought him capable of.

My phone rings. It's Jari. "Hi, little brother," he says. "I haven't spoken to you since we left your house in a rush. I'm sorry about that."

It amuses me when he calls me "little brother," since I'm almost twice his size. "It's okay, just a little culture clash. It happens."

"I wanted to check on you. How's your migraine situation?"

"Better today. Kate gave me a healthy

baby girl this morning, both of them are fine, and my headache went away."

"You have a baby! Wow! Congratulations! You busy right now?"

"No. Kate's asleep and I'm at home."

"Then we're going to have your *varpa-jaiset*."

"Now?"

"Now."

"Do I have to?"

"Yes."

I smile and sigh. "Okay, then meet me at Hilpeä Hauki and we'll do it."

His voice is full of glee. "I'll meet you in an hour."

We hang up.

"Come on, John," I say. "We're going out. It's time for my *varpajaiset*."

"*Varpajaiset?*"

"*Varpaat* are toes. A *varpajaiset* is a party. When a man becomes a father, he's supposed to have a drink for every toe his child was born with. So I'm required to have ten drinks. I suspect you will, too. I'm sure you'll enjoy it."

We tramp through the snow over to Hilpeä Hauki and sit at a corner table. My phone rings, it's Milo. "Arvid Lahtinen murdered Filippov," he says. "That's fucking awesome.

You have to tell me the story."

"Not now," I say. "Kate had a baby girl, and I'm having a *varpajaiset* at Hauki."

"That's great news," he says. "Can I come?"

His voice is so full of enthusiasm that I can't say no. "Sure. Come over. Buy me a drink."

Within a few minutes, Jari and Milo are sitting with us, and our table is covered with beers and shots. Apparently, I'm expected to exceed the ten-drink quota. The mood is gregarious, the jokes are silly.

"All right, Milo," I say, "now I'm ready. Tell me the story behind your Hitler Youth dagger."

He beams, thrilled that I asked him to tell a story. "My great-grandpa took it off a Russian soldier in the war. Which means he must have taken it off a German soldier."

He pauses, once again attempting to build anticipation.

"That's vaguely interesting," I say, "but I was expecting something more."

"I wanted to make you ask. I'm coming to the good part. Great-Grandpa gave it to Grandpa, who gave it to Dad, who had a weakness for women. One day, Mom decided she had enough and stabbed Dad with it."

Milo grins. I'm not sure if I'm supposed to laugh or not. "Did she kill him?"

"No, she stuck it through his leg and ripped a seven-inch gouge in it. He nearly lost the leg, missed weeks of work. Mom got her point across. He quit cheating on her after that."

A good story. It gets a laugh out of me. We toast to Kate, and all of us knock back another *kossu*.

My phone rings again. It's Jyri Ivalo. He also wants to hear about Arvid capping Filippov, and he wants to know if I've got my hands on the evidence against him and certain prominent others. I tell him I'm celebrating the birth of my child, and if he wants to talk to me, he has to come to Hauki and buy me drinks to earn the privilege. I hang up on him, as he's so often done to me.

Milo slams his shot glass onto the table to get our attention. He doesn't have enough body weight to have a good head for alcohol, and his eyes glisten. He claps a hand on my shoulder. He raises his voice, as drunks tend to. "I admire this guy," he says. "I killed a man this week, and it's eating me up. I feel fucking awful. Kari, you don't seem to feel anything about it. You tough motherfucker."

I don't have words of wisdom for him. I

shrug. "It's something that happened. You did the right thing. Time will make it better."

"You killed a man once," he says. "How did you live with it? Did time make it better for you?"

We've been drinking hard and fast, and the booze has gone to my head, too. I feel like I owe him the truth. "When I blew that gangster's head off, I felt nothing but relief that it was him instead of me. I didn't feel guilt, or anything at all. Never have. The only reason I went to therapy for it was because I thought my lack of guilt meant something was wrong with me."

The others look at me for a long minute and try to decide if I'm joking or not. Jari decides that I am and starts laughing, so the others do, too. I'm pleased that Milo feels remorse. It lessens my worry that he's disturbed beyond repair.

Jyri walks in and comes up behind me. "A word, Inspector."

He's disconcerted, uncomfortable. I feel like toying with him. "When you bring a round of beers and shots for the table, we can chat." My voice turns sarcastic. "We'll use veiled and secretive language to keep the others in the dark."

He has no choice, does as he's told. When

he comes back, I ask, "What do you want to know?"

My phone rings again. I don't see the caller on the display, but answer to interrupt and further disconcert Jyri.

"Inspector, this is Sulo Polvinen. Can I talk to you?"

I give him my stock drunken answer for the evening. "I'm celebrating the birth of my daughter at Hilpeä Hauki. The address is Vaasankatu 7. Come here if you want to talk to me." I hang up on him, too.

"What happened at Kämp?" Jyri asks.

He's brought a round of *kossu*. I insist we drink it and toast to Kate again before I answer. Then I give him a most succinct account.

"Arvid Lahtinen murdered Filippov, because if he stands trial for murder in Finland, he won't be extradited to Germany. He also did it as a favor to me, so you and your buddies won't fuck me later. Filippov believed he was murdering his wife, but Iisa tricked him into murdering Linda, the woman he loved. I let Iisa go. She's going to embezzle the funds from Filippov Construction, disappear and live out her life — I believe — as Linda Pohjola, probably in another country."

"Did you retrieve the things we dis-

430

cussed?"

"I know where they are and will retrieve them in due course."

He looks like he wants to reach across the table and choke me. "I want those things."

"No, Jyri," I say, "I think I'll hang on to them for a while. You don't have anything to worry about."

He doesn't know how to answer and scowls at me.

I have pity on him. "You're safe now. Everything has been resolved to your satisfaction. You have my word. And about the job you offered me. I'll take it."

He brightens. "You will?"

"Yes. And now that we're partners in crime, I'll regard you as just that, a partner, rather than my boss."

His brightness withers.

Sulo Polvinen comes in. I tell him to take a seat. "There's no need," he says. "I've come to turn myself in for attacking the bouncers at the Silver Dollar."

"Have you got any money?" I ask.

He looks baffled. "Why?"

"Because the price of admission to sit at this table is a round of *kossu*. Until you bring it and drink with us, I won't even consider arresting you."

He screws up his mouth, doesn't know

431

what to say, goes to the bar and does as he's told. He spreads the shots around the table and sits. "To my lovely wife and my darling daughter," I say.

Our crowd is drunk now, and the toast is loud and raucous. "So, Sulo," I say, "tell me why I should arrest you."

"I tried to kill two men. My father is going to be punished for my crime."

I chase the *kossu* with beer. "Your father is going to jail for murder. He'll get ten years. If you confess to the attack, you go to jail and he still gets ten years. What would it help for you to sit in prison, too?"

"I did wrong. I deserve punishment."

"Your father is a piece of shit who put you up to the attack in the first place. If you go to jail, your mother has no one. Your request for incarceration is denied."

He didn't expect this. It stuns him to momentary silence. "Well," he stammers, "what am I supposed to do, then?"

Jyri sits across from me, still disconcerted. He wanted something, I told him no. He's not used to it.

I say, "What you're supposed to do, Sulo, is get on with your life and make something out of yourself."

He stares down at the table. I slide him a pint of beer. He says, "I don't know how to do anything."

Jyri says he wants a black-ops team. It needs tough guys, and Jyri says I can staff it as I like. I test Jyri's sincerity. "Sure you can. Do something about people like the ones that killed your brother. Be a cop. I'm starting a new unit and could use a mountain-sized kid who's not afraid to take out two bouncers with a box cutter." I look at Jyri. "That's okay with you, right?"

We're playing big dog/little dog again — only this time our roles are reversed. "Sure," he says. "Whatever."

"And you'll see to it that Arvid Lahtinen is released from custody tomorrow. Right?"

Jyri nods.

"Don't you have to go to school to be a cop?" Sulo asks.

I do this because I feel my power, because I can. "Your employment is contingent upon studying while you work." I point at Jyri. "He'll see to your admission into a law enforcement program. I'll pay you two thousand a month cash out of my slush fund while you study."

Sulo can't grasp his sudden change in fortune, toys with his glass, sloshes some beer on the table. "Okay," he says.

"Of course," I say, "I don't know you, and your employment is subject to termination at my whim. You have to prove yourself. Don't fucking disappoint me."

Jari is baffled, can't comprehend the conversation. I guess he thinks the booze is confusing him. Milo gets it all. He loves watching me abuse Jyri, is working hard to keep from bursting out laughing.

I feel satisfied, even giddy. "Well, gentlemen," I say, "I believe I've done my duty pertaining to alcohol here this evening. It's time for me to go home. I have a wife and a child to attend to in the morning."

"Don't forget, you have an MRI in the morning," Jari says.

I had forgotten.

"Is Kate coming home tomorrow?" he asks.

"She should be."

"We have some things to drop off for your family. Do you mind if we come over? It's important to Taina. She wants to make amends."

"Jari, you never have to ask if you can come to my home," I say, and don my coat.

Except for John, who didn't understand the conversation but is content to drink heavily, the men I leave at the table look mystified, furious or amused, each for his own reasons.

# 48

I get up early the next morning. I drank a fair amount, but wasn't out too late, so my hangover is mild, and despite it, the migraine remains absent. The snow has stopped falling for the time being, and the drive to Meilahti hospital isn't difficult. I make my nine o'clock appointment, and technicians roll me into something resembling a thrumming spacecraft. They put earphones on me to dull the MRI machine's cacophony. I lie still and listen to classical music for half an hour while they shoot hundreds of pictures of my brain. As hospital tests go, it isn't so bad.

Afterward, I drive to Kätilöopiston hospital. Kate is up and about, packing her things. "Mary told me you were here most of the day yesterday," she says. "I've never been so tired in all my life. I slept nearly around the clock. But they tell me I can go home now."

Mary has stayed at the hospital with Kate and the baby since I brought her here. I appreciate that, it makes me value Mary more than I thought possible. I sit in a chair with our little girl. She grabs my little finger and hangs on for dear life. "We may have a female wrestler in the making," I say.

I drive Kate, Mary and the wee one home. John is on the couch, sleeping off his hangover. We all follow his example and nap for a while. Our baby lies on the bed between us. I can't sleep, because I'm afraid I'll roll over and crush her. Around noon, we all rouse, and I start to make lunch for everyone, but it isn't needed. Jari and Taina arrive, arms full of food and gifts.

"What's all this?" I ask.

"It's called *rotinat*," Taina says. "In my hometown of Imatra, our tradition is that when a baby is born, all the relatives cook and knit something for the baby. The idea is to take care of the mom so she can take it easy and heal, and also to celebrate the baby. We brought enough food for a few days, baby clothes, diapers, towels and some other little things."

Imatra is in Eastern Finland, and we don't have this tradition in my part of Lapland. I've never heard of *rotinat.* I'm touched and surprised, don't know what to say. Kate gets up from the kitchen table and walks over. She's not wobbling anymore, got her balance back as soon as she had the baby. Kate hugs Taina and speaks for both of us. "That's the sweetest thing anyone ever did for us. Thank you so much."

I look around. John yawns, his hangover is bad. Mary's face is troubled. Jari stares at the floor. I wonder if he's concerned because of the last time he and Taina came here.

I check the thermometer. It's minus thirteen, the warmest day we've had for a long while. I ask no one in particular, "Do you think I should get the stroller out of the closet, bundle up the baby, give her a first taste of winter and put her out on the balcony for a few minutes?"

Mary hits the roof and yells, "What?"

Once again, her anger confuses me. "What did I say?"

She stands up and walks toward me, waggling a finger, spluttering with rage. "Are you insane? You can't take an infant out into subzero cold."

I've had mixed feelings about Mary over the past week, mostly good lately, but I just reached the end of my rope. "Mary," I say, "could I please speak with you in private?"

She storms into the kitchen, which isn't as private as I would have liked, folds her arms and glowers at me. I keep my voice down to avoid embarrassing her. "In this country," I say, "putting infants, dressed warmly, outside in the cold for a little while is considered a healthy practice. Everyone does it. What's your problem?"

She deflates, drops her arms to the sides, looks down and stares at the refrigerator.

"Mary," I say, "I've tried hard to like you, and sometimes I do. At the hospital, I saw your love for Kate and got my first sense of our being family. But you're a guest here, and this home belongs to me and Kate. We have ways of doing things you're not accustomed to, but we're good people and you have no right to criticize us. There are two options. You either accept and respect our cultural differences, or you leave. If you prefer to leave, I'll drive you to the airport today."

She looks at me deadpan, considers her response. Then her anger dissipates and her bravado dissolves. She doesn't cry, but her face falls. In that moment, she looks like an upset young woman of her age rather than the dour middle-aged woman she so often appears to be.

Mary keeps her voice low, stares at the floor. "You have a baby. I'm not able to have one myself. My husband is older than me, about the same age difference as you and Kate. When we married, we planned on having a big family. But after trying for a couple years, I found out that because of something that happened to me when I was young, I'm unable to have children. It makes me worthless in my husband's eyes. I'm a disappointment to him and to myself."

Now she looks at me, teary-eyed. "I've sometimes behaved badly, I know. I'm jealous of Kate, pure and simple. Please don't make me leave. I don't want to go home. I'm happier here."

I don't want her to feel worse than she already does. I give her a moment to collect herself, then say, "Let's go back and join the others."

We go back to the living room. Kate is holding the clothes Taina knitted up against our little girl, saying how lovely they look. Jari is downcast, standing in front of our bookshelf, perusing, with his hands in his pockets. I get it now.

"Jari," I say, "would you come out on the balcony with me while I have a cigarette?"

I see he doesn't want to. I give him a pair of slippers to keep his feet dry, and we step outside together. "Tell me," I say.

He feigns confusion. "Tell you what?"

I light a Marlboro. "I had the MRI this

morning. The results are supposed to take a few days, but you were worried about me and rammed them through. Tell me."

He shakes his head and stares down Vaasankatu. "Not today, Kari."

"Yes, Jari. Today."

"Today should be joyous. You just had your firstborn child. Let it be joyous."

I put an arm on his shoulder. "I just had my firstborn child. No matter what you say, today is joyous."

He can't look at me. "Little brother, you've got a brain tumor."

I had already guessed as much. "Is it malignant?"

"We won't know until you've had a biopsy."

"Look at me," I say.

He manages it.

"Am I going to die soon?"

"It's not a large growth, and because of its placement, we may be able to remove it without causing you cognitive damage. I can't tell you much more."

"Give me a survival percentage. What are my odds?"

He makes himself spit it out. "If the tumor is benign, eighty-five percent survival. If it's malignant, significantly lower."

Poor Kate. She was ambivalent about staying home for months to take care of the baby. Now she'll have to care for both of us. "Jari, we're going back inside now, and you're going to smile and chat and pretend everything is okay. Not a fucking word. Understood?"

He nods. "Leave me here for a minute to compose myself."

I flick my cigarette onto the street below and step in. Kate, Taina and Mary are talking and smiling, all three comfortable together. Taina brought a head of cabbage. She's explaining to Kate that putting a cabbage leaf inside her bra will keep her nipples from getting too sore when she breast-feeds. I pick up our baby girl and cradle her in my arms. She grips my little finger. We sit together and listen.

# ACKNOWLEDGMENTS

With special thanks to historians Oula Silvennoinen and Aapo Roselius, and to the Good Samaritans of Torrevieja, Spain — Lisa Anne Barry, Dominic Shaddick and Stuart Cunningham — for reaffirming my belief in the existence of kindness toward strangers.

# ABOUT THE AUTHOR

**James Thompson,** eastern Kentucky-born and -raised, has lived in Finland for the past dozen years and currently makes his home in Helsinki. Before becoming a full-time writer, Thompson studied Finnish — in which he is fluent — and Swedish, and worked as a bartender, bouncer, construction worker, photographer, rare coin dealer, and soldier.

The employees of Thorndike Press hope you have enjoyed this Large Print book. All our Thorndike, Wheeler, and Kennebec Large Print titles are designed for easy reading, and all our books are made to last. Other Thorndike Press Large Print books are available at your library, through selected bookstores, or directly from us.

For information about titles, please call:
  (800) 223-1244

or visit our Web site at:
  http://gale.cengage.com/thorndike

To share your comments, please write:
  Publisher
  Thorndike Press
  10 Water St., Suite 310
  Waterville, ME 04901